the
Accidental
Bride

**Center Point
Large Print**

Also by Denise Hunter
and available from Center Point Large Print:

The Big Sky Romance series
A Cowboy's Touch

Nantucket Love Stories
Driftwood Lane
Seaside Letters

**This Large Print Book carries the
Seal of Approval of N.A.V.H.**

the Accidental Bride

A Big Sky Romance

DENISE HUNTER

CENTER POINT LARGE PRINT
THORNDIKE, MAINE

The text of this Large Print edition is unabridged.
In other aspects, this book may vary from the original
edition. Printed in the United States of America on
permanent paper. Set in 16-point Times New Roman type.

ISBN: 978-1-61173-284-9

Library of Congress Cataloging-in-Publication Data

Hunter, Denise, 1968–
The accidental bride / Denise Hunter.
p. cm. — (A big sky romance)
ISBN 978-1-61173-284-9 (library binding : alk. paper)
1. Cowboys—Fiction. 2. Single mothers—Fiction.
3. Montana—Fiction. 4. Large type books. I. Title.
PS3608.U5925A63 2012b
813′.6—dc23
                                                    2011041035

For am I now trying to win the favor of people,
or God? Or am I striving to please people?

GALATIANS 1:10
(HOLMAN CHRISTIAN STANDARD BIBLE)

I knew you before I formed you
in your mother's womb.

JEREMIAH 1:5
(NEW LIVING TRANSLATION)

the Accidental Bride

1

The bell above the diner's door jingled and—despite her most valiant effort—Shay Brandenberger's eyes darted toward the entry. An unfamiliar couple entered—tourists. She could tell by their khaki Eddie Bauer vests and spanking-new hiking boots. Look out, Yellowstone.

When her heart rate returned to normal, she checked her watch and took a sip of coffee. Five minutes till she met Miss Lucy at the Doll House, forty till she met John Oakley at the bank. What if he said no? What would they do then?

"Mom . . . Earth to Mom . . ." Olivia waved her hand too close to Shay's face, her brown eyes widening.

"Sorry, hon." The one bright moment of her Saturday was breakfast with her daughter, and she couldn't enjoy it for the dread. "What were you saying?"

Olivia set her fork on her pancake-sticky plate and heaved a sigh worthy of her twelve-year-old self. "Never mind." She bounced across the vinyl bench, her thick brown ponytail swinging. "I'm going to meet Maddy."

"Right back here at noon," Shay called, but Olivia was out the door with the flick of her hand.

The diner buzzed with idle chatter. Silverware clattered and scraped, and the savory smell of bacon and fried eggs unsettled her stomach. She took a sip of the strong brew from the fat rim of her mug.

The bell jingled again. *I will not look. I will not look. I will not—*

The server appeared at her booth, a new girl, and gathered Olivia's dishes. "On the house today."

Shay set down her mug, bristling. "Why?"

The woman shrugged. "Boss's orders," she said, then made off with the dirty dishes.

From the rectangular kitchen window, Mabel Franklin gave Shay a pointed look.

So Shay had helped the couple with their foal the week before. It was the neighborly thing to do.

Fine. She gave a reluctant smile and a wave. She pulled her wallet from her purse, counted out the tip, and dragged herself from the booth, remembering her daughter's bouncy exit. Lately her thirty-two years pressed down on her body like a two-ton boulder.

She opened the diner's door and peeked both ways before exiting the Tin Roof and turning toward the Doll House. She was only checking sidewalk traffic, not hiding. Nope, she wasn't hiding from anyone. The boardwalks were busy on Saturdays. That was why she hadn't come to town for two weeks. Why their pantry was emptier than a water trough at high noon.

She hurried three shops down and slipped into the cool, welcoming air of Miss Lucy's shop.

" 'Morning, Miss Lucy."

" 'Morning, dear." The elderly woman, in the middle of helping a customer, called over her rounded shoulder, "It's in the back." Miss Lucy's brown eyes were big as buckeyes behind her thick glasses, and her white curls glowed under the spotlights.

"Okeydoke." Shay forced her feet toward the storeroom.

A musty smell assaulted her as she entered the back room and flipped on the overhead fluorescents. She scanned the boxes of doll parts and skeins of yarn until she found what she was looking for. She approached the box, lifted the lid, and parted the tissue.

The wedding gown had been carefully folded and tucked away. Shay ran her fingers over the delicate lace and pearls. Must've been crisp white in its day, but time had cast a long shadow over it. Time had a way of doing that.

Her fingers lingered on the thin fabric. She remembered another time, another dress. A simple white one that hung on her young shoulders, just skimmed the cement of the courthouse steps. The ache that squeezed her heart had faded with time, but it was there all the same. Would it ever go away?

Shaking her head, Shay turned back to the task at hand. The gown seemed too pretty, too fragile to disturb.

Oh well. She'd promised.

She pulled it out and draped it over the box, then shimmied from her jeans. When she was down to the bare necessities, she stepped carefully into the gown. She eased it over her narrow hips and slid her arms into the long sleeves. The neckline was modest, the gathered skirt fuller than anything she ever wore. Here in the air-conditioning it was fine, but she would swelter next Saturday.

Leaving the button-up back gaping, she hitched the skirt to the top of her cowboy boots and entered the store.

Miss Lucy was ushering the customer out the door. When she turned, she stopped, her old-lady shoes squeaking on the linoleum. "Land sakes."

Shay took two steps forward and dropped the skirt. It fell to the floor with a whoosh.

"Fits like a glove," Miss Lucy said. "And with some low heels it'll be the perfect length."

Shay didn't even own heels. "My boots'll have to do. Button the back?"

Miss Lucy waddled forward, turned Shay toward a small wall mirror flecked with time, and began working the tiny pearl buttons.

Shay's breath caught at her image. She forced its release, then frowned. Wedding gowns were

12

bad luck. She'd sworn she'd never wear another. If someone had told her yesterday she'd be wearing this thing today, she'd have said they were one straw short of a bale.

Miss Lucy moved up to the buttons between her shoulders, and Shay lifted her hair. The dress did fit, clinging to her torso like it was made for her, wouldn't you know. Even the color complemented her olive skin.

Still, there was that whole bad luck thing.

And what would everyone think of Shay Brandenberger wearing this valuable piece of Moose Creek heritage? A white wedding gown, no less. If she didn't have the approval of her closest friends and neighbors, what did she have? Not much, to her thinking.

She wanted to cut and run. Wanted to shimmy right out of the dress, tuck it into that box in the storeroom, slip back into her Levi's and plaid button-up, and go back to her ranch where she could hole up for the next six months.

She checked the time and wished Miss Lucy had nimbler fingers. Of all days to do this, a Saturday, when everyone with two legs was in town. And she still had that infernal meeting with John Oakley.

Please, God, I can't lose our home . . .

"I'm obliged to you, dear. I completely forgot Jessie was going out of town."

"No problem."

"Baloney. You'd rather be knee-deep in cow dung." The woman's marionette lines at the sides of her mouth deepened.

"It's one hour of my life." A pittance, after all Miss Lucy had done for her.

Miss Lucy finished buttoning, and Shay dropped her hair and smoothed the delicate lace at the cuffs.

"Well, bless you for being willing. God is smiling down on you today for your kindness."

Shay doubted God really cared one way or another. It was her neighbors she worried about.

"Beautiful, just beautiful. You'll be the talk of the town on Founders Day."

"No doubt." Everyone in Moose Creek would be thinking about the last time she'd worn a wedding gown. And the time before that.

Especially the time before that.

Third time's a charm, Shay thought, the corner of her lip turning up.

"Stop fretting," Miss Lucy said, squeezing her shoulders. "You look quite fetching, like the gown was made for you. I won't have to make a single alteration. Why, it fits you better than it ever did Jessie—don't you tell her I said so."

Shay tilted her head. Maybe Miss Lucy was right. The dress did make the most of her figure. And she had as much right to wear it as anyone. Maybe more—she was born and raised here, after all. It was just a silly old reenactment anyway. No one cared who the bride and groom were.

The bell jingled as the door opened behind her. She glanced in the mirror, over her shoulder, where a hulking silhouette filled the shop's doorway. There was something familiar in the set of the man's broad shoulders, in the slow way he reached up and removed his hat.

The sight of him constricted her rib cage, squeezed the air from her lungs as if she were wearing a corset. But she wasn't wearing a corset. She was wearing a wedding gown. Just as she had been the last time she'd set eyes on Travis McCoy.

2

*T*ravis McCoy stopped just past the threshold of Miss Lucy's store. He paused, waiting for his eyes to adjust to the light before letting himself believe it. Shay Brandenberger really was standing in the middle of the doll shop in a wedding gown. He pulled off his hat even as his stomach dived for his heels.

In the mirror, her green eyes turned toward him. A split second later they widened in recognition.

She turned, as if double-checking. Her features had matured. Time had been her friend, had rounded out the sharp angles, filled out the curves. But it had also stolen the sparkle from her eyes, the easy smile from her lips.

Or maybe he'd done that.

Shay's mouth flattened and her spine defied gravity. She faced the mirror.

Okay. He deserved that. His gaze swept over the gown, his mouth going dry as Sandstone Creek in the middle of August.

"Travis," Miss Lucy said, "what brings you in? Did you come to see my girls?"

He scanned the rows of handmade dolls. "Ran into Mrs. Teasley at Pappy's Market. Asked me to tell you about an emergency meeting tonight at seven."

Shay was fussing at the high collar with those long elegant fingers. Fingers that used to—

"Land sakes, what can that woman want now?"

It wasn't like he hadn't known Shay still lived in Moose Creek. That he'd run into her sooner or later. In fact, that had been the plan. But not here. Not today.

Not with her in a wedding gown.

He squeezed the brim of his best hat as he nodded. "Shay."

She tossed her head, flipping her mahogany hair from her eyes, not looking. "Travis."

He'd heard rumors of her and Beau Meyers. But they were just going out casually, was the way he heard it. Having some fun. Kicking up their heels on a Saturday night.

"She say what it's about?" Miss Lucy asked.

"No, ma'am."

A wedding gown, just like the last time he'd seen her. Only this time she wore it for another man. He tried to quell the panic rising high and fast. The rumors had been wrong. Dead wrong.

"That woman." Miss Lucy fussed with the dress. "Mountain out of a molehill. I think that'll do, Shay." She made one final brush on the skirt.

"Little late, aren't you?" Shay met his eyes in the mirror for a split second, long enough to make her point. "Fourteen years, that about right?"

"I'll just be in the back room," Miss Lucy said.

His girl still had fire. The thought kicked up the corner of his lips. Then he remembered she wasn't his girl anymore. That she'd be unleashing that fire on someone else.

"Who's the lucky guy?" The words nearly jammed in his throat.

She stopped her fidgeting. Met his gaze in the mirror, and he saw something. Just as quick, it was gone.

"Not you."

Tell him something he didn't know. All these years. All the waiting, the wishing. Hope rushed down the drain. He tried to plug the hole, but it was useless.

"Beau Meyers?" The name tasted sour on his tongue. Shay was a Thoroughbred, Beau a Clydesdale. He'd never be able to handle her. Maybe that's the way she liked it now.

"Been chewin' the fat with our neighbors?"

Beau would never make her happy—couldn't she see that?

She turned toward the back room. "If you'll excuse me."

Desperation propelled him forward. He had no right anymore. No right to take her slender arm. No right to touch her, no right to say it. "Don't do it, Shay."

Her eyes challenged him. "What's it to you, McCoy?" The question hung in the air between them, a loaded shotgun.

"Sure you want to know?" She wasn't ready to hear his answer, and she wouldn't believe it anyway. Not that he could blame her.

She pulled away, surprisingly strong, and he released her.

"Cool your heels. I'm not marrying Beau, I'm playing Prudence Adams in the Founders Day ceremony."

The reenactment. Relief flooded through him, leaving his legs rickety. *Thank You, Jesus. Thank You*.

She pulled open the storeroom door, then turned back suddenly, her eyes sparking. "And for the record, Travis McCoy, if I do choose to marry Beau Meyers, or anyone else for that matter, it's no business of yours." She hitched up her skirt, crossed the threshold, and slammed the door behind her with a force that shook the frame.

Travis stared at the door while his thoughts searched for a new gear. This was not the way he'd planned their first meeting. Not even close.

It was hotter than a furnace inside the infernal dress. "Unbutton me, please."

It took everything in Shay to keep her voice level. She turned her back to Miss Lucy and held her hair off her damp neck, still shaking. She felt the woman's fingers at the buttons.

Sweet merciful heavens. Why'd he have to show up today—with her in a wedding gown, of all things? The irony would've made her laugh if it didn't make her feel like her bones were disintegrating.

It didn't help that Travis McCoy had transformed from lean, wiry boy to brawny cowboy, complete with bull-wide shoulders, slim hips, and long legs. And those stormy gray eyes . . . those hadn't changed at all. They still had the power to suck her under. Cussed man.

She wiped the dampness from her forehead. Could Miss Lucy be any slower?

"Pretty tough on him out there," the older woman said.

"He left me high and dry."

"It was years ago, child."

"At the *altar*."

"Courthouse steps, I recall."

"Same difference."

"It was foolish and selfish."

"Blame right." She had returned to Moose Creek alone. The whispers and stares were almost as bad as losing him. The rejection. Almost as bad as lying on Miss Lucy's couch night after night smothering her sobs in her pillow, yearning for his touch.

"Figured you two would've run into each other by now." Miss Lucy finished the last button and helped Shay peel the dress from her arms. "But I guess not, with you buried away at your place like you've been."

"I wasn't hiding."

Miss Lucy's brows popped over her frames. "Didn't mean that, dear."

The woman's soft voice tweaked Shay's conscience. "Sorry. I'm touchy." She stepped from the gown and removed her boots.

"Don't be. You got a lot of troubles, and you surely didn't expect chemistry to come waltzing through the door this morning."

"That wasn't chemistry, it was animosity."

"Enough sparks between the pair of you to light the town at midnight."

Shay snatched her Levi's off a box. "Hogwash."

"Had me a hot flash and I'm way past that."

Shay heaved a sigh, torn between frustration and humor.

Miss Lucy folded the gown, tucked it into the box, and slipped the lid back on while Shay finished dressing. She still had the meeting at the bank, and she needed a moment to gather herself before she faced that particular hurdle.

Who was she kidding? She'd had fourteen years to get over Travis McCoy, and it still hadn't been long enough.

3

$\mathcal{S}$hay tucked her hands under her legs and forced her gaze to John Oakley's beady little eyes. She'd had about two minutes to recover from her encounter with Travis, and her nerves were shot. The bank had just closed up for the day and was silent as a tomb.

John laced his fingers, rested his hands on his desk, and gave her the look. She'd seen it the last three times she'd been in. Had to beg for this meeting today.

Please, God. I need some help here. A miracle would be good.

"We've been through this before, Shay," he said in his nasal voice.

"I just need more time."

"You've had time." The look turned smug. He poked his glasses up with his index finger.

Shay pressed her lips together. She wanted to remind him he was no older than she was, no more important just because he had money. She wanted to remind him of the time he peed his pants on their first-grade field trip and point out that his hairline had receded two inches since graduation. But none of that would help her cause.

"May I be honest, Shay?"

She bit the inside of her mouth. Hard. "Sure."

"I know the property's been in your family awhile—"

"Three generations."

He tucked his weak little chin. "Right. A long time, no one's arguing that. Your folks both worked it hard and barely kept it afloat."

"I made regular payments for years. I wasn't so much as a day late—"

"Until a year ago. I'm not the enemy here, Shay. When your husband was here running the place, the payments weren't a problem, right? Now, it pains me to say it, but Garrett's desertion, not my bank, put you in a bind. God rest his soul."

He did not just go there.

"It takes two to handle a ranch the size of yours. We've given you plenty of notice, and you're months behind. The bank demands payment in full or an auction date will be set in thirty days, just as the letter said."

A public auction. Could there be a more humiliating scenario? She imagined her neighbors walking the property, judging the upkeep—or lack thereof—and putting in low bids on the property that she and her ancestors had sweated and bled over.

She'd beg if she had to. "I can't lose it, John."

If Olivia wasn't going to have a father, she was at least going to have a place to call home—a place with roots that went deep.

"Please. It's the only home Olivia's ever known . . . the only home I've ever known. And I have a hand to consider."

"Manny's just a part-time high school kid. And as for your daughter . . . children are very resilient."

What did John Oakley know about children? He hadn't even managed a date for the high school prom. Shay wanted to smack the smug look from his face.

Instead she tried again. "Just sixty days, then. I'll come up with the money somehow." She could sell her truck and some cattle.

John's chuckle made her neck hairs stand on end. "Shay, honey, I'm sorry. I've done all I can." He checked his watch.

"Please, John. As a friend." That was stretching it.

"Best thing you can do is start packing your things. Look for an apartment here in town. You could make those little baskets full-time."

Her barbed-wire baskets were hardly going to put a roof over their heads and food on the table, and John knew it. Besides, the ranch was her legacy, such as it was. Her home.

John stood, his chair rolling backward as he extended his hand. "Wish you the best, honey."

Begging had gotten her nowhere. Shay gritted her teeth as she stood and shook his hand. She lifted her chin and straightened her back as she left the bank, a posture she'd perfected long ago. She heard John locking up behind her.

What now, God? I need money and soon. A burning started at the back of her eyes. *You have to do something. Anything. Please!*

She was going to have to let Manny go. Somehow she'd find a way to pay him for the last two weeks. But it wasn't fair, his working for nothing, not with his own family struggling. It was why she'd hired him to begin with.

Shay crossed the street, narrowly missing a sedan with an Idaho plate when it didn't yield at the pedestrian walk. She restrained the impulse to scream. She was dangling by her last thread. She wanted to yell or kick something. Or better yet, crawl into bed, pull the covers over her head, and sink into oblivion.

Instead she hopped the curb and entered the bustling diner. Olivia was seated at the counter sipping a chocolate milk. A dollar twenty-five.

Her daughter turned at the bell. "You're late, Mom, and I—What's wrong?"

"Nothing," Shay said, then caught sight of Travis in a nearby booth.

"Your eyes are red," Olivia said.

Shay fished in her purse for her wallet, her fingers clumsy. "Ready to go?"

"Mrs. Franklin said it was on the house. I didn't even order it."

"You thanked her?"

"Yep."

"Let's go, then."

"Hold on." Olivia slurped her milk.

Shay could feel Travis's eyes boring into her back. At least she was wearing her best shirt and jeans. At least she wasn't in a wedding gown. The confrontation in the shop returned to mind, piling on top of the disaster at the bank. The weight of it tugged at her shoulders.

"Come on."

"Sheesh, Mom." Olivia drained her cup and then hopped off the stool.

Shay hooked her arm around her daughter's shoulders and hustled her from the diner. "Got work to do."

Lots of it. Not that it would do any good.

As she crossed the street to her beat-up truck, she could swear she felt Travis's eyes on her every step of the way.

4

ravis dismounted Buck and led him into the barn. He wasn't sure why his folks had been so reluctant to leave the Barr M all these years, or why they'd asked him to watch over it while they went on their long-term mission trip. The place ran like clockwork under the foreman, Jacob Whitehorse.

Jacob entered the barn as Travis pulled the saddle from Buck. Jacob had the thick black hair and strong bone structure of his Indian ancestors.

They worked in silence like two men born to the job. Two men who were weary after a long day in the saddle.

"Good weather today," Jacob said.

"Not bad for June."

"Must be tame compared to Texas."

"In more ways than one." The rodeo circuit had been good for Travis's wallet and good for his ego. But pulling his truck into Moose Creek was coming home.

"Heard from your parents?"

"When they arrived in Guatemala. Told 'em you had everything under control. Not sure why I'm here."

"You know your dad. 'Sides, someone has to keep up the books. Math's not my thing."

His dad liked all his ducks in a row. That was

one reason the Barr M had prospered while so many other ranches had gone under. Ranches like Shay's.

The sight of her leaving the bank three days earlier pricked at him like a burr. Even through the diner's smudged window he'd seen her distress. It was written in the rigid set of her shoulders, in the straight line of her spine. She was a proud girl, always had been.

After he'd left the diner, he stopped to see Miss Lucy, hoping to find out what was going on. If Shay was in financial trouble, maybe he could help. John Oakley clearly hadn't offered any assistance. But Miss Lucy had been a closed vault.

Travis and Jacob finished grooming their horses, left the barn, and parted ways at the lane that headed toward Jacob's place. The sun had set over the Gallatin Range, silhouetting them against the pink-streaked sky. Travis had missed those mountains. Missed the towering trees, the grassy valley, and the loamy smell of dirt. He'd left it on his own accord, but he hadn't realized the mistake until it was too late.

He was on the porch steps when he heard a car rolling down the lane. A cloud of dust plumed behind a vintage yellow Volkswagen. He pocketed his hands as he approached the vehicle.

Miss Lucy stopped her car, turned it off, and rolled down her window.

Travis removed his hat. "Evening, ma'am."

"We need to talk." The furrows above the notch in her glasses deepened.

He reached for her door. "Come on in, sit a spell."

"Thank you, but I can't be long. The girls have been home alone all day."

"The girls" were made of fabric and stuffed with polyester, but Travis didn't comment. "What can I do for you, then?"

"You can play Joseph Adams in the Founders Day ceremony."

She couldn't be serious. Miss Lucy's request tied his tongue in a slipknot. The woman had been there three days ago. Hadn't she seen the way Shay had looked at him, heard the way she had spoken to him?

"Cat got your tongue?"

"I thought . . . Riley Raines was doing that."

"He has a girlfriend this year—Missy Teasley—and she's a jealous one. Her mama asked me to find someone else."

"And you thought you'd honk Shay off real good by asking the man at the top of her Most Hated list."

"She doesn't hate you."

"Could've fooled me."

"Well, you haven't fooled anybody, least of all me." Miss Lucy's eyes, magnified by the bottle glasses, narrowed knowingly.

Travis looked toward the darkening sky and clamped his jaw. "Don't know what you're talking about."

"Don't be contrary with me, Travis McCoy. I've known you since you were running around this place in nothing but a diaper. You're still in love with Shay."

His eyes drifted back to hers. "That's crazy." If Miss Lucy had seen right through him, what about Shay?

Okay, so it was true. He'd never forgotten her, and by the time he realized what he'd lost, she'd fallen hook, line, and sinker for some musician patsy. But then the guy up and left her.

Just like you, McCoy. The thought tasted like dust.

Plainly, Shay put him in the same category with her ex-husband. "You saw how she was."

"Can you blame her? You hurt her. She's had a hard life, and the last thing she needs is the likes of you stomping all over her heart again."

"Then why're you asking me—"

"Because sometimes true love needs a little help. Shay still sees you as the stupid young boy who threw her away like yesterday's garbage."

Ouch.

"I see the man you've become. You just might be worthy of her now. Maybe."

He wasn't so sure. He knew he didn't deserve a second chance, and he wouldn't hurt Shay for the world. She'd been his best friend. His first love. He'd missed her every day since he left. Had spent nights dreaming about their talks by the creek, their clandestine meetings in her barn when her parents thought she was in bed.

He remembered the way she looked in that antique gown. Beautiful. The thought of another man standing next to her, taking those vows—even if they were pretending—rankled.

"Shay know you're asking me?"

" 'Course not. You think I'm crazy?"

Half the town did, but Travis liked to think of Lucy Bowers as eccentric. "She's gonna be ticked if we spring it on her." When had he agreed to this?

"That . . . or she'll look into your warm gray eyes and see the truth. How vulnerable are you willing to be?"

"I haven't even apologized." He'd planned to do that first thing. Then he'd seen her in that gown, and his brain turned to mush.

"There'll be time for that later."

"If she doesn't leave *me* at the altar this time."

The woman cackled. "Now, wouldn't that be a Founders Day ceremony for the record books."

On second thought, maybe that wouldn't be so awful. Might do Shay good to turn the tables on him. Maybe she'd even slap him for good measure. On the other hand, did he want to do something so public when he was uncertain of her reaction?

"I don't know, Miss Lucy. She seemed awful sore."

"Now, you listen here. That girl's been at the top of my prayer list since you left her to face her future all alone. I don't know how she might react right off, but I've put in hours on my knees for Shay, and I've got peace about this plan of mine."

"Glad *you* do."

The woman started her car. "You just show up and let those eyes tell her what you feel, young man. Leave the rest up to me. Deal?" She stuck her age-spotted hand out the window.

Travis took her hand in his and squeezed gently. He was in for it now, for better or worse. Literally.

The wry grin slid from his face as he watched Miss Lucy's car roll down the lane. He was pretty sure, in all the ways that mattered, that he was the crazy one.

5

ow about Cocoa?" From her spot on the ground, Olivia gripped the bottle. The calf sucked greedily, almost wrestling it from her daughter's hands.

"You know how I feel about that," Shay said. First a name, then a pet, then she was one cow shy of a herd. Besides, barring a miracle, the calf and everything else would soon belong to someone else. She continued raking out the stall, the pungent odors of cow flesh, dung, and straw filling her nostrils.

"Her spots look like spilled cocoa. Not that I would know what that looks like." Olivia shot Shay a mischievous glance. "Man, she's hungry."

The calf's mama hadn't survived childbirth, but Olivia was standing in just fine. She'd been nursing the baby like clockwork. Off in the distance in town, the Moose Creek marching band struck up a tune. The Founders Day parade had begun.

"Where's Manny?" Olivia asked. "He said he'd show me how to win the ringtoss game. I'm coming home with a stuffed animal so big it takes up half my room."

That wouldn't be hard. "I had to let Manny go."

"Why?" Olivia pulled the empty bottle from the calf's mouth and scrambled to her feet, a frown drawing her brows together.

"Can't afford the help."

"But he needs this job. He's saving for Mr. Ryan's old truck."

It had about killed Shay to do it. But there was no money, and she wouldn't have him working without pay anymore. "He'll get another job, munchkin. I'll give him a hearty recommendation."

She could feel her daughter's glare on her back as she set down the rake and began spreading fresh straw. The faint strains of "Yankee Doodle" faded as the band turned a corner in town.

"Can I go meet Maddy now?" There was a remnant of anger in her voice.

"Finish your chores?"

"Yep."

"Go ahead, then. When will you be home?"

"Aren't you coming?"

Shay scanned the rows of dirty stalls. When those were finished, she had to do laundry and finish the books. "Seen one Founders Day, seen them all. I'll meet you at the ceremony, if that's okay with Abigail and Wade."

Her daughter shrugged, gave the calf one last pet, and hopped on the bike Shay had gotten her for Christmas from a used bicycle shop in Billings. It was a bike that had brought Olivia and Maddy together. As in, her daughter stealing Maddy's.

Shay sighed. Offspring had countless ways of humiliating you. But God had brought something good from that mess. He'd brought Maddy into Olivia's life and Abigail into hers. She hadn't had a best friend in years.

In a nearby stall, Brandy nickered.

"No time for a ride today, girl."

Shay never missed Founders Day. No one did. The history of Moose Creek's beginnings had been meticulously documented with dates, names, and details. The particularity of the stories had given rise to uncommon pride in the little town's heritage.

Which was all just fine and dandy, except this time she was the one wearing Prudence Adams's wedding gown. It had hung in her closet all week, mocking her every time she opened the door. How had she gotten herself into this?

A picture of Miss Lucy, her eyes wide and frantic, appeared like a cartoon balloon.

Oh yeah.

At least her chores were an excuse to avoid Travis McCoy. Maybe she could avoid him completely if he didn't attend the ceremony. He'd missed it for fourteen years, what was one more? He probably wouldn't be there. After all the big-time stuff he'd done in Texas, this little rinky-dink town probably bored him silly. By the time his folks came back in six months, he'd be itching to return to his exciting rodeo life where women no doubt dropped at his feet like flies.

Not that she gave a hoot.

She'd heard countless tales of the rodeo circuit from Maddy's dad, Wade. He'd reached national celebrity status before he escaped it in favor of anonymity in Moose Creek. Then God had led Abigail here to be Maddy's nanny last summer, and the rest, as they say, was history. Now they were married and living happily ever after, and Wade's notoriety had done nothing but help the local economy.

But Travis wasn't like Wade. Whereas Wade had run from the trappings of fame and fortune to settle here in relative peace, Travis had left the tranquility of Moose Creek in search of fame and fortune. And he'd leave again, even though he'd already found both. Let other cowgirls fawn and flatter all they liked, Shay preferred a man with staying power. But since there didn't appear to be any of those left, she'd settle for no man at all.

Her cell rang, and she pulled off her gloves and answered.

" 'Morning, sunshine." The blaring band in the background left little question about his location.

"Hey, Beau."

"Where ya at?"

"In my barn."

"I saved you a seat."

He was getting too presumptuous. Beau was a fun distraction come Saturday night, but that was all. Last thing she'd meant to do was lead him on. "Thanks, but I've got too many chores."

"Meet me later? There's a band onstage at three, supposed to have a great guitarist."

If she never saw another strutting guitarist, it'd be too soon. "Gotta get ready for the ceremony."

"Aw, you're breaking my heart."

"I'll see you at Bridal Falls."

"Not my idea of fun, watching my gal say vows to another man."

My gal? She had to put an end to this. "It's pretend, goofy."

"Yeah, yeah, I heard. Say you'll be my date for the picnic, and all is forgiven." There was a smile in his voice. "The Silver Spurs are onstage afterward. We can dance the night away."

She wasn't planning to go, but she had to break the news sometime. "All right, fine."

"I'll save you a seat on the fairgrounds. When you get out of that fancy getup, meet me over there."

The phone buzzed. "All right. Gotta go, another call coming in."

She said good-bye, then she glanced at the screen to see Abigail's name and answered. The band blared in the background. Good grief, she may as well be there.

"Hey there," she said.

"You're not coming?"

"Too many chores to catch up on."

"Aw, rats."

She'd never meant to burden her friend with babysitting. "You want me to come get Olivia?"

"Of course not. They're having a blast." A tuba sounded as it passed by. "Literally," Abigail shouted.

"I'm going to the picnic with Beau later, but no reason we can't all sit together." She'd squeeze in a chance to break his heart at some point. "And of course, I'll be at the reenactment."

"Should I bring 'something borrowed'?"

"You're killing me here."

After they got off the phone, Shay finished the barn, grabbed a quick lunch, and spent the early afternoon with her head in the books—the picture wasn't pretty. By the time she finished, she had an hour to clean up and present herself at Bridal Falls.

She'd grown progressively nervous as the day waned. By the time she was showered and ready to slip into the gown, she was shaking.

She'd been a failure at marriage, and the whole community knew it. Scared off her first groom and chased away her second. Well, they had nothing to worry about. Both times the rug had been jerked from under her, and she wouldn't be subjected to that again, thank you very much.

Shay pulled the gown from its hanger and

stepped into it. Would the ceremony stir it all up again? The gossip around her husband's desertion, the humiliation of being second to the rodeo circuit and a musical career?

Somehow, despite the fact that Garrett's desertion was more recent and seemingly more heinous, it was the memories of the one before it that made her hands shake as she pulled the dress over her hips.

It hadn't helped that she'd returned from her disgrace in Cody, Wyoming, by bus. That she'd had no change of clothes and had stepped off the public vehicle into the busiest intersection in Moose Creek on a bustling Saturday night in her wedding dress. Alone.

It had taken years to live that down. People still told the story to their young daughters, a cautionary tale against premature marriage. She was going down in the Moose Creek annals just like Prudence. Maybe someday they'd do a reenactment of her bus stop arrival.

Bridal Falls was situated eleven miles south of town, just across the Wyoming border. As the story went, Joseph Adams had ordered himself a bride after striking gold in nearby South Pass City. When his bride-to-be, Prudence Wilcott, arrived by stagecoach, it was love at first sight—or so the legend went.

With no permanent church in the settlement,

the couple exchanged vows at Bridal Falls before a handful of friends. Their honeymoon took them north a short distance, where they camped by a bubbling brook in Paradise Valley, snuggled between the Gallatin and Absaroka Mountain Ranges. The first morning they awoke to find a moose and her young in the middle of the creek and named the stream Moose Creek. Later they settled in the area, and the name stuck.

Shay cared about none of this as she made her way down the wooded path beside Miss Lucy. All she wanted was to get through the next fifteen minutes. She hiked the dress to her knees, careful of the delicate fabric. Last thing she needed was to be known as the woman who destroyed the town's most precious relic.

Judging by the cars lining the road and filling the grassy meadow, all of Moose Creek had turned out. When she and Miss Lucy emerged from the forest, Shay stopped, dropping the skirts to the ground. Folks were gathered on the grassy shoreline, a short distance from the falls, leaving a path down the middle for her.

Someone spotted her. "She's here!" All at once, the mass of people turned to stare.

Shay's spine stiffened. "They're staring."

Miss Lucy tugged her forward. "Of course they're staring. You're the bride."

"Pray for me," Shay said.

"I always do. And don't forget . . . you look beautiful!"

As they approached the rear of the group, Miss Lucy left Shay to walk the grassy aisle alone. She pulled her shoulders back and lifted her chin.

I don't care what anyone thinks. I. Do. Not. Care.

Whispers tickled the air. She blocked them all and focused on the gentle whoosh of the distant falls. On the call of a magpie from a nearby branch. On the swish of her boots through the grass. *Don't let me fall, God.*

"Oh my word . . ." The whisper, so close, was impossible to miss. "Does she . . . groom?"

Warmth flooded her cheeks. She looked toward the groom's spot but couldn't see Riley Raines for the crowd. She forced her eyes to Pastor Blevins's round face at the end of the pathway. At the tuft of hair the wind pulled across his balding head. At the black Bible in his hands, burgeoning with papers and bulletins and notes.

She wondered if Missy Teasley's eyes were shooting darts into her back. It was no secret Missy had gotten her mama's possessive genes. She'd probably made poor Riley wish a thousand times he'd just said no. Why hadn't Miss Lucy just asked Missy to fill the role? But of course, the dress would hardly fit her plump frame.

A paper slipped from Pastor Blevins's swollen Bible, and he stooped to retrieve it. His shoulder knocked into a wooden pedestal. It wobbled precariously, then he grabbed it, steadying it. That was new, the pedestal. Pastor Blevins poked his spectacles back into place with his index finger.

Fifteen minutes. Just fifteen minutes and this will be over.

On the other hand, if the preacher became distracted, he had a tendency to go down bunny trails. He could stretch this into thirty, easy.

By the time it was finished, Shay would be ready to go home and hide. She was already regretting her decision to join Beau and the others at the picnic.

But the quicker she walked, the sooner it would be over. She picked up her pace. Almost there. The only other person who wanted this thing over with was nearly in view. She turned a sympathetic smile in Riley's direction as his plaid sleeve came into view.

Yeah, I know. Me too, her grin said.

The sleeve became a shoulder, and the shoulder became a face.

But the face wasn't that of Riley Raines.

6

*G*ravity plucked at the corners of Shay's mouth. At her shoulders. At her heart.

Her step faltered, and Travis's hand went out. But she caught herself before he touched her.

She wanted to smack the cocksure grin right off his face.

How could he do this? How could Miss Lucy?

"Isn't he the one . . . ?" someone whispered.

"Did she know?"

"Maybe he won't run for the hills this time."

She stopped in front of the lopsided pedestal, facing Pastor. Her jaw clamped down. She felt her nostrils flare and wondered if steam was rising from the top of her head.

Pastor started talking, and the whispering quieted.

Please, God. Get me through this.

He began a message on the sanctity of marriage, droning on. For heaven's sake, it wasn't even a real wedding. *Thank God,* she thought, remembering who was at her side.

Travis stood close, his arm touching hers. Its warmth added to the furnace inside the dress, and a sweat broke out on the back of her neck. Her shallow breaths challenged her heart to a race. Hard to say which was in the lead.

Breathe, Shay, breathe.

How did this happen? He must've talked Miss Lucy into it somehow. Lied to her or something. The woman would never put her through this agony intentionally. She was the one person who knew the depth of pain Travis McCoy had caused. Knew exactly how the gossip and rumors had about been the death of her.

She was going to kill him. As soon as this was over. As soon as the crowd left. She would tighten that bolo tie until his face went tomato red.

No. She would hold him under the falls until he begged for mercy.

Better yet—

"Face one another, please," Pastor Blevins said.

She turned and followed the pearly white buttons up Travis's shirt. Up past his stubborn jaw, past his crooked nose, to his gray eyes.

She narrowed her own and hoped he could read her every thought. *Self-absorbed, bigheaded, egotistical—*

"Joseph Edward Adams," the pastor continued, "wilt thou have this woman to be thy wedded wife, to live together after God's ordinance in the holy estate of matrimony? Wilt thou love her, comfort her, honor and keep her, in sickness and in health; and, forsaking all others, keep thee only unto her so long as ye both shall live?"

You man enough to say it this time?

"I will." His voice boomed, deep and certain.

Easy enough when you're pretending, isn't it?

"Prudence Jane Wilcott, wilt thou have this man to be thy wedded husband, to live together after God's ordinance in the holy estate of matrimony?"

Not a chance in—

"Wilt thou love, honor, and keep him, in sickness and in health . . ."

Ha!

". . . and, forsaking all others, keep thee only unto him so long as ye both shall live?"

Won't be long for you, anyway. She unlocked her jaw and squeezed the words out. "I will."

"Joseph, take your bride's right hand."

Travis took her hand. The grin had slipped from his mouth and wariness had crept into his eyes.

"Say after me the followeth: I, Joseph Edward Adams, take thee, Prudence Jane Wilcott, to be my wedded wife."

"I, Joseph Edward Adams . . ."

She had to pull it together. Her profile was in full view of the crowd. She lifted her chin. *Don't let them see how riled you are. Do not dig your nails into his palm.*

Pastor Blevins fed the next lines, and Travis continued. Shay forced herself to look him in the eye.

"To have and to hold, from this day forward,

45

for better, for worse, for richer, for poorer, in sickness and in health."

The steadiness of his gaze, the words, spoken softly and firmly, reached deep into her core. Despite her best efforts, the knot of anger began to loosen.

She remembered their times down by the creek, just the two of them, when they had a lifetime of love stretching ahead. Remembered the first time he'd kissed her, at sixteen, in her parents' barn, on a dare.

"To love and to cherish," Travis continued. "Till death us do part, according to God's holy ordinance; and thereto I pledge thee my love."

How could graceful words sound so masculine? How could she be so angry with him one minute and want to fall into his gray eyes the next?

He's only acting, Shay Brandenberger, and don't you forget it. The man had a future in Hollywood.

But the real problem was plain to her now. The hold he'd had on her way-back-when hadn't gone away. Not after a painful desertion, and not after a fourteen-year separation. It was like he'd never left. Like her emotions had picked up right—

A squeeze on her hand pulled her to the present. Pastor Blevins and Travis stared expectantly. "Oh, uh . . ."

Words! A trail of sweat trickled down the center of her back.

"I—" she began. "Prudence Jane Wilcott, take thee, Joseph Edward Adams, to be my wedded husband."

The pastor fed her the remaining lines, and she repeated them, taking care to steady her voice.

As she spoke, Travis's face softened, his eyes taking on a sadness she hadn't seen in forever. Not since his dog Sparky had been trampled by a horse when he was sixteen. He'd shed actual tears as he'd told her, then she'd cradled his head in her lap and had run her fingers through his hair.

There were no tears now, but she wondered if that wasn't regret mingling with the sadness in his eyes.

"Let us pray."

She closed her eyes. Wished she could keep them closed until her neighbors were gone. Until Travis was back in Texas where he belonged. How could his parents have asked this of him?

". . . through Jesus Christ, our Lord. Amen. Joseph, take the ring and repeat after me. With this ring, I thee wed, and with all my worldly possessions, I thee endow."

Travis placed the cheap gold band on her finger and repeated the words. The ring. That's where all this had started. Or rather, where it all had ended.

Pastor Blevins handed her a band and instructed her to do the same. She placed the ring on Travis's thick, squared ring finger, then wetted her parched lips and repeated the vow.

As she finished, a gust of wind blew, and a paper on the pedestal sailed off. They both reached for it, but Travis caught it and replaced it.

"Forasmuch as Joseph and Prudence hath consented together . . ."

The ring on her finger felt cool and alien. She thought back fourteen years and wondered if Travis had ever gotten her that ring at all. If he had, he'd probably sold it at the nearest pawnshop on his way to fame and fortune.

Had he even wondered how she'd get home from Cody, or had she disappeared from his mind the instant he'd left? Had he grieved the end of their love? The end of their friendship?

Her eyes swung to his. *Did you even love me? How could you end what we had? You were my first love, my everything. Was it really that easy to give me up?*

Time had etched fine lines at the corners of his eyes, and the sun had permanently stamped them. His face was more angular, his jawline square and strong, and his hair longer. He'd always turned heads, but he was handsomer now than ever.

A breeze came and ran its fingers through the

dark strands, taunting her. She used to do the same thing. He had a ticklish spot behind his ear—

Stop it, Shay.

She had to be on guard. He was her Achilles' heel. Her kryptonite. Her—

"Those whom God hath joined together, let no man put asunder." Pastor Blevins's smile bunched his chubby cheeks.

Almost over. Almost over. Almost—

"Joseph," the pastor said, "you may now kiss your bride."

7

*T*ravis watched the emotions flicker over Shay's face and wished they weren't standing in front of the whole town. Wished they weren't in the middle of a solemn occasion so he could say something to erase the hurt in her eyes.

Instead, he tightened his hand on hers and prayed for a quick ending.

Minutes ago she'd been mad as a hornet, his little wildcat, her olive eyes spitting amber sparks. In her younger days she would've smacked him then and there. Anger had always been her default, and that hadn't changed.

And she had plenty to be angry about.

Her composure had fallen as the pastor spoke words of love, and that's when the hurt surfaced. Now he just wanted to take her in his arms and say he was a hundred kinds of sorry.

Sorry he'd hurt her. Sorry he'd been too young and foolish to realize how special she was. Sorry, he thought, watching the ache wash across her face, that "sorry" might just be too little, too late.

"Those whom God hath joined together, let no man put asunder."

It was almost over, and he felt the moment slipping through his fingers like floodwaters through a barbed wire fence. His hand tightened on hers.

"Joseph," Pastor Blevins said, "you may now kiss your bride."

She widened her eyes, parted her lips.

Founders Day tradition dictated a peck on the cheek, but Travis had never been a follower.

He lowered his head and took advantage of her surprise. Her lips were soft as a rose petal and just as pliable.

He'd meant it to be a quick, comforting brushing of lips, but then she responded. Just the faintest movement. The yielding lit a fire in his belly that wouldn't be extinguished anytime soon. He went back for seconds.

I've missed you so much.

He took her face in his hands, wanted to thread his fingers through that long thick hair and pull her closer.

But then two palms planted into his chest and pushed hard.

Her eyes spat sparks. She dragged the back of her hand across her lips as if wiping the kiss away.

Won't be as easy as that, darlin'.

Her eyes narrowed as her chin lifted.

"May the Lord shower this blessed union with love and peace, and may you abide in His love all the days of your lives. Amen."

At the pastor's nod, Travis took Shay's hand, cold as ice, tucked it in his arm, and led her down the aisle.

Halfway down, a stage whisper, loud enough to be heard from the next county . . . "You'd think she'd learn . . ."

Shay's fingers dug into his arm.

Priscilla Teasley. Old busybody. He found her in the crowd and silenced her with a glance.

Anyone else? His eyes scanned the assembly. *Didn't think so.*

Shay's pace had quickened. They were at the back of the crowd, which was now beginning to disperse and buzz with chatter. He could only imagine what they were saying. Why had he let Miss Lucy talk him into this? Despite Shay's bravado, he knew the truth. He'd done nothing but humiliate her. And kissing her like that . . . what was he thinking?

As they entered the coolness of the woods, her foot caught on a tree root. He drew her arm close to his side.

She jerked away, pulled free, then hiked her dress and stalked down the path.

"Shay, wait."

She whirled, shooting him all kinds of angry. "Don't you say one more word to me. Not. One. More. Word." She removed the ring and flung it at him.

He caught it against his chest.

She wiped the back of her fingers across her mouth again.

He felt her pain. *Not so easy, is it, sweetness?*

She turned and walked away, dress hiked to the top of her boots, a sliver of her legs showing.

A hard pit formed in his gut as he watched her stalk away. If she wasn't angry enough before, she sure as shooting was now. The apology would have to wait. He pocketed the cheap ring and followed the path toward his truck, not wanting the others to catch up just now.

When he reached the clearing, he made his way to his truck. Shay was long gone, just as he figured. He put the vehicle in drive and pulled onto the highway as the crowd began trickling from the woods.

The cool air felt good on his skin. He pulled at the bolo tie and unfastened the top buttons of his shirt. Least this ceremony wasn't as bad as the last one. Of course, the last one had never happened. He remembered the day like it was yesterday.

Shay looked so beautiful, sitting beside him in his truck. Her silky dress flowed over her perfect body like a glistening waterfall. She had saved all summer for the gown, and it fit her to perfection.

Everything was set. Travis didn't know why his heart kicked him in the ribs, why his palms stuck to the steering wheel. They'd planned this for weeks. When they returned to Moose Creek, they'd be husband and wife.

He swallowed hard.

"We have everything, right?" Shay laid her hand on the wedding license on her lap.

"Think so." Why did he suddenly feel like a cow stuck knee-deep in a muddy bog?

They were due at the courthouse in twenty minutes, though they were only two minutes away. Two minutes. He gripped the wheel until his knuckles turned white.

"You okay?"

He gave her what he hoped was an encouraging smile. "Fine. Did I tell you how beautiful you look?"

Her lips stretched. "About a dozen times."

The light ahead turned red, and his brakes squealed as he stopped.

Thirty minutes from now they'd be married. They'd head back to Moose Creek and face her irate parents. And they would be irate, though not for long. After all, they needed Shay to keep the ranch going. His own parents wouldn't be too thrilled either.

And then there was the whole rodeo thing. That dream was over, killed like an eagle midflight. But he had Shay. Loved her. He'd work on his dad's ranch and someday save enough to start his own spread.

Someday.

The light turned green. Green meant go. Go directly to the courthouse and pledge his life to

Shay. He applied the gas, and they advanced one block at a time through Cody, his breath feeling stuffed and hot inside his lungs.

When he reached the building, he drew up to a meter. Eighteen minutes.

Shay took his hand in hers and he squeezed, trying for a smile.

She stretched out her fingers, laying them flat against his, palm to palm. "We never got rings."

They'd meant to, but everything had moved so quickly once they'd arrived in Cody. He looked at her hand, small and delicate against his. She deserved a ring, for pity's sake. It was her wedding day.

"I'm going to get you a ring," he said, sure once the words were out.

"Someday . . ."

"No, now."

"What? Our appointment is in seventeen minutes. We won't be able to get another if we miss it."

He needed to get away anyhow. Take a deep breath, gather himself so he could be fully present and accounted for when they exchanged vows, not in some fog of disbelief.

"You can go on in and let them know we're here, just in case I'm a few minutes late. Shouldn't take long. We passed a Kmart on the way." He cringed a little. Shay deserved a wedding ring from the finest jeweler.

"You sure?"

"Positive. Have to hurry, though." He started up the truck again. Just the rumbling engine made him feel better somehow.

"Wait. Let's do this first." Shay laid the license on his leg. "Get all the legal, unromantic stuff outta the way."

Maybe she sensed his nerves. Or maybe she just wanted to keep this unfairytale wedding as romantic as she could. He was sure no girl dreamed of a courthouse wedding.

Shay signed the document and handed him the pen. He scrawled his name, more eager to pull away from the curb than he could say.

Shay gave him a peck on the lips. "Hurry back, now." She gave a cute little wave from the concrete steps as he put the truck in gear and gave it some gas.

All right, McCoy, come on. Pull it together.

This wasn't like him. He didn't ruffle easily. But then, he'd never run away to elope at eighteen either. It seemed like such a fine idea three months ago, right before graduation, when the subject came up. He couldn't remember which of them voiced it first. All he'd been thinking at the time was how beautiful she was with the light shining off her mahogany hair, how lucky he was to be in love with his best friend. How she made his engine hum whenever she was near.

He hadn't been thinking about the fact that Shay was tied to Moose Creek tighter'n paint on a barn. Or about how he'd never compete in the PRCA or own a spread in Texas like he'd dreamed of since he was a boy. Shay would never leave her family in a bind with the ranch, with her mom nearly bedridden. She'd always been loyal. It was one of the things he loved about her.

He'd stuffed his own disappointment, figured he'd get over it eventually. Settle in a little apartment somewhere near town and start saving some money.

Travis tightened his hands on the steering wheel. He did love Shay, did want to spend the rest of his life with her. But he wanted Texas too. Wanted the rodeo life and a chance to put his skills to the test. His friend Seth had moved there straight out of high school, was making his dream come true.

He'd called just the day before. "Loving it down here, man. Got a rodeo coming up end of the month. You'd have a better shot at winning it than me, but you'll be an old married man by then. Don't know what you're missing."

Only Travis did know. It was sinking in now like water into fresh soil. His breaths dried his throat, struggled to keep pace with his racing heart. Was this what a panic attack felt like?

Come on, McCoy. Cowboy up. He took four deep breaths.

Kmart was just ahead, a sprawling, dingy building with a cracked sign in the empty parking lot.

"Sure you know what you're doing, pal?" Seth had asked.

"I'm sure." And he was sure, when he was holding Shay in his arms by the creek, her back curled into his chest, his arms tight around her.

But when he was lying in bed at night, imagining the future, the existence they'd eke out one day at a time, he faltered. His parents were well off, but he was determined to make it on his own. He hadn't drawn an allowance since he was thirteen, when he'd gotten his first job as an extra hand on the O'Neil ranch, and he sure wasn't going to start accepting handouts now.

He worked for his dad now, a fair wage, but hardly enough to support a family. And Shay's family couldn't pay her a decent wage.

He looked around and realized he'd just passed the Kmart entrance. He'd have to turn around at the next intersection. Turn around. Go back to their Kmart future. Turn away from Texas and everything he'd dreamed of.

When he reached the intersection, he saw a No U-turn sign. The light turned green, and he continued ahead. A sign for the upcoming highway caught his eye: State Route 120 Casper.

He was already in the left lane. His truck seemed to take the route of its own volition. He was on Route 120, headed south toward Casper. South toward Texas.

His heart rate dropped and his fingers relaxed on the steering wheel. His breathing slowed, the knot in his stomach loosened. He felt better already, just pointing the truck in a different direction.

Pointing his life in a different direction. A giddy feeling welled up inside him at the thought of all that lay ahead. But it was immediately choked out by thoughts of Shay.

Shay, waiting for him at the courthouse. He had to call her. How could he explain this drastic change? But it wasn't drastic really, was it? He'd been waffling since the moment they'd dreamed up this plan.

She had to know he was struggling. Hadn't he tried to talk to her about this weeks ago? Hadn't she asked him a dozen times if he was sure? Hadn't she asked him just this morning?

And you said you were.

He stuffed the thought back down. He'd made the decision, and it felt right. Felt freeing. A marriage couldn't be God's will for them, not right now. They didn't even have their parents' blessings. That wasn't honoring, was it?

Now he just had to break it to Shay.

He'd stop at the next pay phone, call the courthouse. He'd tell Shay he loved her, that this wasn't about her at all. That they were too

59

young. They could get married later, after he'd had a chance to chase his dreams.

He scanned the roadside and saw a phone booth outside a convenience store. He pulled in and entered the booth, racking his brain for the right words. He didn't want to hurt Shay, but no matter what he said, that was unavoidable.

The number was in the government section. He deposited some coins and placed the call. The receptionist picked up on the fifth ring.

"Uh, yes, I have an appointment for—" He checked his watch. "Well, right now. I need to talk to Shay Monroe. She should be there in your office."

"She checked in a few minutes ago, but she went outside to wait for her fiancé."

"I'm her fiancé. There's been a—uh, change of plans. Can you get her, please?"

"I'm sorry, sir, I can't leave my office."

"Please, I have to tell her I'm not coming."

A second line rang. "Hold, please."

"No, wait—" But the line clicked and she was gone.

Blast it! He hated the thought of Shay waiting outside for him, watching every car as it turned the corner. Had she sensed his agitation? Surely she had. He twisted the cold metal cord around his hand.

"Hello?" the woman said.

"Yes, I'm here."

Another line pealed in the background. "I'm afraid I can't leave my desk. We're quite busy."

"Please. It won't take but a few minutes, and I have to tell her—"

"Sir. When the phone stops ringing, I'll run out and get her, but I don't know when that will be. Call back in fifteen or twenty minutes, and I'll see that she's here."

It was the best he was going to get. "Thank you."

He hung up the phone. He should put the truck back on the highway headed north and handle this face-to-face like a man. He knew it was the right thing to do.

But if he went back, he knew he wouldn't have the nerve to leave again. Even now he felt pulled, like he needed more distance between them to think with his head and not his heart.

He'd keep heading south, just for fifteen minutes, then he'd pull off and call back. He ripped the number from the phone book, stuffed it in his pocket, and exited the booth, the accordion door creaking with neglect.

He started the truck and got back on the highway, his mind whirling. How would Shay react? She'd be spittin' mad, that was for sure. If he were there, she'd shove him, her eyes shooting fire. She'd rail on him; then, after a while, her face would start to crumple and he'd try to hold her. She'd push him away at first, then she'd fall apart and sob in his arms.

He had to stop this. Had to start thinking of what to say. How to put words to his thoughts.

Ten minutes later he had his monologue memorized. He was half wondering if she'd hang up on him when his truck made a noise. A half mile later he began losing speed. The truck sputtered, and that's when he remembered. Gas!

He'd meant to get it on the way to the courthouse, but he'd been so lost in his own misery, he'd forgotten. Stupid!

He pulled the truck onto the emergency lane and turned the key, looking around. He'd left town miles ago, maybe six or seven?

He got out and started jogging back toward Cody. By the time he reached a gas station, his shirt was wet with sweat, but the only thing he cared about was reaching Shay. He approached the phone, bolted to the side of the building, and placed the call.

How long had it been? An hour and a half. He wiped the sweat from his forehead while the phone rang.

When the woman answered, he identified himself.

"I'm sorry, sir, your fiancée left a little while ago."

"What do you mean she left? What did you say?"

"Sir, I don't care for your tone."

Travis rubbed his face. "I'm sorry. I'm sorry. I'm just . . . upset."

"She asked me what you'd said, and I told her you'd changed your mind and you weren't coming."

Awww . . . blast it! He ground his teeth together and kicked the concrete wall twice. Three times. Then he took a steadying breath. "What'd she say? Where'd she go?"

Another phone pealed in the background. "She was visibly upset. She waited awhile and then she left. I don't know where she went. I'm sorry, sir, but I have to go."

"No, wait—" But the click sounded in his ear.

He holstered the phone in its cradle with enough force to break it. Then picked it up and did it three more times. She was probably on her way home by now. She would've called her folks to come after her. There was no way to reach her at the moment.

He bought a container, filled it with gas, and hitched a ride to his truck. Once it was running, he continued south, stopping to call Shay's house at every town he hit. Shay's dad finally picked up four hours later.

"You have some nerve, buddy."

"Did Shay make it back?"

"No thanks to you."

He begged to speak with her, but her dad said she wasn't there. He decided to keep trying.

She'd pick up eventually, and then he could explain. But at every stop, every time he called, her dad picked up. The last time he'd gotten a blistering earful.

Travis kept driving, determined, now that he'd set his course, on crossing the Texas line before stopping. It was after midnight when he pulled into the first Texas motel he came across, La Siesta. It was a dimly lit U-shaped building with two cars in the lot. He opened the truck door, and when the interior light came on, he noticed something black on the passenger floor. He reached for it, his heart sinking.

Shay's purse.

He'd left her with no money, no identification, nothing! He groaned and drove his palm into the steering wheel. Idiot! But surely she'd had . . . Then he remembered her suitcase. She hadn't taken it out of the pickup bed—why would she? They were supposed to be married and driving home together.

He called himself every name in the book as he checked in, then lay awake half the night berating himself for his thoughtlessness. But even in the darkness of night, even while he regretted what he'd put Shay through, he didn't feel he'd made a mistake in calling off the wedding. The real mistake had been planning it in the first place.

It would be months until he realized that some mistakes could never be undone.

8

"Okay, spill," Abigail said as soon as Beau lumbered away.

The two women were sitting on a blanket on the town square lawn. Darkness was falling, and the lamps along the street flickered on one by one.

Shay pulled her knees into her chest. "Don't know what you mean."

"You've been acting weird all evening," Abigail said. "Was it the wedding? It must've reminded you of Garrett."

Strangely enough, she hadn't thought of her ex-husband once. "Ancient history."

She tapped her toes to the country-and-western music. Across the wide expanse of lawn, the Silver Spurs jammed onstage. The guitarist moved forward, showing off his skills, and a gaggle of girls gathered at the foot of the stage. Musicians. Oh brother.

"You and Beau all right? He seems tense."

"There is no me and Beau."

"I know that, I just . . ." Abigail heaved a sigh. "Come on, are we friends or what? It took a lot of creativity to grab a few minutes alone, and if you don't spill soon, they'll be back."

Fine. Whatever. "If you must know, the groom was Travis."

"Yeah, I know. Wade said they used to compete sometimes on the—" Abigail's eyes popped open. "Travis? *The* Travis?"

"The very one."

"Holy cow, Shay, I had no idea—why didn't you tell me he was back?"

"All Moose Creek knows he's back."

"Well, I'm new here, remember? Oh my goodness. Your first love. Your soul mate. No wonder you—oooh, that kiss . . . No wonder Beau's all prickly."

"He's not prickly."

"He's livid. He's so handsome . . ."

"Beau?"

Abigail nudged Shay's foot. "No, silly, Travis. It's all making sense now."

Shay was glad it made sense to someone. Her own thoughts were a tangled knot of barbed wire.

"I'm surprised you agreed to it."

"Didn't know Travis was the groom. That was your aunt's little surprise." A breeze tugged at her hair, and the smell of roasted pork wafted by, turning her stomach.

"I should've known. Aunt Lucy's such a matchmaker."

"Well, she's wasting her time."

"Not if that kiss was anything to go by." Abigail winked.

Shay knew her friend was teasing, but Travis

had never been a joking matter. "Last thing I need is another cowardly man."

Last thing she needed was another man, period.

"Sorry." Abigail smiled sheepishly.

Shay and Olivia were fine on their own. The girl had been devastated by her father's desertion. She'd asked him every time he called when he was coming back. When he died, she cried daily for three months while Shay stifled her anger. Only when the anger wore off had she shed tears of sadness at his loss. In the end, she'd decided the anger was easier.

No, they didn't need some man strolling into their lives and breaking their hearts again, humiliating them in front of the whole town.

Abigail nudged her foot. "So what are you going to do? Wade said he's here until his folks return from Guatemala, and that's not for—" Her eyes swung upward, over Shay's head.

"His being here is no concern of mine."

"Shay . . ."

"I got plenty to keep me busy and—"

"Uh, Shay."

"—last thing I'm worried about is—"

"Travis McCoy!" Abigail stood to her feet. "I'm Abigail, Wade's wife."

He is not standing behind me. Shay turned and followed a long denim leg upward.

Travis stood behind her with Wade. Towering

over her. She stood, dusted off her rear end, and crossed her arms. She wasn't going to look.

"Shay, I'm sure you know Travis," Wade said. "Seeing as how you just got married and all."

"Ha, ha," Abigail said, a bit too animated. "Cute, honey."

"We went to school together," Shay said.

"Actually," Travis said, "we were high school sweethearts."

She looked. He'd changed into a black T-shirt and faded jeans and wore his cowboy hat. Too bad the bolo tie was gone. She'd missed her chance.

"Actually"—Shay fixed her eyes on Travis—"we were engaged. He left me at the altar."

"Oh, uh, I see." Wade pocketed his hands, looked helplessly at Abigail.

"Now, where'd Maddy and Olivia run off to?" Abigail said. "Those girls. Always running off somewhere."

"You asked them to fetch you a lemonade." Beau approached the group and handed Shay the Coke she'd requested. He looked between the three of them. "Did I interrupt something?"

"No."

"Not a thing!" Abigail said.

Travis nodded Beau's way. "Meyers. Good to see you."

"McCoy." Beau gave him a reluctant nod and draped his arm around Shay's shoulders.

The action was ornery and gutsier than she would've given Beau credit for. Just because she could, Shay let his arm rest there. Her eyes flickered to Travis, but he'd turned to watch the Silver Spurs. A shadow flickered across his jaw.

The moment drew out, none of them wanting to sit because doing so would be rude without issuing Travis an invitation. And no one wanted that kind of awkwardness.

Abigail surrendered to the pressure first. "Travis, would you like to—"

Shay cut her off with a sharp glance.

"I should take off," Travis said. "Promised Mrs. Teasley I'd judge the huckleberry pies."

"Tough gig," Wade said.

Travis shrugged, backing away. "Somebody's gotta do it. See y'all later."

His gaze swung to Shay one last time, that lazy grin tugging one side of his mouth.

A big butterfly flopped over in her belly.

Then he turned and walked away, fading into the darkness.

"Some nerve," Beau muttered.

They sank down onto the blanket, and Shay put enough space between them to fit a pregnant hog.

9

Shay got out of the truck and stepped out into the tall grass. Coming around the other side, Olivia wiped away the trickle of sweat that rolled down her temple.

She only had a few more salt blocks to drop, then the cattle would be set on minerals for the week.

"You're done, munchkin. Why don't you run home and see if Maddy wants to come over?"

Olivia hopped into the bed and pushed the heavy salt block toward the tailgate. "We're not finished."

Her daughter had done nothing but work all day, all week. Some summer vacation. And soon they'd be booted off their property. Shay hadn't broken the news to her yet, didn't know what she was waiting for.

She grabbed the fifty-pound salt block. "I'm almost done. Go do something fun."

It wouldn't take her long to finish, and the smile on Olivia's face as she wheeled away and jogged toward the house was worth it.

Shay walked the block over to the cattle and set it on the ground. "Lick away, girls."

She'd forgotten how much Manny had done around here, but it was coming back to her in the form of sore muscles and calloused hands.

Long as her hours were, they did nothing to alleviate the growing pile of bills. She'd put off her creditors as long as she dared, and still the foreclosure loomed. At this point, selling cattle was pointless, nothing but a downhill slope to ruin. Without the cattle, she'd have no means of income.

Twenty minutes later her cell vibrated in her pocket. She pulled the last block to the edge of the bed, then checked her phone.

"Hey, sweetie."

"Maddy invited me to supper. That okay?"

She could hardly blame her daughter. Rice and beans were getting pretty old. "It's okay with Wade and Abigail?"

"Yeah."

"All right. Be back before dark or call for a ride."

"Thanks, Mom!"

Shay said good-bye, turned off the phone, then hoisted the salt block. She didn't deserve her daughter's gratitude. She'd promised herself she wouldn't give Olivia more chores than she already had. Yet the girl had been out here all week while all her peers were swimming in the creek or taking shopping excursions to Billings.

She knew just how that felt, and darned if her daughter was going to live that way. *Help me, Jesus. Provide what we need soon. We're down to the wire, You know.*

Her phone pealed. Probably Olivia again. It took a few seconds to balance the salt block on her thigh and check the caller ID. *Unknown Number*.

Another collector. They just wouldn't leave her alone. Wasn't she trying her best? She could only do so much.

She shifted the block on her thigh and pocketed the phone. The salt block teetered on her leg, then slipped from her gloved hand. It hit her foot with a dull thud.

The pain came a full second later, shooting through her foot with a force that buckled her leg. Shay bit down on her lip, stifling a groan as she lowered herself to the ground. She pulled her knee to her chest and grimaced.

She'd really done it now. She propped her foot on the cussed salt block, hoping to alleviate the throbbing. She'd likely just bruised the muscle or something.

It was already feeling a little better, wasn't it? She clamped her teeth down hard. *Help me, Jesus. I do not need an injury right now, and I sure as shooting don't need a doctor bill.*

If she just breathed, focused on something else, the pain would ebb away, and she could get back to work.

Travis removed his hat, wiped his forehead, and replaced the hat. Buck started toward the pen, but Travis pulled the reins the other direction. "Not today, buddy. Got an errand." Not a fun one, but necessary. And long overdue.

He cut across the pasture, then crossed the shallow creek that divided their properties. The creek where they used to meet on hot summer days and cool autumn evenings. They'd carved their initials on a big oak on the day he'd asked her to be his girl. It still showed; he'd already checked.

He wondered if Shay had cooled her heels. He'd given her nine days, but now he wondered if the anger had only festered since he'd left her on the town square lawn with Beau Meyers.

He nudged Buck into a canter as they peaked the slope of the creek bank—as if saving two minutes was going to help matters. In the old days when she got her dander up, he just let her get it all out. She kicked up a ruckus and eventually the anger drained away, leaving her spent.

Once during their junior year, she'd caught him flirting with Marla Jenkins. When he'd tried to steal a kiss from Shay after school, she'd shoved him into his locker.

Later, by the creek, she'd broken into tears, and he'd held her while she sobbed, feeling like all kinds of fool for hurting her. Her emotions had always run high. But not until you got close. Until then, she was a tall, prickly fence.

He'd broken through that fence, and two years later he'd gone and hurt her good. His gut ached even now just thinking about what a royal fool he'd been, leaving her in Cody. His errand to Kmart for cheap rings had turned into a desertion of the worst kind.

And fourteen years later you're going to ask for her forgiveness?

Not that he hadn't tried before. But after waiting alone on the courthouse steps and then finding a ride back to Moose Creek, Shay hadn't been in the mood for apologies.

And could he blame her?

Just ahead, her ranch came into view. There was a small house sitting in front of the trailer where she'd grown up. A new barn. Shay and her ex must've done okay for a while. The thought reminded him of Shay's exit from the bank and the distress he'd seen on her face.

None o' your business, McCoy. Miss Lucy had set him straight on that.

He rode through the grassy meadow toward the house. She was probably sitting down to supper 'bout now, with her daughter. As he neared the structure, he saw signs of neglect. Peeling paint, weeds run amok in the garden, a hanging porch planter that sprouted a fern's brittle skeleton.

He thought of his own parents' ranch, running like a well-oiled machine even with the owners gone, while Shay's place ran into the ground. He wished he could help.

Yeah, like that's going to happen. The woman had enough pride in her little finger to supply the town for weeks. As he neared the barn, he saw that the corral fence was in disrepair. Didn't she have any help around here?

A noise in the barn had him pulling on his reins. A grunting, a human sound. He dismounted and tied Buck to the fence post. Inside, the barn was dark. The smells of fresh straw and horseflesh greeted him.

He heard movement in the tack room and took a few steps forward. Shay was carrying a saddle, and hefted it upward toward the wall peg. She missed and groaned as she lowered the heavy equipment, staggering. She was favoring her right leg.

Travis stepped forward and relieved her of her load. She jumped and lurched away, tottering on one leg.

He hung the saddle and reached out to steady her.

She swatted his hand away, catching her own balance. "What are you doing here?"

"What's wrong with your leg?"

She set her left foot down on the dirt and flinched. "Nothing."

"Like heck."

A trickle of sweat ran from beneath her hat

down her temple. Her face was flushed with exertion. She grabbed a brush and turned toward her horse outside the tack room, limping.

He followed. "What happened?"

"Bruised my foot. What do you want, McCoy?"

That was no bruise. Not the way she was limping. He grabbed the brush, wrestled it from her. "Sit down, take off your boot."

Shay jabbed her hands on her hips. "I have work to do."

"I'll do it." He started brushing the horse, holding eye contact with Shay until she huffed and hobbled out the barn door.

He brushed her mare until her mahogany coat gleamed, then returned her to a stall.

When he left the barn, Shay was sitting in the grass, her back against the red wood, her face as white as a February pasture. Her boot was still on.

Blast it, woman. He reached for the boot.

"Don't!" She jerked away.

He heard the panic in her voice. She'd gone and hurt herself good and was too blame stubborn to admit it.

He hunkered down next to her. "Gotta come off, Shay."

"It's fine." She tried to stand. "Go away."

"Sit." He grabbed her arm and held on until she relented, letting her weight sink back onto the ground, but not without a glare.

He reached for her boot and gave a gentle tug.

"Stop!"

He saw a flash of fear in her eyes before she blinked it away.

"I can't get it off," she squeezed out between teeth that were clenched in pain or anger, he wasn't sure which.

"Where're your shears?"

"You can't cut my boots."

"Wanna bet?"

"They're my favorite pair!"

Way she was looking at them, one part desperation, one part fear, he wondered if they were her only pair. Something inside him softened. Darned if she couldn't get him every time. "I'll buy you another."

"I don't want your money." This she spat with a little venom. The money he'd left her for. She didn't have to say it.

"I ruin 'em, I replace 'em." He owed her more than a pair of boots, and they both knew it. "Come on, Shay. What're you gonna do—wear them to bed? They have to come off."

He watched the emotions play out on her face as the battle waged inside her. She knew he was right. She was mule-headed, but she wasn't dumb.

She crossed her arms and gazed out across the pasture. "In the tack room, left side."

"Atta girl." Travis retrieved the shears and returned. She'd pulled up her jeans, exposing that sliver of skin below her knee. There was a day he would've reached out and drawn his finger across the softness of her skin.

"Can you just do it already?"

Her hands were knotted on the ground at her side.

He began cutting away the tough leather. The blade was dull, making the cutting difficult and slow. She tensed as he approached the ankle.

"Where's it hurt?"

"Outside of my foot."

He slowed down, taking his time, careful of the tender area. Tried hard not to jostle her as the blades sliced down on the leather. "Easy now . . ."

"I'm not a horse," she snapped.

He bit back a grin he knew she wouldn't appreciate. Maybe a distraction was in order.

"The other day I was remembering that time Sparky got in a fight with your mom's cat." He made another cut. "He thought he was so tough. Came slinking back to us with his tail between his legs." Over the arch . . . easy . . .

"Wasn't even hurt." She spoke between gritted teeth.

Almost there. "Just his pride. Didn't go near your mom's cat again. What was her name?"

"Jasmine."

"That's right. Jasmine. She was a prickly one." He pulled the blade out and eased what was left of the boot from her foot.

Even with the sock on, the swelling was obvious. "This is the easy part."

He eased it down over the heel and off, lowering her foot to his lap. The purplish-blue bruising wrapped around her foot and toward the arch. Looked a lot like his foot when he broke it in Houston falling from a particularly feisty bull.

"How'd it happen?"

"Dropped a salt block on it."

"Needs an X-ray."

"It's just bruised."

"It's broken, Shay."

She pulled her foot away. "You're no doctor."

"That's right, I'm not."

"Thanks for your help." She made to stand. Braced her weight on her right foot and inched up the barn wall.

"I'll take you now."

"I'll wait and see how it is in the morning."

"No, you won't. You'll go right on with your chores."

"You don't know me, Travis McCoy."

"I know you more than you think. You haven't changed at all, that much is clear."

"What's that supposed to mean?" She tottered on one foot. Sweat dotted her forehead, and she looked ready to pass out.

Stubborn woman. He fetched her hat and set it back on her head. "Nothing. It means nothing."

He took a few breaths, looked around the

property, listened to a starling sing a quick song. "If it don't set up right, you'll have permanent damage."

"How would you know?"

"Broke my foot a few years back, and it needed a pin. You don't want surgery, now, do you? Or a permanent limp? Make it hard to get around. 'Sides, I'd have to start calling you Hop-along."

He could see the indecision in her pain-glazed eyes.

"Dr. Garvin can give you something strong for the pain."

"Clinic's closed."

"I'll call him on the way over. Where's your daughter?"

"At a friend's."

"Perfect." He held out his arm. "Your chariot awaits."

She looked toward the dusty new pickup and let out a feeble grunt. The paleness of her skin frightened him. He'd pick her up and throw her over his shoulder if he thought she wouldn't put up a fight and hurt herself worse.

Plus, the feeling that coursed through him when she willingly took his arm . . . well, that was worth more than money could buy.

10

Dr. Garvin hung the X-ray on the wall and pointed with his crooked index finger. "Right there."

"It's broken?"

"No doubt about it. See here where this hairline runs . . ."

No, no, no, she couldn't have a broken foot. She had a ranch to run—money to raise, somehow. A daughter to feed and animals that depended on her. *God, what are You doing? You're killing me here.*

Shay closed her eyes and breathed deeply. The antiseptic smell choked her. Her foot throbbed despite the painkiller Dr. Garvin had given her. She'd just have to load up on the stuff and hobble around. What choice did she have?

She could do this. How long could it take to heal anyway? A couple weeks? It was just a tiny little hairline break. The worst of it would be facing the I-told-you-so she had coming from Travis when she left the exam room.

"Can you just wrap it or something?"

Dr. Garvin's hand fell from the X-ray, then he pushed back on his oversized spectacles. She'd interrupted his monologue, but she didn't care about the fifth metatarsal and whatnot.

"You are your daddy's girl, Shay. Bottom line,

you'll be in a splint six or seven weeks. You'll need to stay off the foot for at least a week. After that, crutches."

"Wait, stay off the foot?"

"Completely off."

Ha! And who was going to feed her horses and clean the stalls and put out salt blocks and chase the bulls back to their pen and fix the fences they plowed through?

"I know that's going to be hard, but it's imperative that you stay off it."

"And who's supposed to run my ranch while I lounge around the house?"

"Hire it out, Shay."

She pressed her lips together. Right. And what was she supposed to pay a hand with—a smile?

She couldn't make her mortgage payments now. Not to mention she was running up a medical tab she'd be paying off till she retired unless Dr. Garvin accepted payment in the form of barbed wire baskets. She could only pray he wouldn't charge extra for off-duty hours.

"Listen, I won't charge you for my time tonight, just the medical supplies and such, if that'll help you out any."

The old feelings came back with a rush. Teachers bringing her a pair of jeans because they'd noticed Shay's inching upward. The cafeteria cashier setting a milk carton on her tray even though she had no milk money that day. She knew she should be grateful for charity, but she hated it. Hated the way it made her feel, like she was lower than everyone else. Like they pitied her. She hated being pitied most of all.

Shay ground her teeth together. Oh, to have the luxury of saying, *Don't be silly. Just put it on my tab, and I'll settle up when the bill comes.*

She pried her teeth apart and forced herself to speak. "Thanks, Dr. Garvin." The words tasted like wet sawdust.

"Now, let's get that foot splinted up so you can get home to your girl."

Thirty minutes later Shay was settled in the passenger side of Travis's truck, a packet of information in one hand, a bottle of pills in the other, and a set of crutches in the bed behind them.

Travis pulled onto Main Street, his thick fingers wrapped around the vibrating steering wheel. She had to give him credit. When she'd hobbled out to the lobby, there hadn't been one hint of I-told-you-so.

It was dark now, and the streetlamps twinkled in a long line that reminded her of an airport runway. She'd called Abigail and told her what had happened. Her friend had offered to keep Olivia overnight, but Shay had asked Abigail to bring her home later instead. Shay was going to need her daughter's help in the morning, like it or not.

They turned out of town, heading toward her place.

"What're you gonna do?" Travis's voice seemed deep in the dark cab.

"I'll manage."

Was she going to ask her twelve-year-old to do a man's job? Shay could barely manage herself. Could she ask Manny to come back, promise to pay him later, after she sold off some cattle? That wasn't fair. He needed money now, not weeks from now.

God, You've got to step in here. I can't do this alone.

She could feel her pulse in her foot, now splinted and throbbing. Why weren't those painkillers working?

"Listen, I've got extra time. God knows the Barr M practically runs itself. I'm basically deadweight—"

"No." She couldn't afford to refuse Doc's help, but she couldn't afford to accept Travis's.

"You said Dr. Garvin told you to stay off your feet for a week. He may not know what that means to a rancher, but I do."

"That's my problem."

His hands tightened on the steering wheel.

Fine, Travis, be upset. He had no idea what upset was, with his money and privilege and, no doubt, women 'round every corner.

"Beau will give me a hand." She didn't know

where the words came from. Didn't know she had the thought until it was out.

"Beau . . ." He huffed, shook his head.

"Got something to say?"

"Not a word."

"Good."

Who was he to mock her choices? Not that Beau was her choice. She had no doubt he'd be happy to help, but she couldn't take advantage. Travis didn't have to know that, though. She didn't ask herself why that gave her satisfaction.

"He's all wrong for you," Travis said.

"You're the expert? Last I checked, you resigned from that position." The pain was making her testy, making her say things she shouldn't. She clamped down on her lips.

"You're right. That's why I came over tonight." He rubbed his jaw, set his hand back on the wheel. "But that's for later. You've had enough for one day."

Like she was going to let him leave it at that. "Go ahead. Spill it."

"Another time, Shay."

"I'm too cranky, that it? Can't handle it, McCoy?"

"I can handle you just fine, and we both know it."

His eyes burned into hers, and she was remembering that night just as he'd no doubt meant her to. The night she'd dared him to kiss her, and he'd wrestled her to the ground and set her lips on fire right there on a haystack in her parents' barn. She'd put up an honest fight, thinking he liked Marla Jenkins, not her, but he'd taken her down like she was a feather and had her melting in his arms in two seconds flat.

Blast the man. Her cheeks burned, and she tore her eyes from his. She was a grown woman now, and she'd learned plenty along the way. Such as, a man who broke your heart once will surely break it again.

When they finally arrived home, Travis pulled the truck to the porch steps. "Stay there."

Like she had any choice. She opened the door while he retrieved the crutches. If he had his way, he'd be carrying her, but she wasn't letting that happen. As it was, she couldn't get away soon enough.

He handed her the crutches and followed her up the porch steps. She kept her knee bent, her broken foot well off the ground. She was going to take another pill as soon as she got inside.

"Maybe I should stay until your daughter—"

"I don't need a babysitter."

He opened the door and held it while she hobbled through.

"Thanks for your help." She turned awkwardly and took hold of the door.

He opened his mouth, then closed it again. Instead, he touched the brim of his hat, but the furrow between his brows said everything his mouth wouldn't.

It wasn't until later, foot propped on a foam pillow, daughter tucked in her bed across the hall, that Shay realized Travis never did tell her why he'd come over in the first place.

11

When Travis got home from Shay's house, he picked up the mail and settled behind his dad's desk. After tackling the bills, he opened the final letter, addressed to him, and unfolded the document.

He frowned at the certificate. Strange. He leaned back in his father's chair and looked at the envelope the letter had come in. The county clerk's office. Why would they be sending him a marriage certificate? Made no sense.

He looked closer at the document and saw his name, his signature. On the next line was Shay's name, Shay's signature, and below that . . . he squinted hard . . . *Pastor Blevins's?*

A shot of adrenaline rippled through him. He didn't understand. He turned the paper over, blank on the other side.

He and Shay hadn't signed anything during the pretend ceremony. He looked closer, looked at the date, and felt the heavy weight of dread sink like a boulder in his stomach.

It was their marriage license, the one they'd filed for fourteen years ago. But how had Pastor Blevins gotten hold of it? And why was the clerk's office mailing it to him?

He looked up the pastor's home number and

dialed. Voice mail kicked on, and he hung up. He'd have to wait until morning.

He stood and paced the length of the office. Where had that license come from? Surely Shay hadn't kept it all these years. It was a mistake of some kind. Maybe Miss Lucy knew what happened. He stalked back to the desk and called her at home.

"Hi, Miss Lucy, it's Travis. Hope I didn't wake you."

"Oh no, dear. The girls and I were just getting ready for bed. What can I do for you?"

He rubbed the back of his neck. "This is going to sound strange, but do you know whatever happened to Shay's and my wedding license?"

"Oh, that. Well, I do, actually. I found it in one of my boxes and—remember that pedestal at the Founders Day reenactment? I set the license there, hoping to jog Shay's memory. Give her a little nudge, you know. But I don't think she even noticed it."

Man, oh, man. Travis rubbed his face.

"Why do you ask, dear?"

"What did you do with it after the ceremony?"

"What did I—Oh dear, I don't know. I forgot all about it. Did you want to save it? I hope it didn't blow away."

"It didn't blow away."

"Oh good."

"Miss Lucy, it arrived in the mail today."

"Well, isn't that lucky!"

He rubbed his face. "Shay and I seem to be officially married."

"Oh my! Congratulations, dear!"

"This is not good, Miss Lucy." It had to be a mistake. Shay would kill him if it wasn't. "I mean, the license must've expired, right? Anyway, we applied for it in Wyoming, and the wedding was in—Wyoming. But we don't reside in Wyoming, so that should make it null and void. The clerk's office just missed it."

"I don't know anything about all that—let me ask the girls." She muffled the phone while she talked to her dolls. Heaven help him.

The Internet. He marched to the computer and typed in a search, then drummed his fingers while the links came up. He clicked on a government site and began skimming.

Must be eighteen years of age or older. Check.

The license must be used in the state of Wyoming. Check.

Any licensed or ordained minister may perform ceremony. Check.

Do not have to be a resident of Wyoming. Check.

"The girls don't know either, Travis. Oh my, this is all my fault."

"I'm sure it's a mistake. The license is fourteen years old. It can't be any—"

License is valid indefinitely.

Gulp.

"What is it?"

Travis cleared his throat. "A Wyoming license has no expiration date."

"Oh my."

He kept reading, looking for something. There had to be something. "This is not good."

"Not finding anything?"

"Nothing. I'll call the clerk's office in the morning and explain."

"Of course. I'm sure they'll understand it was all just a silly mistake." Her confident tone was reassuring. "That is what you want, isn't it?"

"Of course that's what I want."

He wanted this to go away. To make the call, explain the mistake, and have their records incinerated. *Poof!* Marriage over. And everything would be back to normal. He and Shay would be officially single. She would hate his guts. She would keep seeing Beau Meyers.

That was what he wanted.

Right?

"Travis?"

"I'm here. I'll call the clerk's office in the morning. Thanks for your help, Miss Lucy."

"I'm sure it'll all work out just as God intends, dear."

"I'm sure you're right."

Travis hung up, then went upstairs and went through all the motions of getting ready for bed.

But instead of sleeping, he stared at the wood beams running across the ceiling. His mind traveled back two months.

He and Seth had just won the team roping competition, and they were celebrating at Clive's with their buddies from the circuit. This year had been his biggest windfall yet, and his others hadn't exactly been shoddy.

Travis took a chunk from the southwestern nachos the server had delivered minutes earlier along with a flirtatious smile. Ella Reynolds was with him, a pretty cowgirl and decent barrel racer in her own right.

She leaned over and kissed his cheek, her blond hair tumbling over her shoulders. The sweet scent of her perfume filled his nostrils, killing his appetite. She had green eyes almost the same color as Shay's. But something about Ella's seemed flat, like a mirror with nothing inside, only a reflection. Shay's eyes were like a mountain stream, deep and mysterious.

But why was he thinking about Shay? She was some other man's wife and had been for years, since about two seconds after he'd left her in Cody.

"You were something tonight, Trav," Ella said over the din of chatter. "You and Seth make a great team."

"Here it is!" one of his friends called, pointing

to the big screen in the corner where the replay of today's rodeo was being broadcast. The air was so smoky, it cast a fog over his view.

Travis watched the screen, watched himself and Seth work together to take down the steer, Travis heading and Seth heeling. Cheers went up when the event ended with their quickest time ever, and his friends raised their mugs to them.

He had everything he wanted. Fourteen years of hard work, and he was practically set for life if he was careful. He had money, a touch of fame, and a pretty filly on his arm.

And yet something was missing. He felt it often, lying in bed after a date, when his apartment was quiet, his body still. But now the emptiness filled him with an ache that spread wide enough to engulf him, almost taking his breath away. Strange that he felt it now, when the din of celebration and the excitement of reaching the record win should've left him high and heady.

What is it, God? You've blessed me like crazy. I have everything I ever wanted. Why do I feel so . . . alone?

He wasn't alone. He had God. He had buckets of friends and no shortage of women.

But as soon as the thought trotted through his head, he knew what was wrong. What he tried to deny, tried to shove back deep inside where he didn't have to think about it. Because thinking about it was useless.

Seth appeared in the seat beside him where Ella had been moments before. "What's with the long face?"

Travis shrugged. Took a drink.

"It's a celebration, and we're the men of the hour. Perk up—we'll make it to the finals this year for sure."

Travis had been to the finals half a dozen times; being a top fifteen earner gave him that privilege. But it would be a first for his best buddy. "Might be right. But December's a long ways off."

"We're way ahead of the others. Shoot, we could sit out awhile and still break the top fifteen."

Seth was right. Still, it wasn't the thrill it used to be.

"Ella getting on your nerves?"

Travis searched the room and found her at the jukebox, searching the selections. "Ella's cool."

The smoky air was heavy, and the room was too loud. He felt a headache coming on.

"You've got that look again, Trav. Tell me this isn't about Shay Monroe."

It was Brandenberger now, but he didn't feel like correcting his friend. His lips tightened.

"Dude."

Seth should understand. He'd been there when Travis and Shay were together. But he'd never understood how Travis could miss someone he hadn't seen in years. Travis wasn't sure he understood it himself. It was like a piece of him was missing, and all the pieces he'd tried to put in its place didn't fit. Not even close.

"You don't understand."

"She belongs to another man."

That one hurt. Nothing he hadn't reminded himself of a thousand times, but having it out there, so blunt, was a bitter wakeup call. What kind of jerk was he, longing for someone else's wife? Not like he hadn't blown his chance.

He stood abruptly, his chair darting out behind him. Ella was there, a drink in each hand. "Where ya going?"

"I have to go. I have . . . something I gotta do."

A song kicked on, loud and familiar. The tune they'd danced to the week before.

Her smile drooped at the corners. "Oh."

"Need a ride?" he asked belatedly. Some date he was.

"Callie can take me home. You're kinda the guest of honor, Travis."

He didn't care at the moment. He had to escape this place before the emptiness ate him alive.

"Call you tomorrow, okay?" He offered what he hoped was an apologetic smile and headed toward the door, barely aware of the conversations around him, of the peanut shells crunching under his boots, the pungent smell of fried onions.

"Hey, McCoy!" a voice called, but he was at the door by then and leaving, escaping into the hot Texas air, making his way toward his shiny new truck.

He had called Ella the next day, good as his word, but the emptiness had taken up residence and wasn't budging, not even with the extra hours he was putting in at his boss's ranch. He should quit, start his own operation, now that he had the money. But did he really want to lay down roots in Texas? Besides, there was more money to be made on the circuit, and he was in his prime.

Two weeks later he was heating a can of beans on his stove top when his cell rang.

"Hi, honey," his mom said, her voice sounding older than he remembered.

"Hey, Mom."

"I didn't interrupt anything, did I?"

"Just my fancy dinner for one."

"Pork and beans?"

He laughed at his own predictability. "Everything okay? Dad feeling all right?"

"Right as rain. Getting along just fine, and the ranch is doing great. How 'bout you?"

His mom heard things other people didn't. He forced some energy into his tone. "Great. Won first in a big rodeo a couple weeks ago, me and Seth."

"It was in our paper. I called, but kept getting voice mail."

So he hadn't felt like talking lately. "Sorry 'bout that." He gave the beans another stir and removed the pot from the stove.

"Dad and I called to ask you something. Well, actually to tell you something, then ask a question."

"What's up?"

"We're going on a mission trip—to Guatemala."

"That's great, Mom. You've always wanted to do something like that."

"We figured we'd better do it before we get old and decrepit. We're tired of the ranch holding us hostage, and when God tells you to go, well, you go."

"Good for you." He meant that. His parents never left their place except for quick trips to see him. A mission trip was right up their alley.

"We'd like for you to come look after things while we're away."

"What?"

"We'd feel good about leaving it in Jacob's care—"

"Mom—"

"—if we weren't going to be gone so long. But he can't do the books, and your dad—"

"Mom, you know how I feel about that."

Just the thought of seeing Shay again . . . Shay with her husband and their daughter.

"It's been so long."

And he missed Shay more than ever. He wanted to help his parents. He owed them everything. He tried to imagine going home. Seeing Shay with her husband, his arm draped possessively over her shoulder.

His heart seized. "I can't."

It was hard enough here, hundreds of miles away. What would it be like to see her again, knowing he could never have her? Knowing he'd thrown away the one thing that mattered most?

"I can't."

"She's not married anymore, Travis."

He hadn't heard right. What did she mean?

"He up and left her months ago. They divorced."

Divorced? How did he not know this? The creep left Shay and his own daughter? Travis felt for her, for the hurt and embarrassment it must've caused her. The selfish jerk . . .

"Next thing I heard, he died doing some fool rock climbing thing in Utah."

He died? Shay's husband was dead? Ex-husband, he reminded himself. His heart started beating again. Felt like the first time it had beat normally in months. Years. He should feel sorry, sorry that Shay's marriage was over, but all he could find inside were relief and hope.

Hope. That was what set his heart beating hard and steady.

"Travis."

"All right, I'll come."

"I didn't even say when or how long."

"When and how long?"

His mom chuckled. "We leave at the end of May, and we'll be gone six months."

"Done."

"What about your apartment, your job, the rodeo . . . ?"

Seth was going to kill him. But they were so far ahead, they'd still have a shot at the finals. "I'll figure it out. It's time for me to come home."

He couldn't believe it. Maybe he'd have a second chance. Was it possible she didn't hate him anymore for what he'd done? Was it possible she still missed him too, even after all these years?

"I always did think you made a great couple," Mom said. "Your dad and I both."

"I blew it."

"You were awful young. If it seemed we didn't support you, it was only because we were afraid you were too young. We feel partly responsible for what happened."

"Got no one to blame but myself." But he was ready and willing to set things right.

He'd used his remaining time in Texas tying up loose ends and preparing for his return to Moose Creek. He'd prayed until his knees were sore, seeking God's will.

Now Travis punched the pillow and turned onto his side. He couldn't have foreseen the crazy set of circumstances that had transpired. But the longer he lay there thinking, the more he realized that an incredible opportunity had fallen into his lap.

It was almost as if God had reached down and given him a helping hand.

That wasn't so hard to believe, was it? That God saw his heartbreak, heard his prayers? What could he do but take the opportunity and hope for the best?

12

$\mathcal{S}$omething was wrong.

Shay glanced down at the lump under the quilt. Her foot throbbed like the dickens, but that wasn't it. She glanced around the room. Then it hit her.

The light was all wrong. Golden yellow sunshine bounced off the beige walls, reflected from her bureau mirror.

Her eyes snapped to the clock: 10:15.

Olivia . . . the animals . . .

She threw off the quilt and lowered her feet to the floor, an action she instantly regretted.

"Olivia!"

The house was quiet. Too quiet. Why had Olivia let her sleep so late? She'd promised to milk the cows, but that had been done hours ago.

Shay hobbled across the room on her crutches and dressed awkwardly in gray sweatpants, grimacing against the pain in her foot. She hadn't slept so late in years. She vaguely recalled waking in the middle of the night and taking more pain meds. She must've turned off her alarm and gone right back to sleep.

"Olivia!" Where had the girl gotten to?

Dressed now, Shay grabbed her crutches and left the room. "Olivia?"

The TV and lights were off. She'd better not

have gone off on one of the horses. Or ridden her bike to Maddy's. Or gone swimming in the creek. She was only twelve. Too young to be running around the countryside alone.

Shay hurried her steps as all manner of trouble crept into her thoughts. She maneuvered to the front door and nearly tripped over the threshold. After catching her balance, she tottered to the porch's edge.

"Oliv—!"

From her spot in the vegetable garden, her daughter's head snapped up. A streak of dirt smudged her cheek, and a cluster of weeds sprouted from her gloved hand. "Hey, Mom."

"What are you—Why didn't you—" She couldn't think with her foot throbbing.

Olivia sprang up and dusted off her hands. "You shouldn't be on that foot."

"Why are you weeding?"

Olivia hated yard work. She always put it off.

"Mr. McCoy said if I did we could go—"

"Mr. McCoy?"

Movement near the barn caught Shay's eye. As if his name had conjured him, Travis appeared in the doorway.

Shay clamped her teeth together. She'd told him—Why was he—Cussed man.

"Hey," he called, approaching. Strutting, really, with those long thick legs of his. "What're you doing up?"

"Go home, Travis."

"Mom, he—"

"Stay out of it, Olivia." Shay instantly regretted her tone. "Please . . . go inside and fetch my pills."

Her daughter looked to Travis as if for permission, which only raised Shay's hackles further. Olivia shrugged and headed inside.

"I told you not to come," she said when Olivia was out of earshot. What she'd really said was that she'd manage. But the only thing she'd managed to do so far was sleep.

"And Dr. Garvin told you to stay off that foot." He was close now, almost to the porch.

She hated the way she was suddenly conscious of her snarled hair and sleepy eyes.

Focus, Shay. She had to get him out of here. She didn't like what he did to her insides, making them feel all curdled, like month-old milk.

"I don't have the luxury of lounging on the couch all day, McCoy. The cows—"

"Are already milked."

"The horses—"

"Are fed."

She glared. "Well, the stalls need—"

"Clean." He crossed his arms and cocked his head. *Anything else?* his posture said.

All that and he'd gotten Olivia to weed too? She wanted to smack the smug look from his face. Instead, she nodded sharply. "Thank you. I can take it from here."

"I promised Olivia I'd take her to the creek."

She didn't know which galled her more. That he'd done her chores or that he was making promises to her daughter.

"Come on." He ambled up the porch steps. "Let's get you settled."

She stifled the urge to back away.

"Here, Mom." Olivia appeared with a glass of water and her pill.

"Thanks." Shay took the pill and gulped it down, then realized belatedly she'd be drowsy for hours. Perfect.

"I have to finish the weeds," Olivia said. "You really should take a load off."

Olivia scampered down the porch steps and plopped back down in the vegetable garden. "Mr. McCoy's gonna show me where he carved your initials in a tree when you were boyfriend and girlfriend."

Shay narrowed a look at Travis. She had a few choice words for Mr. McCoy. But the words would keep till they were inside, out of Olivia's earshot.

Shay jerked the screen door open and hobbled through. Her foot was throbbing like a son of a gun, and she felt like screeching at the top of her lungs. Once inside, she faced him, scowling. "Who do you think you are—"

"Sit down."

"Coming over here, doing my chores, making my daughter promises?"

"Sit down, Shay."

"First of all, the initials are probably long gone—"

"Do I have to pick you up and put you on that couch?"

Fine. She sank onto the sofa and glared. *Happy?*

He pushed over the ottoman, and she propped her splinted foot on it before he could do that for her too. Then he perched on the edge of the recliner.

Her head was beginning to throb now, and she just wanted him gone.

"Actually, our initials are still there, but we have more pressing matters to discuss."

"I can't imagine what."

"I'm sure you can't." He ran a hand over his jaw, his trademark move.

She wondered what was troubling him. Had Olivia done something? Confessed something? She remembered the bike her daughter had stolen the year before and felt a moment's panic. But Olivia had been truly sorry. Shay was sure she'd learned her lesson.

"What's wrong?" she asked.

"Hang on to your hat . . . It's about the Founders Day thing. There was some kind of mistake."

"Founders Day thing?"

"The ceremony."

She thought about the way he'd looked at her at the end of the ceremony. Then she recalled the way his lips had thoroughly ravished her own. Warmth flooded her cheeks.

"It seems we're legally married."

It took a moment for the words to sink in. "What?"

"Our marriage license was there—it blew off the pedestal, remember?"

She shook her head, trying to clear the fog that was closing in.

"Pastor Blevins sent it to the county office by mistake, with a few others he'd found clumped in his Bible—you know how he is."

"What are you saying?"

"I'm saying I got the official certificate in the mail." His gaze went right through her. "We're married, Shay."

It was just a silly mistake. "Well, call and tell them what happened."

"I did. The certificate has been validated and filed."

"Well, tell them to unvalidate it!"

"It doesn't work that way."

She shook her head. "Our license was fourteen years old."

"There's no expiration date on a Wyoming license."

"Well, it's a *Wyoming* license, and the ceremony was in—"

"Wyoming. Bridal Falls, remember?"

"Of course I remember." She rubbed her temple. "This is absurd. There must be something—the whole town was there, and everyone knows it was just—"

"Doesn't matter."

"How could our intentions not matter?" Like she'd ever marry him on purpose. Choose to blend their lives together, to wake up beside him every morning.

That was it. That was their out. "We didn't consummate the vows!" She felt a smile building and looked at Travis.

His gray eyes dimmed, like someone had turned down the lights. "Don't have to be so happy about that."

She realized what she'd said, and her face burned hotter at the thought of him . . . of her . . . of them. She swallowed hard. *Focus, Shay.*

She'd stumbled upon something important. Something vital. Relief flowed through her, making her limbs go weak. "That settles it, then. It's just a matter of going down there and straightening this out."

Travis removed his hat and dangled it between his knees. He rubbed his jaw again.

Then he looked at her. "Wyoming doesn't require vows to be consummated. I turned over

107

every stone, Shay, believe me. I was on the phone with the county office for an hour first thing this morning. Like it or not, we're officially husband and wife."

It couldn't be. It. Could. Not. Be. She shook her head. *Denial*. What she needed here was a little healthy denial.

But the look on Travis's face refuted it. The way he stared calmly at her, as if it were a done deal. As if waiting for that reality to set in for her.

And then it did. It came and sat on her like a two-ton cow.

She was married to Travis at last. It would be funny if it weren't so blame pathetic. Oh, the town would have a heyday with this one. She'd be the butt of every joke from now till Jesus returned.

Now would be good, God. Can You just come back now?

She waited, closed her eyes, just in case her prayer activated the whole end-times sequence.

But no, she was still sitting here, head and foot pounding angrily. She opened her eyes, and there Travis was too. Still looking at her with those deep eyes that saw everything.

A shadow danced across his jaw as he clenched it. In these few moments, she'd been so wrapped up in her own feelings, she hadn't considered his perspective. Not until now.

Her laugh came out harsh, sardonic. "Well, this really blows for you, doesn't it, McCoy. Getting out of wedlock this time is going to be a little harder than putting your truck in gear and heading south. You might have to fill out some paperwork, shell out some money. Oh, and our neighbors! You might have to face them like a man this time. Might have to see them whispering behind their hands and looking at you with pity. These things are public, you know. Even an annulment will be made public—and I'm assuming we qualify for that since we have not and will *never* consummate those stupid vows—"

She didn't run out of steam. She had plenty more to say. But her voice was starting to wobble, and her eyes were starting to burn, and she would not let him see her cry.

Pull it together, Shay. Quick. She swallowed past the fist in her throat and distracted herself by counting the pulse beats in her foot. *Bom-bom. Bom-bom. Bom-bom.*

"I'm really sorry."

"What are you sorry for?" She wasn't so blind with anger that she didn't see he was a victim here too.

"Not about this."

There was a new look on his face, one she hadn't seen before. His eyes turned down at the corners. Sorrow? Frustration? Regret? She couldn't quite put her finger on it.

"I'm sorry about before. Sorry for the embarrassment I caused you. I was young and immature and—"

"Stupid."

A corner of his lip tucked in. "Yeah. Plenty of that."

"A little late for apologies."

"Way overdue."

"Got that right."

So he was sorry. So what? His apology didn't undo the pain and suffering. Didn't change how his bad choices had led to her bad choices.

"How do we get this ridiculous farce-of-a-marriage over with?"

He turned his hat in his hands. Got up, ambled over to the picture window, and looked out over the yard, where her daughter was probably still hunkered over the weed-ridden garden. He crossed his arms, taking his good ol' time. His silhouette was long and sturdy. He was a good six inches taller than Garrett had been. Brawnier.

She looked away.

"How's your foot?"

His question took her aback. "Fine." Maybe not fine, but the pill was starting to kick in. She had to get him out of here before she was slumped over the sofa with drool trickling from her mouth.

"Travis. What do we have to do?"

She wanted to get this over with as quickly and

quietly as possible. Why was he taking all day to answer? Why was he looking out the window as if they had all the time in the world? As if—

He walked back, sat beside her on the sofa this time. Close enough she could smell his shampoo, far enough she couldn't protest.

He turned toward her. "Just hear me out."

She studied his gray eyes. "Why do I get the feeling I'm not going to like this?"

"Got an idea, something that would benefit us both."

That look in his eyes, that expectant tone in his voice . . . it sent dread snaking through her veins.

She shook her head. "No. Whatever it is, no."

"Are you in danger of losing your ranch?"

His gentle tone didn't soften the effect. She wondered if John Oakley had leaked her private business. "My finances are no business of yours, McCoy."

"What if I could help?"

She had her pride. It was about all she had sometimes, but still. "I can manage on my own, thank you." She'd manage all right. In a short time she'd manage herself and Olivia right off the property.

"Where's Beau? I half expected to see him here this morning."

She didn't want to talk about Beau. Not to Travis. "I forgot to call."

"How serious are the two of you?"

"That's your business, how?"

He shrugged. "Wondering how the news of our marriage was going to hit him."

"It's not a marriage, it's a mistake."

"I've got a proposal, Shay."

She tilted her head. "Last one didn't stick too well."

"Just hear me out."

Shay stifled a yawn. Durn pills. She may as well suffer through whatever he had stuck in his craw. That was the only way she was gonna get him out of there.

"Spill it."

He leaned forward, and his hair fell over his forehead. Her fingers twitched with the impulse to reach out and push it back. She knotted her fist.

"You already had your hands pretty full. Now you're under doctor's orders to stay off your foot a week. Even after that, you'll be on crutches awhile."

"Thanks for the recap."

"I have the time and know-how to run things until you're back on your feet."

It was true. She didn't have to like it, but it was true.

"And I'm willing. I also have the wherewithal to carry this place through the summer and beyond. Feed, fencing supplies, groceries, whatever you need."

He had no idea how much she needed and how quickly. "I don't need your money."

That wasn't true. She didn't *want* to need his money.

But she had Olivia to think of. Olivia who needed a roof over her head, Olivia whose jeans were inching farther north each week, Olivia who would need milk money and school supply money and a heated house come fall. But money didn't grow on trees. Shay was fresh out, and no one else was offering.

Still, nothing was free. "What's the catch?"

There was one. She could see it in the way he eyed her warily, as if appraising her readiness to hear whatever he was about to say. The look sped her heart and dried her mouth. Before she could stop him, his words filled the thick space between them.

"I want us to stay married."

13

Shay's head was fuzzy, her thinking cloudy. The pills. She hadn't heard right. He hadn't just suggested they make this marriage real.

"Hear me, Shay? I want us to stay married."

"What the *heck*. Stop saying that."

"Give it five months. Think about it . . . I can fill in around here, relieve you of financial strain, offer some stability for Olivia. Wouldn't it be nice not to worry about money for once?"

"Stop it! What kind of harebrained idea—This was a *mistake*."

"It doesn't have to be."

"You're crazy."

"Am I?"

He had to be. Because from her perspective this seemed awful one-sided. She got the help. She got the money. Maybe he was lonely for a woman and weary of the unwanted strings necessary to get one. Maybe he remembered the chemistry they'd had once upon a time, the sizzle that arced between them whenever they'd touched.

He was out of his mind if he thought she was joining that circus again. She crossed her arms. "What's in it for you, McCoy?"

He looked down at his fingers, toying with the brim of his hat. Then he shot her a look that made her breath catch. That set her veins on fire and weakened her limbs.

"I want another chance, Shay."

Another . . . what? He couldn't mean it that way. Yet he was looking at her like . . .

Worse yet, an invisible force tugged at her heart, trying to convince her to believe something she knew was reckless and foolish. After all he'd done, after all the pain she'd gone through, she had to admit he still had a hold on her.

Travis watched Shay blink once, watched the confusion dance across her face like ripples over a river. He'd made her speechless, not an easy task.

"I know I don't deserve it," he said. "But I'm asking just the same."

Shay sprang to her feet. Then her broken foot hit the floor beside the other. "Blame it!"

Travis stood, reached toward her. "Shay—"

She swatted his hand away and sank back onto the cushions. "Get out."

Her breaths came hard and heavy. Her face was flushed, whether with anger or exertion he wasn't sure. Still, this was the only chance he was going to get.

"Not until I finish."

She shot him a look. Her nose flared.

She was a captive audience if there ever was

one, and she knew it. But maybe a little space was in order. He paced across the room and leaned against the windowsill.

"I'm only asking for five months. I'll run things around here till you're back on your feet. After that we can work side by side. I'll foot the bill—pardon the pun—for anything you need. Anything at all."

Did he sound too desperate? Because he was. He'd take her back at any cost, but he couldn't let her know that.

"What kind of game is this?"

"It's no game, Shay." If she only knew how serious he was. "I have regrets."

He'd already scared the tar out of her. He could see it in her eyes, in the way she'd shot from the sofa. She was as spooked as a cornered cat. Maybe he shouldn't have told her he wanted a second chance. Maybe he should've made something up.

But he wasn't going into this with trickery. He was shooting straight, right from the get-go. If that spooked her, so be it. Lucky for him, she didn't have many options.

"Don't you ever wonder what would've happened if we'd gotten married?" he asked.

"No, I don't."

He hoped that wasn't true. If it was, he really had his work cut out. "Five months. A real effort to make this work."

"And when it doesn't?"

He didn't like her pessimism. "*If* it doesn't . . . I'll leave. I'll give you an annulment—if that's still an option . . ."

She was shaking her head, clutching the pillow against her stomach like her life depended on it. "No."

What did he go and say that for?

"Don't need your answer now. Mull it over." He put his hat on his head.

"Don't need to."

He glanced out the window. "Olivia's 'bout done with the weeding. All right if I keep my promise?"

Her lips pressed together. She was tempted to say no, but she wouldn't. "Fine. Have her back in an hour. And not one word of this."

"Yes, ma'am." He touched the brim of his hat. "Stay off that foot now." He left just in time. The pillow hit the door right behind him.

14

$\mathcal{M}$r. McCoy showed me how to skip rocks."
Olivia moved her bowl closer on the TV
tray. She'd fixed a corn and black bean salad for
them after Shay had insisted that Travis finally
leave.

Shay hadn't had a pain pill in hours, not
wanting to doze off again, but she was taking one
before bed, that was for sure.

"He can make 'em skip, like, ten or twelve
times. I'm not that good yet, but he told me if
you pick a real flat one . . ."

Shay set the fork on her empty plate and
resisted the urge to roll her eyes. All she'd heard
since Olivia had returned was *Mr. McCoy this,
Mr. McCoy that*. She was going to gag at the next
mention of his name.

". . . and Mr. McCoy said . . ."

Heaven help me.

She'd been napping when they returned—
hadn't woken until afternoon. By then Travis had
fixed the corral fence, organized the tack room,
and apparently held the world on its axis.

She couldn't get his offer off her mind, crazy as
it was. She even called the county clerk's office,
making sure it was just as Travis said.

Still, they could file for an annulment. A little
paperwork, a little time, and all this would be

over. Only one thing had stopped her from doing it.

Her ranch. She needed the money and the help. They'd only managed today because of Travis. Her friends had ranches of their own, financial problems of their own. The recession had hit everyone hard.

Everyone except Travis, apparently.

One minute she'd find herself thinking this was the perfect solution. It would give them half a shot at stability, if only for five months. But if she was smart, she could set them up for the future. Could make some investments that would pay dividends down the road and give her enough operating capital to keep things going long term.

Then she'd remember the look in his eyes.

She didn't need that. Didn't want his . . . whatever it was. How could she protect her heart for five long months? Waking to him every morning, working side by side, sitting across from him meal after meal after meal.

And then she'd decided, no. She couldn't do it. Wouldn't risk her heart with a man who'd already cut and run once before. Wouldn't face the whispers when everyone thought they were together again. The looks of pity when—

The lights went out, and the whirring fan of the air conditioner went quiet.

"Mom?"

The tray rattled as Shay set her spoon in her bowl.

"What happened, Mom? It's not storming . . ." Her daughter's voice sounded younger than her years.

Maybe it was a breaker. Or someone hitting a pole. "I'm not sure." Shay pushed her tray back. Who was she kidding? It wasn't a breaker, and there was no accident. "We're a little behind on the electric bill."

And the mortgage. And the phone. And the credit card. Did she really think they wouldn't follow through on their threat to shut it off?

"What are we gonna do?"

Shay had exactly $72.54 in the bank. She was saving that for groceries, but she wondered if it was enough to get the electricity back.

"Let me make a phone call." She pulled out her cell, dialed the number.

Ten minutes later she turned off her phone and set it on the TV tray. Now she had to pay a turn-on fee in addition to her bill. If she'd had the cash for that, wouldn't she have paid it already?

And what about the other bills? What about the mortgage? This was only electricity. What was going to happen when she lost the house too? When the bank came and collected everything they owned to pay back what she owed?

"They shut it off?"

She tried for calm. " 'Fraid so." She'd tried so

hard to shelter Olivia from their financial problems. Intercepting creditor calls, taking them in the other room or just not picking up the phone. But there was no hiding it this time. And there would be no hiding it when they showed up to take the house.

"What're we gonna do?" Olivia asked again.

Shay hated the anxiety that had crept into her daughter's voice, the worry that puckered her brows. "We'll figure something out. God's always taken care of us, hasn't He? We've never gone a day without."

"But what about—"

"Shush. That's Mom's problem. Go on outside and find something to do while I figure this out."

Olivia cleared the plates and then went outside, hopefully forgetting about the fact that her mom couldn't manage things on her own.

Things had never been easy, but she'd spoken the truth. God had always provided. This time, though, Shay wondered if His provision would turn out to be the biggest mistake of her life.

Travis was brushing down Buck when his cell vibrated in his pocket.

"Yeah," he answered.

"All right."

It was Shay, and she didn't sound happy.

"It's a deal."

He lowered the brush as he realized what she

was saying. He didn't question it, knew he'd better accept her consent before she took it back.

"I'll be right over."

"Wait!" Her voice shook on the command. "Some rules first . . ."

"Shoot." Terms didn't matter a lick. He'd agree to anything.

"There'll be no . . . funny business."

His lips twitched. "Not unless you—"

"I *don't*. Another thing . . . when this arrangement ends—"

"*If* this arrangement ends."

"Fine. *If*. It needs to be clear it was my doing, my choice. If everyone thinks our marriage is real—"

"It is real."

"You know what I mean. If they think we're splitting, it was my decision. Understand?"

"I'll take out an ad in the *Moose Creek Chronicle* if you want."

"And I'm keeping my name."

If she wanted to keep that mouthful-of-a-last-name, more power to her.

"I'm only doing this because I'm desperate, you know," she said.

That was a hard kick to the solar plexus. "Now, Shay, don't go flattering."

"This is business. That's all."

Full disclosure, McCoy. "It's business for you, I get that. But you need to understand it's personal for me. As long as we understand each other, I don't see a problem."

The quiet on the other end of the line unsettled him. Maybe full disclosure wasn't such a bright idea.

"Fine."

He couldn't stop the smile. "I'll be right over."

"Hold on. I haven't told Olivia. I'll tell her tonight—and I'm telling her the whole shebang. It's only fair she knows this is temporary. You can come in the morning—and you're sleeping on the sofa."

He'd sleep in the barn if he had to. "Anything else?"

"I'll let you know."

"See you in the morning, then."

"Wait. What are you going to tell your parents?"

"Talked to them this afternoon. I'll keep tabs on the ranch for them. They know about our marriage—said to tell you congrats."

Something like a growl snarled across the line. "Good-bye, McCoy."

"Get used to it, darlin'."

Her answer was a click followed by a dial tone.

15

ravis pulled his truck to Shay's barn and turned off the ignition. It was predawn, and the house lights were off, the property quiet. Home sweet home. At least for the next five months.

He exited the cab and made his way toward the barn on buoyant legs. He loved mornings. The crisp air, the smell of dew. But that wasn't why he could scarcely keep his feet on the ground.

He didn't take this second chance for granted. He'd winged a thousand prayers of gratitude skyward since Shay's call, in between packing his bags and tossing in bed until his alarm sounded.

He entered the barn and flipped the light switch. Nothing. Strange. He felt his way to the tack room and flipped that one. Same thing.

Faulty fuse? Electricity out? It hadn't stormed. There could've been an accident, but he'd had electricity at the Barr M.

Probably just a breaker. He fetched the flashlight in his truck and found the breaker box in the barn. Nothing wrong there. He needed light to work, and the sun wasn't going to hasten its arrival. He wondered where Shay kept her generator.

Travis scanned the barn but didn't see one. He hated to wake her, but chores were waiting.

Making up his mind, he lit out for the house.

The darkened structure took on a new meaning. Electricity probably went out in the middle of the night. Shay's alarm wouldn't have gone off.

He turned off the flashlight as he reached for the doorknob. No sense spooking them. The door was unlocked, just as he expected. If he'd thought the barn was dark, the house was a cave. He closed the door quietly. The air was cool. The girls must be freezing.

Two steps in, a phone pealed loudly. Shay's cell lit up across the room. Maybe it was the electric company. No, not this early.

Between rings, he heard the bedding rustle in Shay's room.

Better answer before Olivia woke too. He started for the phone, bumped his leg on a table, and hobbled the last few steps, biting his tongue.

He grabbed the phone on what felt like the twentieth ring. "Yeah," he said quietly.

No response.

"Hello?" he said, louder.

Across the room, there was an awkward *thump-thump* in the vicinity of Shay's bedroom. He pictured her standing in the doorway, crutched, rumpled, and most likely glaring. No wonder, after the ruckus he'd made.

"Who is this?" a voice demanded. Beau Meyers: the riled version.

Travis walked the phone toward Shay's shadow. "For you."

• • •

What was he doing here, in her house, answering her phone? There was no hiding the lack of electricity now. Of course he had to find out. But she didn't have to like it. And she didn't have to like his waltzing into her place like he owned it and answering her personal phone.

Shay snatched the lit-up cell from his hand. "This is Shay." It came out like a croak.

"Was that *McCoy?*"

Beau. Perfect. She cleared her throat. " 'Morning, Beau."

"Don't *good morning* me, Shay. What's he doing there?"

She shouldered the phone, shut the door firmly, adding a glare she knew Travis couldn't see, and hobbled toward her bed. This was not the way she'd planned to tell Beau. Why hadn't she just broken things off at the picnic? It was all Travis's fault. Blast the man.

"Shay?"

"It's a long story. I was going to tell you."

"By all means, go right ahead."

She couldn't blame him for being sore. She was a lowlife, letting him think there was more to their relationship. Her foot had begun throbbing. She propped it on the bed.

"Shay."

"Sorry. Sorry." She had to collect her thoughts,

ease into this. "Thing is, I broke my foot day before yesterday—"

"Why do you think I called? I had to hear it from Hollis this morning."

Hollis was one of his hands—a real blabbermouth. "I'm sorry."

"I was gonna offer to come feed your animals, but I see you got that covered."

Shay ran a hand over her face. "That was very thoughtful of you."

"What's going on, Shay?"

She should just say it. There was no way to make it easy. "Beau . . . Travis and I are . . . married."

She closed her eyes, trying to block the image that popped into her mind. The hurt she knew was on Beau's face.

"This some kind of joke?" She'd never heard that tone in his voice.

"I'm so sorry, Beau."

"What about us, Shay? I thought . . ."

"I should've told you how I felt. I was wrong." *You are such a heel, Shay.*

"Married."

"The ceremony on Founders Day . . . it was real."

"That was . . . but we . . . what the *heck,* Shay?"

"I know. I know. We were planning to announce it today." Sort of true. It was going to get out anyhow. Especially now. "I'm really sorry, Beau. You don't deserve this. I should've told you sooner."

The door to her room clicked open. Travis. She reached out and pushed it shut.

"This is like a nightmare."

She knew the feeling. "I'm sorry."

"You love him, then?"

Shay bit hard on the inside of her lip. What to say? She didn't love Travis, would not love Travis, but she couldn't admit that.

"You never got over him, did you?"

She wished she could lie about that one. "No." She hated to admit it, even to Beau, though it made the marriage seem authentic.

"I can't believe this is happening."

She knew he was probably pinching the bridge of his nose.

Moments later he gave a resigned sigh. "What can I say? Deep down, I hope you're happy, Shay."

Of course he'd be a gentleman. It only made her feel worse. "Thanks."

A minute later she hung up, her throbbing foot the least of her worries. She deserved her throbbing foot. She deserved to be thumped over the head. She dropped back onto her pillows and threw her arm over her face.

A knock sounded on her door. "Shay?"

"Go away."

The door clicked open anyway, creaking on its hinges. "Everything okay?"

"Peachy."

She had a broken foot, was accidentally married to a man who'd broken her heart, and she was stuck with him for months. She'd just hurt a perfectly nice man, and now Travis was going to find out just how destitute they really were.

"It occurs to me we'll need wedding bands," he said.

She hated to admit it, but he was right. It would seem odd if they didn't. "I'll wear my old one."

"I'll buy new ones."

"No, Travis." Last thing she wanted was his thinking this meant anything. "I'll wear my old one. Can't you borrow one from someplace?"

His long pause exposed his disappointment. "I think my dad has an old one."

"Fine." She wished he'd leave. Why was he still standing there?

"Electricity's out," he said.

Could her day get any worse? "You noticed."

"Tried the breakers in the barn, but they're fine."

"The power company shut it off for lack of payment."

There. She'd said it. She reminded herself that the heat flooding her face wasn't fatal. It only felt like it. At least he couldn't see. Wait till he found out about all the back mortgage payments she owed.

"Oh well, no sweat. I'll take care of that when they open."

Why did he have to be so calm? So darned understanding? It would be easier if he dressed her down. Then she could get mad and slam a door or something.

"In the meantime, I'll get your generator running if you could point the way."

Because every ranch worth its salt has a generator. She exhaled loudly. "Don't have one."

"All right. No problem. I'll run home and get ours."

She was a worm. A worthless, fat, slimy, lowly worm. Wanted to close her eyes and sleep away the next five months.

"You okay? Need your meds?"

"I'm fine. Go get the generator," she said, then realized she sounded like a shrew. "Please."

"Be back soon."

She listened to the sound of his footsteps, the sound of the front door clicking shut. That's exactly what she was afraid of.

16

*W*hat are you doing?"

Shay turned from the kitchen sink where she was washing tomatoes for their dinner salad.

Frowning in the doorway, Travis removed his hat and set down a guitar case. His demanding tone of voice set her on edge.

"Not exactly the 'Honey, I'm home' I expected. What's that thing?"

"I picked up guitar."

Of course he did. She wondered if he'd sit around picking the thing when there was work to be done, the way Garrett had. Wondered if he'd someday lose everyone he loved to music and illusions of stardom.

"You're supposed to be in bed."

Shay adjusted her balance on her new knee walker. "He said to stay off the foot, and I'm off."

Abigail had brought the walker over along with a Crock-Pot full of chicken. Bless the woman.

"Shay, you need your rest."

"We may be stuck together, McCoy, but it's my foot, and I'll do as I please." She resumed chopping the tomato. "Where's Olivia?"

"Washing up. Speaking of which . . ." He held out his hands. A layer of dirt caked his knees, and his hair needed a good washing.

Olivia had only a small bathtub. The only shower in the house was in her master bath. Perfect.

If her sigh sounded put-upon, so be it. "Use mine."

"Don't want to be a bother."

"Olivia has a tub, so unless you want to soak in your own filth every night, my shower it is."

He grabbed his duffel and left the room. Moments later she heard her shower kick on. He was even now dropping his clothes onto her tile, stepping under the spray of *her* shower. This was not good. So not good. How was she going to get through 149 more nights like this?

It would be easier when she could get around again. At least then she wouldn't be trapped. She could go out at night, go over to Abigail's or Aunt Lucy's. Join the bridge club. Play Bingo on Thursdays. She banged her head against the cabinet.

"Where's Travis?"

Shay turned. "You mean Mr. McCoy?"

Olivia ran her fingers through her wet hair. "He said I could call him Travis."

Fine. She supposed there was no reason for formality when they were living together like this. "Can you set the table?"

"Sure."

Her daughter went to work. It had been ages since that table was set for three. When she'd

132

told Olivia the night before about the accidental wedding and their plan, her daughter had surprised her. She'd expected her to be put out. Instead, the girl thought the whole thing was very romantic. Romantic!

Shay couldn't think of a less fitting word. She quickly set Olivia straight, but that hadn't dimmed the girl's enthusiasm. Travis had made quite an impression on her daughter, and Shay didn't like it one bit.

What if Olivia became dependent on him? Started thinking of him as a father figure? It wasn't healthy, that's all there was to it. Yet what choice did she have? It was this or lose the ranch.

She was setting out the ketchup when Travis emerged, damp and musky smelling from his shower, looking too broad and masculine in their little house.

She pulled her eyes away. "Supper's ready."

They sat at the square pine table, Travis taking the seat Garrett used to occupy as if he somehow knew it was the head of household's rightful place. If it bothered Olivia, Shay couldn't tell.

"Travis can pray," Olivia said, linking her hand with Shay's automatically.

Travis extended his hand to her. "Glad to."

She gave him a look—*this means nothing*—as she put her hand in his. His hand engulfed hers. It was warm and slightly damp from his shower. The calluses of his palm were softened from the water, and she was suddenly conscious of her own rough palms. Not the silky smooth skin he was undoubtedly used to on the women he courted.

He's not courting you, Shay.

No, he was only married to her, for pity's sake.

"Dear Lord in heaven," he began, "we thank You for this day and for Your bountiful blessings. We thank You for this fine meal and for the opportunity to renew old friendships."

Old friendships? Shay clenched her teeth.

"Please be with us now and direct our steps, that all we do will bring glory to Your name. We ask this in Your name. Amen."

Shay pulled her hand, and Travis caught her rubbing it down her leg. Let him make of that what he liked. She wanted him under no illusions that they were picking up where they'd left off. Old friendships. Regardless of his intentions, she had a high, thick wall in place, and he wasn't welcome on her side.

Her foot was screaming now. She'd been upright for too long and had forgotten her last dose of meds. And she still needed to address her dire financial situation with Travis. It was shaping up to be a lovely evening.

She poured ketchup on her plate and stabbed a piece of Abigail's chicken.

"You still eat ketchup on everything," Travis said.

"Not everything."

"Just meat," Olivia added. "It's gross when she puts it on turkey. Ick!"

Shay made a face at her daughter.

The meal hit the spot, and by the time Shay finished, she was bone weary. Travis and Olivia had kept up the conversation, but supper was winding down. It wasn't even dark yet, and she longed to turn in. But she had to get her bills paid, especially the mortgage.

"Olivia, do the dishes, please?" she asked.

Her daughter stacked the plates and carried them to the sink with Travis's help.

Shay stood, balancing on the knee walker. A pain shot through her foot all the way to her knee. Where had she put her meds?

Travis was there before she released the brake.

"One or two?" He opened the bottle and shook some out.

"Two."

"Thanks," she said after she downed the pills.

Bed. That's all she wanted. But she might not get another chance to talk to him without Olivia nearby. It was humiliating enough to admit her financial crisis without her daughter knowing too.

"Travis, we need to talk."

"Let's get you settled first."

She followed him to her room, where he pulled back the bedding. "I can settle myself."

"No doubt." He set the pill bottle and water on her table as she lowered her body onto the bed and propped her foot.

She stifled a yawn. "We need to talk about money."

"Tomorrow."

If only it could wait. But the bank was starting foreclosure proceedings as they spoke.

She choked back her pride. "I need to pay the mortgage soon." Like three months ago. "I'm . . . a little behind."

Travis pulled the covers over her. She pushed them back down.

"Relax. I took care of it this afternoon. Went into the bank—you're all paid up. The electric's paid up too. I set up a joint account, and if you tell me where your bills are, I'll get those in the mail tomorrow."

"I can pay my own bills." Okay, so she couldn't really *pay* her own bills, but she wasn't so useless she couldn't sit down with a checkbook and calculator. "I'm not helpless, you know."

He didn't deserve her ire. She should be more grateful. It just rankled to need his money. She'd never get out of this with her dignity intact.

He smiled just a little. "Don't know anyone less helpless than you, Shay."

She had mixed feelings about the joint account. What if she got used to this? When he was gone, the money would go too.

"You don't need to open your wallet like that."

"We're married, after all."

"Well, it's bound to be all over town by now, what with you setting up bank accounts."

His grin broadened. "Fine by me. Can't wait to show off my new bride this weekend."

She nearly groaned. Was it just her, or did her foot seem suddenly too wrecked to even think about leaving the house?

He flipped off the lamp. "Sleep tight."

"Yeah, yeah, whatever." Like she was going to do any sleeping at all with him all stretched out on her couch a mere ten feet away.

17

*W*hy aren't you dressed?" Travis asked as he entered the house.

Shay took in his form, his nice yoked shirt tucked into the narrow waistband of his clean jeans, where a trophy buckle gleamed.

"I am dressed."

"You're wearing pj's to the Fourth of July Festival?"

Shay shifted her foot on the ottoman. "Who said I'm going?"

Travis looked away, offering his profile. The afternoon light filtered through the window and flickered on his clenched jaw. "I get it, Shay. I do." There was some look in his eyes that conflicted with the sharp tone of his voice. "You don't want to be seen with me, but you've been—"

"I have a broken—"

"—hiding in this house all week so you don't have to—"

"I am *not* hiding."

"—face our adoring public. But you can't hole up here for five months."

"It hurts."

"You've been wheeling all over the house on that thing."

Her breath heaved. Her foot did hurt, but she

couldn't deny she'd been up and around. A lot. There were things to do. He was already taking care of the ranch, she wasn't letting him do her laundry and cleaning too.

"I'm tired of explaining to everyone why my wife has yet to make an appearance. They're gonna think I buried you out back or have you stuffed in the attic."

"Ridiculous."

"Seriously." His jaw twitched. "I want you to go with me today."

It wasn't the foot and he knew it. Why was facing everyone so hard? Harder than a broken foot.

"Not up to it yet," she said. "All the people, all the questions. Pretending our marriage is real . . ."

"It *is* real."

Why did he have to be so literal? "You know what I mean."

"I've already answered the questions. All you have to do is show up on my arm." His voice had quieted. A lock of hair fell over his forehead. "Is that so hard?"

The look in his gray eyes . . . cloudy with a chance of pain. She'd hurt his feelings. Seeing him standing there, all masculine and . . . built— she sometimes forgot he had feelings.

Well, this wasn't her fault. This whole marriage thing had been his idea.

"Olivia's waiting outside. She'll be disappointed

if you don't go. And you have to face it sometime. Everyone'll be there. You can get it all over with at once."

There would be a lot going on with the festivities. People would be distracted. Maybe they'd hardly notice she was with Travis.

"Fine." She lowered her foot and shot him a look just so he knew she wasn't happy. "Give me twenty minutes."

The smile on Shay's face felt as fake as the stitched grins on Miss Lucy's dolls. No questions, my foot. *How long has this been going on? Were you corresponding with Travis when he was in Texas? How did you keep such a secret?*

Evening had arrived, and the smell of fried pork and funnel cakes filled the town square. A country-and-western tune blared from the distant stage. Friends and families were spread out across the broad expanse of lawn, crowded around picnic tables and checkered tablecloths. Olivia had taken off with Maddy hours ago, and Shay and Travis hadn't seen the girls since.

They'd been lucky enough to score a picnic table on the town square. At least she'd thought it was luck when Ida Mae and Vern, friends of Miss Lucy's, waved them over twenty minutes earlier.

Now she wasn't so sure. The older woman had been waxing poetic about the wedding

140

reenactment like it was Shay's Cinderella moment. Shay avoided Travis's eyes, wished he weren't sitting across from her.

"And, oh my, that kiss . . ." Ida Mae fanned her pudgy cheeks. "I just knew it was real. I looked right over at Vern and said, 'Vern, that kiss was for real!' I did, just ask him."

"She did," Vern said.

Memories of the kiss surfaced, and Shay felt her face warm. *Do not look.*

She took the last bite of her sandwich. Travis was probably eating up every minute of this bunk. Enjoying her misery. *Do. Not. Look.*

She looked.

His lips twitched, and his eyes sparkled like the fireworks that would go off later on the town square. He took a bite of his sandwich, holding her gaze.

You're enjoying this, aren't you, McCoy?

Every minute, his eyes replied.

"You two always did know how to light up a room," Ida Mae said. "Isn't that something, you being back together. Just goes to show true love never dies. I always say that, don't I, Vern?"

"She does."

"And there is just something about that first love, you know, everyone says so . . ."

Shoot me now.

"The feelin's are so strong, and you got all those hormones humming through your veins . . ." Her

141

jowls shook as she nodded. "Remember that, Vern? All those feelin's?"

"Yep."

Any minute now the woman was going to bring up the past. Shay's hands went clammy in her lap, and she looked around for an escape.

"I can see them in you two clear as a bell, just clear as a bell, always have. I was so surprised when y'all didn't elope. I was there when you stepped off that bus in that pretty little gown, remember, Shay? I took your hand, pulled you right into Pappy's Market, and called your daddy for you—"

Shay popped to her feet, scrambled for the crutches she'd graduated to. "I have to go. The pie bake-off . . ."

Travis abandoned his sandwich and stood. "Right. The bake-off. Pies." He smiled at Ida Mae and Vern. "Thank y'all for sharing your table."

"Our pleasure, kiddos. Best of luck to y'all," Ida Mae called.

Shay struggled across the uneven ground. Travis tried to help, but she shook off his hand.

By the time they finally reached the boardwalk, perspiration dotted her forehead. Her crutches thumped on the planks, interrupted by the step of her good foot. The sun had sunk behind the mountains, and twilight was falling like a hazy curtain.

"You took the bus?" Travis asked.

"How'd you think I got home?"

"I didn't know—"

"That's right, you didn't." He hadn't thought about her at all. Didn't know the first thing about love.

"Why didn't your dad come?"

She gave a harsh laugh. "He said I'd managed a way to Cody and I could manage my own way back. They didn't speak to me for weeks. Wouldn't even let me back in the house. I lived with Miss Lucy for three months, McCoy."

She was just getting warmed up. "And did you realize, while you were busy turning yellow, that you had my belongings in the back of your truck? That I had not a stitch of clothes other than the gown on my back? I had no money, nothing, did you realize that? Did you know I had to beg a stranger for bus fare to get me home?"

He pulled her around a corner, away from the crowded walk. They came to a stop in the long narrow alley between the post office and Pappy's Market. So close to where she'd been unceremoniously deposited that day.

Shay's breath came fast and hard, her hands clenching the handles of the crutches. Travis stood too close, and she fixed her eyes on the pearly buttons of his plaid shirt.

"I'm so sorry."

She could tell he meant it, but it would've been real nice to hear it sooner, like fourteen years ago when she thought he didn't give a flying fig.

"Shay, look at me."

He tipped her chin up, and she let him, though she was sure sparks were shooting from her eyes. What he'd done was inexcusable, and to wait so long to acknowledge her feelings was worse.

"I wish I could do something. I wish I could make it up to you."

He had all kinds of regret in his eyes. That stubborn lock of hair protruded from under his hat, falling across his forehead and tangling with his lashes. His eyes were bold, almost burning her with intensity.

She lowered her gaze, following the straight line of his nose. A fine layer of stubble covered his upper lip and jaw. Her fingers twitched with the desire to feel its roughness against her skin.

The familiarity of him made it way too easy to slip right back into their old roles.

Drat the man. He was too darn handsome for his own good.

She was suddenly weary. So tired. Today had been wearing. She closed her eyes and leaned against the wood siding.

"We should get you off your feet. Let's find a seat for the fireworks."

The thought of more people, more questions,

was overwhelming. "I want to go home, Travis. I'm so tired . . ." Of being married. Of people staring. Of fighting the pull of Travis McCoy.

"I have the perfect spot. No people, just wide-open sky. You can lie down and watch in peace. I promise."

Like she'd get any rest with Travis stretched out beside her. Sleep had been nothing but fitful since his arrival. Maybe that's why she was so worn out.

"Come on, Shay . . . I haven't seen Moose Creek's display for years. I've missed it."

At the tone in his voice, she opened her eyes and fell right into his. *I've missed you,* they seemed to say.

"What d'ya say? I'll call Wade and ask them to bring Olivia home after the show."

Wasn't like Shay could drive herself home. "Fine, whatever."

Several minutes later they were pulling into her long drive. "I thought we were—"

"Shh." A hundred yards into the drive he eased the truck to a stop, put it in park, and shut off the engine. "Wait here."

Like she had a choice. She heard him fumbling around in the bed of the truck and then her door was opening.

She turned on the seat, but he was empty-handed. "My crutches?"

He turned his back to her. "Hop on."

Wrap her arms around his neck? Her legs around his waist? It was the last thing she wanted to do.

He backed his tush up to the seat, and she fought the urge to scoot away.

"Sometime tonight?"

"How far we going?"

"Five whole feet to the back of the truck. Come on, night's a-wasting."

Just around to the back. A three-second ride was all.

She huffed, then put her hands on his shoulders and curled her legs around his middle, attaching herself to him like an awkward backpack. "Just so you know, I'd rather be in bed."

"Music to my ears, darlin'." He bumped the door closed with his knee.

She thumped him on the back of the head, and his hat fell to the ground. He just chuckled and hitched her higher.

Up close, she could smell the faint hint of musk, feel the warmth of his back against her belly, the strength of his shoulders under her. He'd always been strong and capable. And protective. He'd gotten in a brawl over her their senior year when Zack Torrell cornered her by the boys' locker room.

A second later he was lowering her onto the tailgate. She inched back over what felt like a lumpy sleeping bag.

"Go ahead, get comfy. We should have a perfect view."

She lay down, clasped her hands on her stomach while he retrieved his hat. Overhead, stars flickered in the velvety night sky like a million fireflies. They already had a perfect view. The air smelled of sweet hay, and grasshoppers chirped their high-pitched calls. A light breeze blew, rustling the tall grass.

The truck dipped as Travis hopped in. He settled beside her, his movements loud and clanging against the hollow floor of the truck. His body was a hair's breadth from hers. The warmth of his arm brushed hers. The truck seemed narrow as a twin bed. She could feel her heart thumping against the metal floor and wondered if she was imagining the vibrations.

It was surreal, being here with him. A month ago he'd been a distant memory, and a bad one at that.

Come on, Shay, that's not quite true.

He'd been her best friend. They'd spent hours together fishing, laughing, talking. And little by little, she'd fallen in love with him. She'd kept her feelings to herself, sure he liked Marla Jenkins, not her. But then she'd dared him to kiss her that day in her parents' barn and had walked away with more than she'd bargained for.

"Wasn't so bad, was it?" His voice was low and quiet under the moonlit night.

"What?"

"Today, being together."

She turned her head. "You kidding me? I feel like I've been through a shredder."

"They're just curious."

"Do you have any idea how many questions I fielded today? God only knows what they really think. Folks never say what's really on their minds."

"Who cares what people think?"

She scowled in the darkness. "Easy for you to say."

He looked at her. "What's that mean?"

Could he really not know? His face was too shadowed to read. She looked away. "Never mind."

How could he understand? He'd never worn secondhand clothes or had to borrow textbooks from friends. He'd never worn boots until they squeezed his toes or rolled up his shirtsleeves to hide how short they'd gotten.

The fireworks began, a starburst of red exploding overhead, followed by white fizzles of light. She was grateful for the interruption.

Everything came so easily for Travis. He was the Golden Boy. Always had been and always would be. She didn't resent him for it, but it kept him from understanding the likes of her.

"You still don't understand," he said.

She looked at him. "*I* don't understand?"

"That's right, you."

She wished she could see his face.

"You never understood how special you are."

She pressed her lips together and stared at the sky. Oh yeah, she was special. So special he'd ditched her in favor of a dusty ride to Texas. Or had he forgotten?

Green and white bloomed overhead.

"What was your husband like?"

The question, coming out of nowhere, took her aback. "None of your business."

Two booms followed, and a slow-burning sizzle filled the silence.

"Fair enough." He clasped his hands under his head. His elbow rested against the top of her head.

"I almost came back, you know. Six months later."

Six months. She'd just gotten married. "Oh?"

"Took me awhile to realize what I'd left, Shay, but not fourteen years."

She tried to swallow and found her throat dry. Her heart echoed the booms of the fireworks. "What changed your mind?"

"My folks told me you were married."

She'd wondered at the time if he knew—when he'd found out and how. Funny thing was, she'd convinced herself he wouldn't care. But he made it sound like he did. She wondered what would've happened if she hadn't married Garrett. Was Travis saying he would've come back?

"In the back of my mind, when I left, I thought we'd be together someday."

She humphed, barely a sound.

"Arrogant, I know. To think I could just drop you and get you back again at my own whim."

"Blame right."

"Well, I didn't expect you to fall right into some other guy's arms."

Who did he think he was?

"You leave a girl at the altar and she's free to fall into whoever's arms she wants." Never mind that she'd been completely humiliated. Of course she'd snatch up the first attention thrown her way, try to prove to everyone she was worthy of a man's love.

"Yeah, well, he's gone, and you're stuck with me now."

"Stuck is exactly the right word."

And yes, Garrett was gone, as Travis so bluntly pointed out. He didn't have to remind her of that. She and Olivia had hardly had time to grieve Garrett's desertion before they were hit with his death. Olivia slept in Shay's bed for almost eighteen months, and Shay wondered if her daughter feared she would leave her too. She held on to her extra tight through those months and begged God for strength to get them through.

They watched the fireworks in silence for five minutes, ten, awkwardness hanging around them like a heavy summer fog.

Her phone buzzed in her pocket. Probably Olivia. She shimmied it out and looked at the screen.

Beau. Could this night get any worse? She'd seen him today from a distance and had managed to steer Travis a different direction. She shut off the ringer and pocketed the phone.

"Not gonna answer?"

"Nope."

The fireworks picked up overhead, colorful blooms with thunderous booms and pops. The sounds ricocheted off the mountains. She'd never been so glad to see the finale.

"Was it Meyers?"

She sighed. What business was it of his? It was her phone, her life.

"He has no business calling you."

For pity's sake. "Just a phone call, Travis."

"You're a married woman."

"Barely."

"Can't be barely married—you either are or you're not—and I have a certificate that says we are."

The fireworks fizzled to nothing but darkness and silence.

"It's over." Relieved, Shay sat up and inched toward the tailgate, but not before Travis's quiet response reached her ears.

"Not by a long shot."

18

*S*hay hobbled to the kitchen for water. After the fireworks Travis had gone to check on a sick mare. Shay was glad for the reprieve and thankful when Olivia returned, though her daughter went straight to her room.

Shay filled a sipper cup and put the lid on tight so she didn't spill it as she hobbled to her room. She was crossing the kitchen threshold when she heard something.

She paused.

A sniffling sound came from the direction of Olivia's room. Was she catching a summer cold? Developing allergies? Another sniffle, this one with the unmistakable shuddering that resulted from a good cry.

Shay set down her water, shuffled to her daughter's door, and tapped lightly. "Olivia?"

The sniffling stopped, and a beat of silence filled the house.

"What?"

"Can I come in?"

Shay heard only the ticking of the wall clock and distant booms from a private Fourth of July celebration. "I know you're crying." She opened the door.

Olivia sat on the bed, cradling her pillow. Her nose was red, her eyes glassy.

Shay eased down on the edge of the bed and propped her crutches against the nightstand. "What's wrong, hon?"

Olivia swiped her hand across her face. "Nothing."

"Come on now. You're not one to cry over nothing." She wondered if the girls had gotten into an argument and said hurtful things. It would be a first.

Olivia tossed her hair, her eyes shooting fire. "It's that stupid Katy O'Neil and her sidekicks!" Angry tears coursed down her face.

"What happened?" Shay rubbed Olivia's arm.

"Me and Maddy were just playing with some sparklers Abigail gave us, you know, over by the playground area before the show." She took a shuddery breath. "We were just minding our own business, and Katy started making fun of me."

"What did she say?"

New tears filled Olivia's eyes. "She said I dress like a hobo! All her friends started calling me Olivia Hoboberger!" Olivia cradled her face and sobbed into her hands.

Shay's stomach bottomed out. It was all her fault. She hadn't provided Olivia with all the things the other girls had.

"She asked if I shop at the Goodwill." Olivia raised her face, and the hurt in her eyes about killed Shay. "It's not fair! She thinks she's so hot just because her dad's rich."

It wasn't fair. The injustice of it made Shay's stomach tighten into a hard knot. "What did you do?"

"Maddy told her to be quiet, but Katy wouldn't. She came closer, calling me that name, and I shoved her right on her rear end!"

Shay pursed her lips, holding back a smile. Part of her was glad Olivia had stood up for herself. "Do you think that was wise?"

"It was self-defense—even Maddy said so."

"What happened next?"

Olivia shrugged, wiping her tears. "The fireworks started, and those stupid girls left."

Shay hated seeing her daughter hurt. It made her feel helpless, just like when Garrett had left.

But she wasn't helpless now. She had money in the bank, at least for a while. She could buy Olivia new clothes—could buy her a whole new wardrobe if she wanted. She hated using Travis's money. But it was part of the agreement, and no one had twisted his arm. Besides, one day she'd pay him back. She was set on that.

"I'm sorry, munchkin. Those girls had no right saying that or being mean. You're twice the person Katy O'Neil is, and you have a great friend in Maddy."

"I know." She sniffled.

"No more fretting, okay?" Shay wiped Olivia's face dry. "Try to get some sleep now."

"All right." Olivia slid down on the bed.

Shay tucked her in, pecked her on the cheek, and gathered her crutches before leaving the room. When she entered the living room, Travis was picking out a tune on his guitar.

He stopped when she entered. "What's wrong?"

Shay shuffled to the end table beside him and collected her water. "Some girls tonight—they teased Olivia about her clothes."

Dashes formed between his eyes. "What about 'em?"

"Well, they're not exactly . . ." Shay searched for the name of a fancy brand and came up empty. "They're not what the popular girls are wearing. I'm taking her shopping this weekend."

Travis picked a couple more notes. "They seem fine to me."

Shay pursed her lips. Of course he'd say that. He'd had all the nice clothes he'd wanted when he was a child. Besides, he was a man. "You wouldn't understand."

"Olivia's a smart and loving girl. She's got everything that matters. 'Sides, kids are always gonna find something to pick on."

Shay shifted her weight. "She is smart and loving, but know what? If I can do this one little thing to make life easier, I'm gonna do it."

"I understand your wanting to fix things, but do you think that's wise?"

He was advising her on parenting matters? Did

155

he really think he knew best? Or maybe it was the money.

"Fine. I'll sell a cow and *then* take her shopping."

"That's not what I meant, Shay. You don't want her thinking her worth comes from clothes. Or that those girls' opinions really matter."

"Of course they matter. Were you ever a teenager? I'm taking her shopping."

Their eyes held for a long minute, then finally he nodded. "By all means use the money in your account. It's at your disposal, as promised."

Naturally he wouldn't see her side. But how could he know how hard it was to have so little? Shay turned toward the bedroom, already planning their trip to Bozeman on Saturday.

19

$\mathcal{S}$he's looking real good." Travis squatted down on the mound of fresh straw where Olivia was bottle-feeding a calf. Maddy sat at the other end, stroking the cow's hide.

"I think so too," Olivia said. She and her mom had spent the day in Bozeman shopping. Now Olivia wore a new pair of jeans with fancy stitching on the pockets and a robin's-egg blue scoop-neck blouse with a white shirt peeking out at the neckline.

The calf rolled its eyes up toward Olivia, and Maddy smiled. "She thinks you're her mama. Don't you, Cocoa?"

"I think you're right, Maddy. Doing a fine job, Olivia." Travis rumpled her hair, and she gave him a shy smile.

Travis had grown fond of her in the two and a half weeks he'd been at Shay's. She ate up his attention, and she was a good kid, respectful and helpful. Regardless of what she wore.

"Yoo-hoo!" a female voice called from the yard. "Time to go, girls!"

"Abigail's taking us to the Chuckwagon." Olivia eyed the half-full bottle and then looked at Travis.

"Go on. I'll finish up."

"Thanks, Travis!"

"Have fun, girls." He lowered himself in the hay, listening to their giddy laughter. He wished he could take Shay to the Chuckwagon tonight. Dancing was out, but she was gonna go stir crazy if she didn't get out again soon.

He offered the bottle, and the calf sucked vigorously. "Greedy little thing, aren't you?"

A shadow fell in the doorway. He looked up to see Abigail standing there, her arms crossed.

"Afternoon, Travis."

"Howdy. Glad you stopped in to see Shay. She needed the company."

"She's bored all right." Abigail leaned against the door frame.

"Not easy for her, staying put. I think she gets lonesome."

She nodded. He got the feeling she had something to say, though he couldn't imagine what.

"Wade all right?" he asked.

"Just fine. We're taking the girls to the Chuckwagon."

"So Olivia said."

That meant a whole evening alone with Shay. He'd look forward to it if she weren't so prickly. She'd probably lock herself in her room with a book all night just to avoid him.

"Look, I'll just get right to the point," Abigail said. "I'm worried about Shay."

He frowned. He'd wondered if Dr. Garvin had

really promoted her to crutches after her last appointment. "Her foot hurting?"

"It's not her foot I'm worried about. What are your intentions here, Travis?"

"Beg pardon?"

"First thing I hear she broke her foot, then I find out you've had some kind of accidental marriage, and now you're here 24-7, pretending to be her doting husband. No offense, but from what I hear, you weren't too interested last time."

"My intentions are honorable, Abigail."

"Wade seems to think you're a decent guy. Maybe it's my journalism background, but I require a little more evidence—especially when things are so lopsided."

The calf emptied the bottle, and Travis stood, glad to be on even ground with Abigail. "Not following."

"Shay's getting a pretty sweet deal here. Someone doing all her work while her foot heals, watching over Olivia, and apparently helping her out financially too . . . ?"

If she was fishing for information, she was wasting her time. If Shay'd wanted her friend to know the details, she would've told her.

"Obviously you're under no obligation to tell me a thing, but I can't help but wonder what's in it for you."

"What's in it for me."

Abigail raised a brow. She wasn't feisty in the way Shay was, just direct. Despite his discomfort, he was glad Shay had a friend like this in her corner.

Hadn't Shay told Abigail why he was doing this? Or did Abigail not buy in? "Shay knows the answer to that."

"You love her."

He felt heat rise on his neck and he rubbed his jaw. He'd never used that word, exactly. Maybe it was true—okay, it *was* true—but a guy liked to keep a few cards to himself. A cowboy had his pride.

"That so hard to believe?"

"You don't exactly have the best track record."

He was a little tired of his past hanging over his head, following him around like an ugly storm cloud. "Give me a break. I was eighteen, a kid."

"You hurt her."

"Think I don't know that? I lost the best thing I ever had, lost her to another man for fourteen years. I come back here thinking I might finally have a chance to win her back, and I end up accidentally married to her. So if you think I'm taking advantage of that, if it seems like I'm taking my best shot at getting her back, you'd be right. If that makes me the bad guy, so be it."

He tipped his hat back and pocketed his hands while Abigail seemed to assess his words.

"Mom, let's go!" Maddy called from the yard.

Travis remembered what Shay had told him. How Wade had hired Abigail as Maddy's nanny last summer, how they'd fallen in love against all odds. Now they were married, and Maddy was calling her Mom. He only wanted what Abigail had found for herself. He wondered if the woman saw the parallel.

She straightened, tossed her blond hair over her shoulder. The look in her eyes assured him she was every bit as astute as he imagined.

"I just want what's best for her."

"Then that makes two of us."

She regarded him an extra second before she gave a nod and left the barn. She was a tough cookie, a skeptic despite her own happy ending with Wade. But Abigail wasn't the one he had to convince.

Shay felt like crying. The brief visit with her friend had been the highlight of her week. She was bored out of her skull sitting around this house day after day while Travis fed her stock, rode her circle, mended her fences.

She pulled herself upright and hobbled on her crutches to the window where a plume of dust billowed behind Abigail's car. And there went her daughter, off for a fun night. Shay liked the way Olivia's new clothes looked on her, the way they made her carry herself differently.

She didn't fault Olivia for getting out of Dodge. She'd go herself if she didn't think Travis would be right behind her, hand on the small of her back. All her elderly neighbors would cluck over what a sweet couple they made while everyone else laid down bets on how long it would be before she sent Travis running for the hills.

One thing was sure: she had a long night ahead of her. Olivia would be out late, and the house was going to seem small and quiet with just Travis and her filling it up. What had she been thinking, letting Olivia go out?

She heard the back door open and shut.

"Got an idea," Travis called from the kitchen.

"No." If he thought he was taking her out tonight, he had another think coming.

"Shoot, woman, hear me out. Fishing. Bass are biting up by Boulder Pass."

She hadn't fished in a month of Sundays. "Says who?"

"Jacob Whitehorse." Travis appeared in the doorway between the kitchen and living room. "Said he took home enough for a week of suppers. What d'ya say?"

It was tempting, but as her eyes lingered on his sturdy form, she realized the last thing she needed was an outing with Travis. She faced the window. "Why don't you go on? It's too hard to get around."

"Not leaving you here alone. Come on, I'll help. You need out of this house. Can't tell me you're not getting restless."

If they had to be alone, she'd just as soon be outdoors than trapped in the house with nothing to do but stare at each other.

"Fine. Abigail brought sandwiches for supper."

"We'll take 'em with us. Wait here and I'll load the gear."

Twenty minutes later they were pulling up to the Yellowstone River in Travis's pickup. Travis had stopped at Jacob's house to bum fishing worms and check on his parents' ranch.

Now he parked under a mammoth oak tree, a stone's throw from the shore, and got out of the cab. "Be right back."

Shay opened her door to let the breeze in while he removed their supplies. She hated this helplessness. She wanted to get her own tackle and food, but the frustrating fact was, she couldn't even get herself to the shore without help.

Travis fetched her crutches, and she worked her way carefully through the tall grass to the bank where he'd spread a large sleeping bag. The sack of food Abigail had brought was dead center, and they wasted no time digging in. Travis had remembered the ketchup, and Shay added it to her turkey sandwich.

"Olivia looks real pretty in her new clothes,"

he said. "She showed me everything you got her."

She couldn't tell if he was conceding that she was right or hinting that she'd spent too much. "Got some great bargains, even at the fancy stores."

"Wasn't worried about that."

Maybe he was only making conversation.

Fifteen minutes later, after they cast their lines into the deep pool of water, she broke the silence. "Heard from your parents?"

"They called last week. Mom's helping with children and Dad's building a new church. They're right where they're supposed to be."

"Mission trips can really change people." Her line had drifted too far, so she reeled in.

"They sound pretty excited about what God's doing down there. Tried to call Dad a couple times this week, but I guess reception's spotty. Have a question about his books, so hope he calls soon."

Travis's bait was drifting fast. He jerked the pole and reeled in a smallmouth.

"Nice." Her own line was as still as an August morning.

He removed the hook and strung up the fish before rebaiting his hook and recasting. "I'm enjoying working your spread, Shay. You've got a nice piece of property."

"My grandparents thought so."

"All those springs and river frontage—prime piece of land."

A quiet moment passed.

When her line drifted too far, she reeled in.

"Mind if I ask you something?" he asked after she recasted, hitting a prime spot.

"Guess not." She felt him looking at her.

"What happened between you and your ex? I mean, did you just grow apart or . . . ?"

Shay shrugged. "We were a bad match from the start. Tried to make the best of it but—well, in the end, he went off to chase his dream of stardom. Never got far."

"I'm sorry. That must've been rough on you and Olivia both."

She tightened her line. "It was, but at least we had each other. God brought us through."

They settled into a thoughtful silence, adjusting their lines and soaking in the peace and quiet.

"Man, I've missed this place." Travis drew in a deep breath of the pine-scented air. "Doesn't smell like this in Texas, let me tell you." He scanned the distant Absaroka Range. "Missed those too."

Shay followed his gaze to the mountains, majestic beasts jutting up from Paradise Valley, painted dusky purple by the evening light.

He may have missed Moose Creek, but not enough to return. It was a point of contention that he hadn't, even if she had been married.

"Missed the people," he said. "Jacob, Miss Lucy, even people I thought I'd never miss."

"Like who?"

The corner of his mouth tipped. "Oh, you know . . ." He switched to a high-pitched twang. "Like, oh my, Ida Mae Perkins. Isn't that right, Vern?"

She smiled. She'd forgotten his talent for impersonations. Once Mr. Orenbeck, their algebra teacher, had interrupted a disturbingly accurate imitation of himself. Travis had spent the afternoon in detention.

"Or our favorite banker," Travis said in a familiar nasal tone. "John Oakley."

Shay laughed. "That was dead-on." Her line began drifting and she tightened it.

"Should've heard him when I paid up your mortgage." He switched to the nasal tone. "Shay's mortgage? Shay Brandenberger? You're what? *Married?*" Travis poked up a pair of invisible spectacles. "Priceless."

Shay laughed at his facial expression, so John-like. "Wish I'd been there. Just to see the look on his face."

"Think he was hoping to rip the ranch out from under you. Little weasel."

"Wouldn't doubt it."

And if she didn't come up with some kind of plan, the man might still have his way. She was going to line up another job after Travis left. She couldn't let the debt pile up like it had before. Next time God might not send a miracle her way.

She felt the weight of a fish on her line and gave the pole a sharp tug. "Got him."

Seconds later she was removing the hook from another smallmouth bass. "I do believe it's bigger than yours, McCoy."

"Night's young, Miss Smarty-pants. In fact, I'm so certain of my fishing prowess, what d'ya say loser cleans and cooks?"

"I say you're on."

Despite Travis's bluster, an hour and a half later when they were bumping home in the truck, it was Shay's string that held more fish, including the largest bass caught.

Shay leaned back against the worn leather seat. "Yep, looking forward to some nice fresh-cooked fish tomorrow night."

Travis scowled. "You never were a gracious winner."

Her lips curled. "And you always were a sore loser."

He humphed. "Like when?"

"Like when you had a conniption over that stupid bottle game at the festival." It had been the summer of their junior year.

"That ring was over the bottle."

"Not the *whole* bottle."

"Well, that's not what Riley Raines said." He

imitated the deep, slow drawl. "Just get the ring 'round the bottle and win yer lady a prize."

Shay chuckled, remembering the brawl that ensued. "Yeah, you got me a prize all right." Shay had stepped between the two boys, trying to break it up, and had walked away with a shiner.

Travis winced. "I was a real knucklehead, wasn't I."

It was humorous in retrospect, though her parents sure hadn't thought so at the time. Travis had fetched a bag of ice from the lemonade stand and held it to her eye in the back of his pickup while they listened to the band play on the town square.

"You had your moments," she said.

And that was God's honest truth. He'd had a way of making her feel like she was one in a million. And his skills in the kissing arena had never been lacking. A fact that hadn't changed, she thought, recalling their wedding kiss.

"I missed you most of all, you know," he said. "You were my best friend."

She felt more than saw Travis looking her way. She wasn't going to look. Wasn't going to take another ride down Memory Lane and ruin the easy companionship they'd found.

"More'n that, of course," he said. "But always my best friend. I could tell you anything."

They'd shared so many secrets, things they'd never told anyone else.

Gravel popped under the tires as he pulled into the drive.

"I enjoyed tonight," he said. "Just being with you, it was almost like old times."

It had been pleasant, once she'd relaxed. He was fun to be with, easy to be with. She'd forgotten that.

"Go to church with us tomorrow?" he asked a minute later as he put the truck in park and shut off the engine.

She'd already made an appearance at the festival earlier in the week. And now that she was mobile, there was no excuse. It was just that she dreaded seeing Beau. And folks at church probably thought she and Beau had been closer than they actually were—Beau had a tendency to exaggerate their relationship. Did they think she'd done him wrong? Would they hold that against her?

"Have to face him sometime," he said as if reading her thoughts. "He ever call back?"

If there was any rancor in his tone, she didn't hear it. "No. But there'll be no avoiding him at church."

Or anyone else. Travis was right, though. She had to face him eventually. Besides, she'd missed church. Singing as a congregation, Pastor Blevins's thoughtful sermons . . .

"I'll go," she said, then wondered suddenly about Travis's life in Texas and the string of women he'd probably left behind. "You haven't mentioned leaving a broken heart in Texas. There some girlfriend you devastated with news of our accidental vows?"

"Nope. No one in Texas, or anywhere else for that matter." He started to say something, then seemed to change his mind. "Part of me pities Beau. I know what it's like, losing you."

She worked to steady her breath, reminded herself it had been Travis who left, his decision. But maybe he had grown up. Least she could do was lower her wall of righteous indignation enough for a little peace to flow across. It would be a long five months otherwise.

Travis exited the truck and brought her crutches around. On the porch, he opened the front door and she hobbled through. She checked the time as a yawn escaped. It was early, but her eyes felt heavy, her body worn from the crutches. Olivia wouldn't be home for a couple hours.

"You're tired," he said. "Go on to bed."

His words prompted another yawn. "Need to wait up for Olivia."

"I'll do it." He emptied his pockets on the end table that had become his nightstand. "Have a passel of fish to clean anyway." The corner of his lip hitched up.

She hesitated in the middle of the room.

"Go on. I'll be up late." He looked unbothered

170

in the dim room, the lamplight casting a yellow glow over his features.

"Okay. Thanks." She shuffled toward her room.

" 'Night," he called.

Once in her room, she closed the door and washed up. His toothbrush and standard black comb sat beside her own toiletries.

Tonight had given her hope. Maybe he had grown up, learned a thing or two over the years. Maybe it was time to put the past behind her. Maybe they could live in harmony for the next several months. If she could just ignore the chemistry and block out his handsome face, maybe they could manage a cautious friendship.

20

*S*hay was trying hard to focus on Pastor Blevins's words, but it wasn't easy. Every minute, someone was turning to look at her. She didn't take her eyes off the pastor's round face, but she could feel their stares.

Her cheeks heated and her insides churned. Suddenly she didn't want to be in church anymore. But Travis had driven them, and he wasn't going anywhere. He was scrawling notes as fast as he could write, oblivious to her anxiety.

She felt the eyes of Beau's best friend burning into her temple. The thought of facing Beau after church in front of his friends gave her palpitations. She had to get out of there. She gathered her crutches, thankful Travis had chosen the back row.

Travis took her arm. "You okay?" he whispered.

She nodded, avoiding his eyes, and hobbled out. Her crutch knocked into the pew's arm, and the loud clatter carried through the open sanctuary.

Her face burned. When she reached the vestibule, she made a quick decision to hole up in the ladies' room. It was too hot outside, and Travis had the truck keys.

She clambered through the restroom's swinging door and had no sooner lowered herself into the sole chair than the door opened. She breathed a sigh when she saw it was only Olivia.

"Travis said I should make sure you're okay." The door eased closed behind her.

"I'm fine." Shay's words wobbled. She cleared her throat. "Just . . . I just needed a break from . . . from people."

Olivia's brows furrowed. Of course she didn't understand.

"It's complicated. I just know what everyone's thinking, what with Beau and I having dated so recently, and now I'm suddenly married to Travis . . . They must think I'm a real jerk. I just couldn't take the looks a minute longer."

"I didn't see anyone looking."

"Yeah?" Maybe she'd made too much of nothing. But then again, Olivia was only twelve and in her own world. "Maybe you're right. But I'm going to stay parked right here till it's over. Why don't you go back to your seat and let Travis know everything's hunky-dory."

"Okay."

Once Olivia left, Shay cleaned out her purse. By the time she was finished she heard the organ strains of "Just as I Am." Several moments later a teenaged girl burst through the door. Shay gathered her crutches, then reached for the door. Hopefully she could make it to the car without any run-ins, and hopefully Travis wouldn't dawdle.

She struggled through the heavy door and came face-to-face with Beau.

"Shay."

"Hi, Beau." She looked for an escape, but he had cornered her between the ladies' room and the drinking fountain.

"Go to lunch with me?" He crunched the brim of his hat in his fingers. "Give me half an hour."

"I'm sorry, but I can't do that. I have to go." Shay tried to hobble around him, but he blocked her path.

"Come on, Shay. I deserve half an hour, don't I? After all we were to each other? I don't understand how you could up and marry him."

She winced at the hurt in his eyes. "I'm really sorry, Beau, but I *did* marry him, and that's all that—"

"Makes no sense." His brows lowered. "You were with *me* after the wedding. Explain that."

He was right. There was no explanation. "I'm sorry." She tried to pass.

Beau took her arm, and she wobbled on her crutches. "Answer me, Shay."

"Let her go, Meyers." Travis was suddenly there, towering over both of them. His tone brooked no argument, and his face was taut.

"I'm fine." She pulled her arm from Beau. "We were just wrapping up."

Beau pulled himself upright, glaring at Travis as Shay shuffled past.

She prayed he wouldn't do something harebrained. Last thing they needed was a brawl in the church vestibule.

They were in the truck before Travis spoke again. He ran his hand over his jaw before turning the key. "He does that again, I'll knock him into tomorrow."

"We haven't even left the church parking lot. Didn't you hear Pastor's message?"

"Didn't Beau?"

Between them, Olivia chuckled. "He was loving his neighbor, all right."

Shay smothered a laugh, then glanced at Travis.

He looked torn between anger and humor. "Yeah, well, he'd better find another neighbor to love. This one's my wife."

"Who can take care of herself," she said, though something pleasant bloomed inside at his words. She wouldn't think too hard about what it was or why it made her feel good.

Maybe Beau would leave her alone now. If he knew what was good for him. She didn't doubt Travis would back his threat with action. He had that protective instinct—even if he was only protecting what he considered his property.

"At least this first time is out of the way," she said. "Hopefully it'll get easier."

"I'd forgotten about your voice," Travis said. "You sing like an angel."

She laughed, but it came out a snort. He'd stood close enough to hear, that was for sure.

"Just say 'thank you,' Mom, like you tell me."

"Thank you," she said with a touch of sarcasm.

"Maybe we can do a duet in church sometime. I'll play guitar and you can sing."

So *not going to happen*. "Uh-huh."

"I'm starving," Olivia said. "What's for dinner?"

"Was thinking about grilling those fish up now instead of waiting for supper. What d'ya think, Olivia?"

"Yum! Will it take long? I'm starving."

"Not if you help."

"Deal!"

Twenty minutes later Travis stood over the hot grill with Olivia, basting the fish with something he'd concocted in the kitchen. Shay watched through the patio door. He was letting Olivia baste now.

Shay set the table and poured three lemonades. When she was done, she checked on Travis and Olivia. The grill was closed, and she spotted the two squatting in the yard by Olivia's upside-down bike. The chain had been falling off lately.

Shay's foot was aching, so she headed to the living room where she sat and propped it on the ottoman. The sofa smelled like Travis now. The pillow at the other end still bore the indentation from his head. On the floor, he'd left his white socks, rolled into balls, and this week's *Moose Creek Chronicle*, open to the crossword puzzle, which he'd helped himself to.

His phone buzzed on the end table beside her. She'd never make it to the door before it stopped. She checked the caller ID and saw an unfamiliar area code. Must be his parents. He wouldn't want to miss the call—he'd said just yesterday he needed to reach his dad.

Shay pushed Talk, eager to greet the McCoys. They'd always treated her like their own daughter.

"Travis's phone."

Silence.

Maybe it was a bad connection. But no, she could hear a country melody, "Party for Two," in the background, clear as a bell.

"Hello?" she said.

Still nothing but music. "Anyone there?"

"Who is this?" a female voice asked.

Shay frowned. "Who's calling?"

"This is Ella. Who's this?"

Ella? The call must be from Texas, she deducted, based on the woman's drawl and unfamiliar area code. And judging by her churlish tone, she wasn't happy another woman had answered.

"Shay Brandenberger . . ." She had the petty urge to add *his wife,* but that wasn't her place. "Travis is busy, but I'll tell him you called," she said, after trying to explain why she'd answered his phone.

"Don't bother. I'll call back."

A click sounded in Shay's ear, and she turned off the phone, frowning. The woman was obviously riled. But why would she be—hadn't Travis said last night that he'd left no one behind in Texas? She had a feeling Ella might beg to differ. And was clearly unaware of their marriage.

It's not real, Shay. Do not forget that.

But if Travis was going to go all Rambo on Beau, didn't Shay have the right to expect loyalty? Or at the very least, honesty?

But candor had never been Travis's strong suit, had it? Hadn't he kept all his real feelings bottled up for three months while they planned their elopement? When all he had to do was call things off? She would've been hurt, especially at the idea of his leaving for Texas, but it couldn't have been worse than finding out on their wedding day.

He hadn't been honest then, and he wasn't being honest now. The gnawing feeling in the pit of her stomach was a lesson learned. It was a reminder to keep her guard up. Even a friendship, like the camaraderie they'd shared the night before, was dangerous. Wasn't that how their relationship had begun, once upon a time?

She couldn't trust herself, and she sure

couldn't trust Travis, who'd been clear that he wanted more than a temporary arrangement. She couldn't let herself trust him again. Because if she did, he'd have the power to hurt her, and there was no way was she going down that slippery slope again.

21

A message was blinking on the phone when Shay emerged from her bedroom, bathed and dressed. Olivia had ridden to Maddy's house on her newly fixed bike, and Travis was out somewhere doing her job. She was feeling restless again, and it had only been two weeks. How was she going to make it another four or five?

Shay shuffled to the phone and pressed Play.

"This is Hank Peterson. Found one o' your bulls in my pasture again, pestering my cattle. I know you're having troubles, but I can't keep hauling 'em back. He's in my pen. Please come and get him."

Shay flinched at his brisk tone. Hank was never friendly, but he sounded more brusque than usual. She'd have to tell Travis about the fence. In the meantime, she'd figure a way to fetch the bull. She wasn't supposed to drive, but Hank was only next door. The hard part would be loading the bull.

It took thirty minutes to hitch the trailer and saddle and load Brandy. Her foot ached from the weight she'd accidentally applied when lifting the trailer onto the hitch.

But now she was all set. Sweat trickled down her temple. She put her window down, hoping for a cool breeze. Hank's property was a large spread to the south. He had three hired men, and she prayed one of them would be on hand to help.

A few minutes later she was backing her trailer to the gate of Hank's stock paneled pen. Her Hereford ran loose. She recognized his markings—this hadn't been his first foray across her property line in search of a hot cow.

She got out of the truck, unloaded Brandy, and, ditching her crutches, carefully mounted. She prayed the bull would cooperate.

"Howdy, Shay." Manny approached on foot.

"Manny . . . you working for Hank now?"

He gave a boyish grin. "Hired me last week."

"That's just great. Congratulations." She was relieved he'd found another job, one that surely paid better.

"Yeah, he's really growing the place. I guess he's expanding even more next spring."

"You don't say." Shay wondered if this was her chance for some extra income after Travis left. Olivia was getting old enough to stay home alone. "Think he'd take on any part-time help?"

Manny shrugged. "Looking for more work?"

"Might come in handy next year. Not sure Hank would hire me, though."

"I'll put in a good word for you."

"Thanks, I'd appreciate that." She gestured to the Hereford. "I came for my bull. Again."

"You should've called. I'd have brought him over."

"Don't think your boss would've been too keen on that."

With Manny's help, the loading went smoothly. Manny offered to follow her to her ranch, but she didn't want to get him in hot water with Hank.

She was still breathing hard as she drove home. She'd gone to seed after only a couple idle weeks. Ranching would be harder than ever when she did get her mobility back.

But her protesting foot told her it was too soon for that. The pain she'd had on the dismount almost made her leg buckle. She turned into her drive, relieved the loading was done. The bull shouldn't put up too big a fuss about coming out. She'd unhitch the trailer, unsaddle her horse, then take the pain meds she'd forgotten this morning.

After backing up to the pen, she shuffled to the gate, sprang it open, then released the trailer gate.

Brandy came out easily, and she led the mare to a nearby stall to wait until she had the bull put safely away. It was hotter'n the dickens already, the sun beating down, not a cloud in sight. Shay hobbled gingerly toward the trailer. Someone needed to make crutches that didn't kill the underarms.

Inside the trailer, the bull was still motionless.

"Ha!" she yelled as she approached the slatted front. She banged her crutch on the trailer's corner, making a clanging sound that apparently didn't impress him.

Her shirt clung to her damp back, and her breaths came hard. "Come on, buddy, move it." She poked her crutch through the slats and nudged. "Ha!"

The bull took two steps back, and Shay lost her balance. She hobbled forward on the one crutch, felt herself twisting. She released the crutch, catching herself as her knee hit the ground.

Shay bit back words she forbade Olivia to say. She braced her weight against the trailer and pushed upright. Her one crutch hung uselessly in her hand. *Stupid thing!* She threw it, and it hit the ground half a dozen feet away, releasing a puff of dirt.

She pulled herself up, bracing her weight on her good foot. Now her crutch was inside, and the bull still hadn't budged. "Ha!" She banged the side of the trailer with her open palm.

Stupid, cantankerous creature! She limped toward the back of the trailer, biting the inside of her mouth at the pain.

Travis nudged Buck to a canter, but even the horse was reluctant to move in the heat. He'd finally managed to push the herd up into the hills so as not to overgraze the streams. He pulled off his hat and ran his forearm over his forehead. It had to be topping ninety already.

He decided to return to the house for grub. Get out of the heat and check on Shay, since Olivia was gone. 'Sides, she'd been acting funny since yesterday. Distant and cranky. She claimed she was fine, but she wasn't. What had happened since their fishing outing?

All he could figure was he'd overstepped with Beau on Sunday. She hadn't seemed sore at the time, but what else could it be? Two steps forward, three steps back. At this rate, he'd be back in Texas before he could say annulment.

He hoped to start mending fences with a shared meal. He planned to heat up the leftover fish and make sandwiches, maybe a side of beans. He was mentally reviewing the pantry when the barn came into view, and with it, the truck and trailer, and Shay.

Shay was banging on the side panel, yelling. One of her crutches lay in the dirt a few feet away. A bull was halfway out of the trailer.

She limped unaided around the trailer, a grimace pinching her face. Was the woman trying to kill herself?

He pulled to a halt when he reached the trailer, dismounting. "What the heck are you doing, woman?"

"Unloading a bull, what's it look like?" A bead of sweat trickled down her temple. Her face strained against the pain of weight on her foot.

"Get off your foot, Shay," he said over the clanging of the bull's hooves.

She faltered as her leg buckled.

He took her arm. "I'll finish here. You're gonna wreck your foot for good."

She shook him off. "Mind your own business."

He ran his hand over his jaw. "You *are* my business."

"Ha!" she yelled at the bull, slapping his rump. When he didn't budge, she turned and limped toward the crutch, her face set.

Stubborn woman.

"I mean it, Shay."

"Go away, McCoy."

She'd be on those crutches for keeps if she didn't stop. Or if he didn't stop her. He followed, arriving as she bent to fetch the crutch. Without thought, he swooped down and caught her hip on his shoulder.

"Put me down!"

He held her legs tight to his chest, careful of her splinted foot. More careful than she was. He started for the house.

She swatted at him. "Put. Me. Down!"

Like a wet cat.

"Put your claws away, woman."

"I have to unsaddle my horse!" *Whack.*

"I'll handle it."

She grabbed the back of his thigh and pinched.

Hard. That would leave a mark. He gritted his teeth.

When the pinch failed to work, she returned to swatting anything in reach.

"Insufferable . . ." *Whack.*

"Egotistical . . ." *Whack.*

"Pigheaded . . ." *Whack.*

"Bully!" The last swat landed on his backside.

"Feeling good, darlin'."

She stopped abruptly, let out an angry roar. He opened the door and eased her through, kicking the door with his heel. When he reached the couch, he lowered his ungrateful load.

She came upright on the sofa, gave his shoulders a good, hard shove. "Jerk!" Blood had rushed to her head, flushing her cheeks. Or maybe it was anger. "Don't you ever do that again."

Leaving her to simmer, he retrieved her pills and a glass of water. What was he supposed to do when she was so reckless? Just stand around while she mangled her foot? She'd be lucky if she hadn't made it worse.

When he returned, Shay jerked the glass from him, sloshing water on the sofa. While she downed the pills, he fetched an ice bag from the freezer.

He returned and dropped the bag in her lap. "Prop your foot and ice it. I'll be back."

She glared, her eyes glossy, her breathing labored. "I can hardly wait."

Travis went outside and unloaded the bull. The Hereford didn't seem so stubborn after dealing with Shay. Travis didn't have to throw it over his shoulder or tiptoe around its pride. When the bull was penned, Travis latched the gate, then unsaddled Buck and Brandy.

Why hadn't she just called? He'd have been happy to retrieve the bull. He wondered how she'd even hitched the trailer. Probably took her ten times as long as it should've.

His stomach rumbled as he closed the stall door. He headed toward the house, grabbing Shay's crutches and her hat that had fallen when he'd tossed her over his shoulder. Hopefully she'd cooled her heels, but knowing Shay, she was in there stewing. She'd been on the verge of tears when he left. He'd thought they were angry tears, but now he wondered if she'd been hurting.

He entered through the front, letting the screen door fall in place behind him. Shay was lying on the sofa, tucked into the space between the seat and back. Her splinted foot rested on the sofa's arm, the bag of ice balanced precariously on top. Her chest rose and fell with deep, peaceful breaths. Her face was relaxed in sleep, her lips slightly parted. Long dark lashes fanned the tops of her cheeks.

Seeing her now, all soft and vulnerable, he could hardly believe she was the same she-cat he'd just hauled into the house. She looked gentle as a lamb, harmless as a dove.

His heart stirred with a yearning desire. Desire to protect her, desire to hold her and love her. *Please, God, someday. I know I'll have to earn her trust. I'll be as patient as I need to be, only please let her know how much I love her.*

Judging by today, he had miles to go. He eyed the sliver of space on the edge of the sofa. He longed to stretch out beside her, curl her body into his, and hold her against him for the rest of the afternoon. His arms ached with the longing. He was her husband, and she was his wife. They were married.

Yet he had no right. He had no doubt she'd set him straight on that if he tried.

He sighed, too loud. She moved in her sleep, crossing her arms against the air-conditioned room. Travis grabbed the blanket that was draped over his guitar case and set it carefully over her, drawing it to her shoulders.

Her hand peeked out from the top, and his eyes caught on the flimsy gold wedding band. He wanted to wrestle the ring from her finger. Every time he saw it, he thought about her marriage to Garrett. She was married to *him* now.

He wondered what her relationship with her husband had been like. Wondered how the man could've left so much behind . . . a beautiful wife and daughter. Shay must've been devastated.

Was likely leery of men in general, and Travis wasn't exactly faultless in that.

But he wasn't fool enough to make that mistake twice. He wanted so much more than five months' room and board. He wanted to help her heal, to fix all the broken parts.

Show me how to love her, God. Give me patience.

Travis watched her slumber, remembering the fight she'd given him just minutes before, and knew he might have to reach real deep for enough patience to win Shay's heart.

22

The next Saturday Shay and Olivia accompanied Travis into town for supplies. When they reached town, Olivia saw a schoolmate headed into the Tin Roof. Travis gave her money for a milk shake, and she scampered off to the diner. Travis needed some things from Timberline Hardware, so Shay went to visit with Miss Lucy at the Doll House. The store was busy with tourists popping in every few minutes, but she was glad to see business going well for her elderly friend.

After leaving the shop, Shay stopped at Mocha Moose and chewed the fat with Tina and a few other neighbors. The smell of brewed coffee tickled her senses, and the loud espresso machine whirred to life every few seconds as tourists and locals placed orders.

Figuring Travis must be about finished, Shay made her way out the door and onto the boarded walk. She began to realize how foolish she'd been to order a to-go cup as she tried to juggle the crutches and the coffee. Thank God the truck was close. The coffee sloshed through the lid, and she felt the hot liquid through her jeans.

"Howdy, Shay." Beau stepped out of the Hair Barn, replacing his hat. "Let me get that for you."

She was wary after their run-in at church, but her armpit was killing her, and she was going to lose half her coffee getting to the truck.

"Thanks." She handed over the cup. "Don't know what I was thinking, getting coffee. I'm headed that way." She nodded her chin toward the truck, parked diagonally in front of the hardware store.

"Glad I ran into you," he said. "I owe you an apology for Sunday." Sincerity shone in his brown eyes, and the chagrined smile he wore reminded her why she liked him.

"That's all right—this was sudden. I can see why you're confused."

They'd reached the truck, and he passed her to get the passenger door.

"Well, anyhow, I do wish you the best, you know. You're a great gal. McCoy's a lucky man."

As she navigated the curb, Shay's crutch caught on something. She'd already begun her swing forward, and her weight was on a crutch that had found no hold. Her arms buckled.

"Shay!" Beau reached out, but not in time to stop her fall.

She landed awkwardly on her rear end between the vehicles.

A dazed second later she felt the damage. Her backside would have a heck of a bruise, but her foot wasn't banged up. There was no pain radiating up her leg. She pulled her palms off the ground to dust away the bits of gravel and opened her mouth to assure Beau she was fine.

But just then a body flew past. A rush of air smacked her face as Travis grabbed Beau by the shirt and shoved him into the side of the truck. The coffee went flying.

"What'd you do, Meyers?" Travis slacked his hold long enough to allow another shove into the cab. "What's wrong, can't take on a man? Get your thrills outta—"

"Stop, Travis!" Shay tried to stand but couldn't find a hold.

Beau pushed back, to no avail. "Get your hands off me, McCoy!"

"It was an accident." She grabbed the fender and pulled to her feet. "I fell, that's all."

Travis glanced at her. She could see the wheels turning. His face was as hard as stone, his lips pressed into a taut line.

"I tripped over the wheel stop." She gestured toward the block, hobbling on one foot. "Beau was helping me to the truck, carrying my coffee." The empty cup rolled in the wind toward the street. "Which is gone now, thanks to you."

Travis's hands were still clenched around a wad of Beau's shirt, his knuckles gone white.

"Get off me." Beau shoved Travis away, his nostrils flaring.

Travis loosened his grip and his hands dropped

to his sides. His shoulders heaved, his jaw twitched.

Men. Shay would've whacked him over the head with her crutch, except it was out of reach.

Beau straightened his shirt. "You need to simmer down, pal."

Travis retrieved Shay's crutches and handed them over. "You okay?"

She snatched the crutches, glaring at him as Beau went to fetch the empty cup.

"You owe him an apology."

Travis glanced at Beau, who'd collected the cup and was now retrieving his hat from the pavement. Then he looked back at her, his jaw picking up slack.

She frowned at him, but he'd noticed the crowd of tourists gathered on the sidewalk.

"Show's over." He waved them away. "Go on . . . scat."

They began dispersing as Beau approached, donning his hat. He looked at Shay. "Sure you're okay?"

"I'm fine." She shot Travis a look, then returned her attention to Beau. "Thank you for your help."

He tipped his hat, gave Travis a look that said plenty, and turned toward his own vehicle. He dropped the empty cup in a trash barrel as he passed.

Shay jabbed Travis in the ribs.

He pressed his lips together like he was swallowing a sour worm. "Meyers," he finally called.

Beau turned, shoulders back, wearing a scowl.

Shay thought she was going to have to jab Travis again before he spoke. "Sorry for the misunderstanding."

Beau sized him up for a full five seconds, then he nodded once and continued on his way.

When Travis recovered from his distasteful task, he took Shay's arm.

She elbowed him away. "I can do it myself." She was beginning to remember why she'd sworn off men to begin with.

23

July galloped into August, arriving hotter and drier than the previous month. From the windows, Shay watched the grass fade from dewy green to brittle brown. The school bus arrived early one August morning to usher Olivia off to her first day of seventh grade.

Each week on their way to church, Shay noted the streams getting lower until soon they were dried gullies, winding through meadows like gray-brown snakes, the dirt cracking and splintering under the brutal sun.

Travis drove the cattle into the hills and cut the bulls from the cows—a hot, tiring job, the bulls fighting amongst themselves like a bunch of high school boys. He found and treated two cases of pneumonia, and both cows were now on the mend.

Shay hated to admit it, but he managed the ranch well in her absence.

Abigail drove her to the clinic at the six-week mark. Shay fairly itched with the desire to be back in the saddle. But instead, Dr. Garvin prescribed another week on crutches.

She stuffed her disappointment and took her medicine with a minimal amount of grumbling. After all, she'd asked for it. She'd expected Travis to point that out, had almost dared him to when she told him the news at supper that night. But maybe he was smarter than she gave him credit for. He'd assured her he and Olivia could handle things until she was back on her feet.

Olivia seconded the thought enthusiastically, and Shay didn't miss the chummy look that passed between the two of them. They'd developed a camaraderie, working together. Sometimes she caught Travis ruffling Olivia's hair or patiently answering her questions, and she wondered if they were growing too close.

One night Shay heard the quiet murmur of his voice, punctuated by Olivia's giggles. She shuffled across the living room and listened around the corner.

He was reading aloud to her, imitating each character's voice. Shay listened to his falsetto, a grin tugging her lips at the incongruity of a cowboy reading *The Princess Diaries*.

Still, it was bittersweet, because bedtime stories were Daddy territory, and Olivia was eating it up. Shay listened until her foot protested, then she returned to her room, heaviness weighing her steps.

A month and a half into their arrangement, and Travis had fit right into their little family. He sometimes fixed breakfast on Saturday mornings. He often grilled out on Sunday afternoons. He kept up her ranch, managed his dad's books, and checked in with Jacob on the day-to-day operations of the Barr M. He took Olivia grocery shopping on Sunday evenings and saw to it there was money in the account for bills. All without a whisper of complaint.

Anyone looking in from the outside would think it was real, this little family. If Shay let herself, she'd believe it too. Already she wondered if Olivia had forgotten this was a short-term arrangement. That Travis would be leaving before Thanksgiving, and then it would be just the two of them again.

The thought set a hollow spot in her middle, but she denied it had anything to do with feelings for Travis. It was a matter of habit. She'd gotten accustomed to having him around, having his help. It was just going to be harder when he left.

Harder to work the ranch, harder to pay the bills. At least she'd have a little extra income in the spring. Manny had spoken to Hank Peterson, and he had offered her a part-time job starting in April. She'd be too busy and tired to notice Travis was gone.

Monday, August thirteenth, marked the seventh week since she'd broken her foot and also her birthday. She couldn't think of anything she wanted more than the freedom to walk unaided.

Abigail drove her to see Dr. Garvin again, and this time he gave her permission to burn her crutches. Tempting as it was, she returned them for the next unfortunate victim and walked gingerly to Abigail's car, beaming from ear to ear.

"You look like you won a million bucks," Abigail said, turning out onto Main Street.

"Happy birthday to me!" Shay sang. "I can drive, I can walk, I can ride, I can take a bath! I cannot wait to soak in the tub again! I can feed my own horses, clean out my own barn, ride my own circle . . ."

"Never saw anyone so eager to get back to work. Or maybe you're eager for time in the saddle with a certain cowboy."

"Ha! Couldn't be further from the truth."

"I don't know." Abigail turned a playful smile her way. "I think there's something there."

"Just three and a half months and it'll be over. That's all I want."

"If you say so."

"What happened to all that suspicion? What happened to 'Be careful, Shay. How do we know his real intentions? Why's he doing this for so little in return?' "

Abigail gave a mock glare. "I do not sound like that. Anyway, that wasn't suspicion, it was caution—always a good thing. But my instincts tell me Travis is all right. I know he hurt you, though."

"Blame right."

"Just don't write him off too soon is all I'm saying. Maybe God brought him back here for a reason."

Shay didn't respond. She wasn't wasting a minute of this glorious afternoon bickering about Travis. She was going to go home and run around the house several times—just because she could.

A few minutes later they pulled into her drive. The sun had sunk behind the mountains, taking its scorching heat with it. Maybe she'd take Olivia somewhere. Fishing or to the Dairy Freeze. She could drive now! She was almost giddy with the thought of freedom.

Abigail pulled up to the house and turned off the engine. "Hey, can I borrow your lawn hose? Our garden's drying up, and our hose isn't long enough."

"Sure." Shay exited the car, and Abigail followed her around back. She could get the hose herself. Her foot didn't even hurt when she put her weight on it, though the muscles felt a little wobbly. That was normal, according to—

"Happy birthday!"

Shay stopped short. Abigail bumped into her, laughing. A dozen people littered her backyard. Olivia, Travis, Miss Lucy, Maddy, Wade, Annie Stevens and her sister Sierra, and Wade's best friend, Dylan.

"Oh my word!" Shay put her hand over her

racing heart. "I did not expect that! Thanks, everyone."

Olivia approached, hugging her. "Are you surprised, Mom?" Her daughter pulled her toward the decorated tables.

"I had no idea." She looked at Abigail. "You trickster."

Abigail shrugged as Wade joined her. He wrapped his arm around her waist. "Lady knows how to keep a secret." He pecked her on the cheek.

Blue tablecloths and colorful balloons decorated the tables. A "HAPPY BIRTHDAY" banner stretched across the old laundry line.

Travis stood at the open grill where, judging by the heavenly smell, he was cooking hamburgers.

"Happy birthday, dear," Miss Lucy said, taking Abigail and Wade's spot beside her.

Her birthday normally passed without fuss. A card from Olivia, a call from Miss Lucy. And she'd never, not in all her life, had a party. "Who did all this?"

"Why, it was Travis. He's been planning it for weeks. And I see you're off your crutches."

"Good as new." She glanced at Travis. He was flipping burgers, laughing at something Dylan said. He wore one of his Sunday shirts, a blue plaid button-up.

Shay made the rounds, thanking everyone for coming. She wasn't much on being the main event, but her spirits were high on her new mobility. Also, she was people-starved from being trapped at home, and this party was just what she needed.

Everyone was talking, laughing, having a great time. Olivia and Maddy lay on their bellies on the patio, writing happy birthday messages with sidewalk chalk.

Travis caught her eye over Miss Lucy's head. He smiled as he scooped the burgers onto a big platter.

Shay excused herself and made her way to the grill. "Word has it you're responsible for all this," she said when she reached his side.

"Oh yeah?"

The fat burgers dripped with thick melting cheese, just the way she liked them.

"Didn't have to go to all this trouble."

"Wanted to." He'd no sooner set the last burger on the platter than Abigail swooped by and took it.

"Well . . . thanks." That wasn't so hard. She could be nice. Especially when he'd been so thoughtful.

He turned off the grill and closed the lid. "See you got your walking license."

"Yep. 'Fraid you'll have to put up with me all day from now on."

His eyes slitted, and he tilted his head. "You're looking to boss me around, aren't you?"

Shay smiled. "Better believe it."

"Come 'n' get it!" Wade called, and the friends swarmed the tables like ants to a cookie crumb.

Her neighbors dived into the food while Dylan entertained them with stories from Texas. He and Travis had known each other from the rodeo circuit and seemed to have hit it off. Shay caught Dylan checking out Annie Stevens whenever she wasn't looking. He flirted with her too, but she rebuffed him at every turn. Shay wondered if the cowboy had finally met his match.

After they ate, Shay opened presents while Abigail blinded her with the flash of her new camera. Miss Lucy had made a doll that looked just like Shay, with long layered brown hair, olive skin, and a miniature splint on her foot.

"A souvenir of your journey this summer," Miss Lucy said.

"Where's the wedding veil?" Dylan asked, making everyone laugh.

Abigail, Wade, and Maddy gave her a basket of Citrus Dream bath bubbles and gels. She opened a bottle and took a whiff. "Mmm, my favorite!"

"Picked it out myself," Wade said.

Abigail elbowed him. "Did not." She addressed Shay. "I know you've been looking forward to your baths."

She opened Olivia's next. Her daughter had made her a beaded necklace, tiny teak hearts on a corded strand, separated by hand-tied knots, with a larger silver heart in the center. "I love it, hon. You know my taste."

"Travis helped me order the silver piece."

"It's perfect." Shay turned around and lifted her hair so Olivia could fasten it.

She unwrapped the rest of her presents: a gift certificate from Movie Magic from her church friends; a coupon for a free cut and style from Ida Franklin, who worked at the Hair Barn; and a bottle of Geritol from Dylan—with a Mocha Moose gift certificate tucked inside the card to ease the blow.

After the presents Travis strummed some songs on his guitar, playing requests, while Dylan made up lyrics that had everyone laughing until their stomachs hurt.

By the time their company left, darkness had fallen. Fireflies twinkled in the yard and beyond, a quiet symphony of light. The cool evening air pebbled Shay's skin. She and Olivia helped Travis clean up. Their neighbors had scarfed down all the burgers, and only a couple pieces of Abigail's lemon cake remained.

After cleanup, Shay tucked Olivia into bed. She raved over her new necklace, and they giggled over Dylan's antics. After she kissed her daughter good night, she drew a bath, filled it with her new citrus bubbles, and soaked until the water grew tepid.

When she was dry and dressed in her nightshirt, she found Travis finishing the dishes.

"I could've done those in the morning," she said.

"Don't have to now."

She watched him dry the hamburger platter and recalled something Abigail had said once. *There's nothing sexier than a man with a dish towel in his hand.* Watching Travis now, Shay had to agree.

He shelved the platter in a high cupboard, and she followed the broad line of his shoulders down to his trim waist and beyond. He always did have a nice—

"This go here?"

She jerked her eyes away. "Uh, yeah."

What was she thinking? She'd been without a man too long, that was all. She missed the intimacy of marriage. She shook her head and turned toward her room.

"Where you going?"

"Bed. I'm wiped out."

"Wait." He dried his hands. "Haven't given you my present."

She stopped. "The party was more than I—"

But he was already past her, in the living room, pulling a bag from behind the sofa. "Happy birthday."

Shay took the large brown sack.

"Sorry about the bag. Not much for wrapping."

He gestured to the sofa, then sank down beside her, his knee grazing hers.

Shay pulled out a box and set it on her lap. She lifted the lid. The smell of good leather wafted upward. Tucked in a nest of beige tissue paper was a luxurious pair of Chippewa boots.

"Travis . . ." She ran her fingers over the supple brown leather. The soles were nonslip, stitched on, not glued. Leather lined the interior of the boots. "This is too much."

She'd never had boots this fancy, had only eyed them in the catalog at Pappy's Market, dreaming.

He lifted one of the boots from its nest. "Look . . . steel toed." He smiled at her. "No more broken feet. Try 'em on."

She wanted to. Bad. But it was too much. A real husband might spend this much on his wife's birthday. But Travis wasn't her real husband. A weight hit the bottom of her stomach. She told herself it was because she had to refuse the boots.

"It was real thoughtful, Travis, but—"

"No way. I ruined your boots, and I promised you a new pair. Now that your foot's not the size of a barn, you'll be needing them."

"Mine were nowhere near this quality and you know it."

"Which is how you ended up with a broken foot. Now put 'em on. Been waiting weeks for this."

He was like a kid on Christmas morning, his gray eyes dancing, an eager grin tugging his lips.

She eyed the beautiful boots. Well, he had promised her a new pair. She bit her lip. And if he really wanted her to have them . . .

"Go on. I wanna see if they fit."

She took the boot and slid her good foot into it, tugging the leather pull-on straps. She slid the other boot on and stood. The insoles cushioned her feet and supported her arches. She took a few steps.

"They're the same size as your old ones, but if they don't fit, I kept the receipt. They said it wouldn't be a problem to send them back."

"You are *not* sending these back." She offered a grin. "I may even sleep in them tonight."

She was rewarded with a smile that reminded her of the boy he'd been way back when. When he was playful and impulsive and more than a little passionate.

She took another spin around the room, appreciating the fine quality and perfect fit. They were heavier than her old ones because of the steel toes, but not cumbersome.

"You like them?"

"Do I ever. Don't know how I'll go backward after these wear out. I'll be utterly spoiled."

"They should last awhile."

She enjoyed the boots for another minute, then sat down and tugged them off. She placed them by the front door, reminding herself she'd be back to her chores bright and early.

A yawn slipped out. "It's late." She put away the bag and box while Travis retrieved his pillow.

She handed him the worn quilt. "Thanks, Travis. For the boots, the party . . . everything." She was going to kiss him on the cheek. Her heels came off the floor. Then she thought better of it. She lowered her heels, balled her hands into fists, and crossed her arms for good measure.

He was looking at her. Or rather, looking right through her, as if he knew what she'd almost done. "My pleasure." His voice was low and raspy. "Hope it was a good birthday."

"The best in years." She wondered if she should've admitted it, but she'd never been one to hold back her thoughts.

He smiled. "Good. You deserve it."

She didn't know about that, but she wasn't looking a gift horse in the mouth. "Well. Good night."

" 'Night."

She felt his eyes on her as she walked toward her room, as she pushed the door closed, and even long into the night as she lay staring at the ceiling, wondering what the future held.

24

He was driving down a long stretch of highway, his foot pressing hard on the accelerator. He had to get there. He was going to be too late. His heart kicked against his ribs painfully. Fear sucked the air from his mouth, drying it.

The green sign said thirty-two more miles, but hadn't the last sign said only seventeen? Made no sense. How could he be farther away?

Then he saw it: the town, just ahead. He flew toward it, the landscape racing past. But it was getting no closer, always just out of reach.

Then he heard a noise, and his truck shuddered. He coasted to a halt, and when he left the truck, he entered a wedding chapel. A crowd filled the church, their backs to him. At the altar, Shay stood with another man, her long white gown trailing behind her.

He had to stop her. A protest formed in his mind, on his tongue. *No, Shay, don't do it! I love you!* But the words were like blanks from a gun.

Hot air stuffed his lungs. He ran toward her, but the aisle had become a treadmill. Running, running, running. *Please! I'm sorry!* Soundless pleas swelled inside him until he thought he'd burst with the pressure.

And then the man kissed her. The wedding was over. She turned around then and he saw something in her arms. A bundle. A baby. She looked directly at him, and that's when he knew—he'd lost her forever.

Something woke Shay. She became aware without opening her eyes. She turned and pulled the quilt up. Even through the closed door she often heard Travis snoring. He liked to play hymns on his guitar before bed, and those sounds also leaked through the door. Instead of annoying her, however, the melodic strumming had become a comforting lullaby, reminding her of God's presence.

Had to go back to sleep. Morning couldn't be far away. She wouldn't open her eyes and check. She nestled into the mattress, turning onto her stomach. In the five weeks since she'd gotten her splint off, she'd relished her old sleeping position. Just as she'd relished hearing the creak of saddle leather, seeing the calves grow before her eyes, smelling the sweet alfalfa and sagebrush on the open range.

Ranching with Travis was different from working with Manny. Way different. Travis was confident, didn't need to be told what to do, not even close. A few times she'd even asked his opinion. She knew her cattle, but he had an affinity with them that belied the time he'd been here. He knew their markings and which calf belonged to which mother.

They'd fallen into a rhythm, working side by side. No need for words.

It was different than it had been with Garrett too. Her ex-husband had a mind of his own and liked to tell her what to do even though she was as competent as he. It used to annoy the dickens out of her. Wasn't it her ranch, passed down from her parents? Hadn't she worked it since she was knee high? But it didn't matter. Garrett wanted her to know he was in charge. She'd argued at first, but as Olivia grew older, Shay had gone along with the program to keep peace. Anything she had to do to hold their marriage together.

So much for that. He'd left anyway, and she'd lost a little of herself in the process.

Another sound came from beyond her door. More like a mumble than a snore. She perked her ears, lifted her head from the pillow. There was nothing but the distant hum of her old refrigerator. The clock read 3:46. She was about to lie back down when she heard it again.

A word, Travis's voice. Who was he talking to? Surely he wasn't on the phone at this hour. She thought of the woman who'd called a couple months before. He hadn't mentioned her, and as far as she knew, he hadn't been calling her.

Unless he was calling in the middle of the night. Sneaking around, pretending to be the loyal husband, all the while carrying on a long-distance relationship, keeping this Ella woman on the sidelines just in case the marriage didn't work out. Or simply biding his time until their arrangement was over.

The thought opened a void in her belly, wide, dark, and aching. She told herself it was nothing, this hollow feeling. It was the thought of betrayal that troubled her, not any feelings she might still have.

Who are you kidding, Shay? The feelings are still there. You can bury them, you can stuff them, but you can't make them disappear.

She'd let her guard down. It was impossible to keep it up 24-7—the man lived with her, for pity's sake. He was doing his laundry in her machine and washing his hair under her spigot.

They'd already been in love once. Plainly they had the chemistry or pheromones or whatever it was that drew two people together. He was always giving her that lopsided smile, throwing her a wink here and there that she'd find herself thinking about when her head hit the pillow.

It was natural those old feelings would creep up. She was only human, after all. It wasn't going to hurt anything—as long as she didn't act on them.

Another sound from the living room. She turned her ear toward the door. It had been just a

211

word or two. If this was a phone conversation, it was pretty one-sided.

She pushed back the covers and slid her feet to the floor. Moonlight washed through the sheer curtains, casting a white glow over the door. She crept toward it, the wooden planks cool against the balls of her feet.

She pressed her ear to the crack between the jamb and the door and waited.

"No."

The word was clear, but it didn't sound right, not like Travis. She pulled open the door, wincing when it creaked. He was a dark lump on the sofa. He moved. His breathing was harsh and shallow.

He was having a nightmare. Not a phone call. Should she wake him or go back to bed?

"Sorry . . ."

At least, that's what she thought he said. He moaned quietly.

Whatever the dream, it wasn't good. She shouldn't let it continue. Besides, she didn't want him waking Olivia.

She crept toward the sofa. The drapes were drawn on the picture window, and only the dim glow of the clock lit her way. As she approached, her feet tangled with the balled-up quilt he must've kicked off at some point. He lay on his side, his legs bent to fit on the sofa.

She touched him on the shoulder, shaking

gently. His breaths continued, erratic and shallow. He jerked in his sleep.

"Travis," she whispered.

He released another low moan. His foot jerked. She squatted down, shook his shoulder. "Travis."

He sucked in a deep breath, like he was draining the room of oxygen. Then he sprang upright on the sofa, nearly tipping her backward.

She grabbed for the sofa's edge to steady herself, but his knees were there instead—solid and warm through the thin cloth of his pajamas.

"Shay." Her name was a sigh of relief. He cupped her cheek with his palm. "You're here."

Her breath caught and hung in her lungs. His palm was warm and rough against her face. She resisted the urge to lean into it.

" 'Course I am," she croaked.

His lifted his other hand, touched her hair as if making sure. The touch awakened a shiver that traveled from her scalp to her spine.

He wasn't awake yet, not quite.

What was her excuse? And did she really want one?

His hand fell from her cheek, leaving a spot that grew cold and lonely for his touch.

"Dreaming, I guess." His voice was low and sleepy.

Her hands were still braced on his knees. She pulled them away, clasped them against her stomach. "Guess so."

She should go. He was awake now. Nightmare over. Mission accomplished.

He grasped her shoulders as if sensing her departure. His hands were warm through her filmy shirt, his hold firm.

"It was awful . . . lost you all over again."

That was what he'd dreamed? What he'd moaned over? Something pleasant and gratifying claimed the hollow spot inside her. Her heart lodged somewhere between her chest and throat.

"Shay . . ." He cupped her face in his palms, his thumbs grazing the tops of her cheeks.

She couldn't read his face in the dimness, but she could read his voice, his touch. And they were saying things she'd longed to hear for so long. Her breaths came in shallow puffs. Feelings she hadn't felt in years filled her to overflowing.

He pushed her hair off her face, his touch as light as a whisper. "I never stopped thinking about you."

His words were water for a thirsty soul. He leaned close, and when she felt his breath on her lips, she closed the distance between them.

His kiss was tentative, restrained. Like she was an iridescent bubble he might burst. His touch was heaven. She could never get enough.

He pulled her closer. Her hands came around his torso, finding the warmth of his bare back. Her touch seemed to unleash something inside him.

He deepened the kiss, his restraint gone, taking hers with it. She'd forgotten how he could make her burn. How quickly she ignited under his touch. But she remembered now. Remembered all too well this feeling he aroused. She was fully awake—more awake than she'd been in years.

Not even Garrett had reached so deeply inside her—no one, ever. There'd never been anyone but Travis. Never been anyone who loved her like he did, who made her feel the way he did.

With that thought, fear wormed into her heart. Loving him would only lead to pain . . .

Travis's lips left hers, and despite the direction of her thoughts, she bit back a protest. But he didn't go far. His lips brushed her forehead, her cheeks, the tip of her nose, loving every inch of her face. When they returned to her lips, she didn't protest.

How could she when she wanted it with every cell of her body? When she ached for more, and more was never enough? Not with Travis. It hadn't been enough fourteen years ago, and it wasn't enough now. She pressed into him, closer still, but not close enough.

He left the couch, easing her back onto the carpet. It was what she wanted so badly. Despite her overwhelming desire—maybe because of it—panic shot through her veins like acid.

This couldn't happen. What was she doing?

She pushed on his chest and turned her face, feeling his hot breath on her cheek. "Stop." The rug felt rough against her cheek after his tender ministrations.

He straightened his arms, bracing his weight. His breaths were ragged.

Or were those hers? She could feel her heart beating against the floor beneath her. She couldn't make out his features, was almost glad of it. Maybe he couldn't see hers either. Couldn't see the flush of desire on her cheeks or the torment of denied longing that was surely scrawled across her face.

"What's wrong?"

She closed her eyes as if she could erase the sound of his anguish. "I can't."

He was suspended above her for the space of a dozen heartbeats, then he eased his hips down beside her, his weight braced on the arm that spanned her torso.

In the quiet moment they caught their breath. Unspent desire coursed through her veins, making her want to whimper.

"Talk to me," he said.

She couldn't find the words. They were there, in her mind, but they danced just out of reach.

"What's going on in that head of yours?"

"I—I don't want this."

"You did a minute ago." His gentle tone made the truth go down a little easier.

"Come on, Travis. We're both grown-ups. What you want and what's good for you are two different things."

He turned her face toward him, and she opened her eyes. "Give me another chance. I know I don't deserve it, but . . ."

There was more he wanted to say. She watched him struggle, wished the shadows would part and reveal his thoughts. But he didn't finish his sentence.

"Nothing's changed." She wouldn't trust her heart to him again. Not after last time. Not after Garrett. She was done trusting her heart to men. It hurt too much when they left, wasn't worth the risk.

"*I've* changed."

She didn't like looking up at him, didn't like being trapped by his arm. She scooted backward, came to a sitting position a safe distance away— if there was such a thing.

"I'm not going anywhere," he said.

But he would. In three months or three years. He'd leave her, and she'd hate herself for trusting him again, for giving herself fully only to be hurt. One time you could excuse. Twice just made you stupid.

"It's late." She stood, tugged her nightshirt into place. "Get some sleep." She turned toward her room. Her body felt heavy, her legs trembling with each step.

"It won't go away, you know."

His words barely reached her, and when they did, she wished they hadn't. Did he speak of the ache that had settled beneath her breastbone? The desire that still coursed through her limbs? Or the flame of love that—she was beginning to realize—had never been fully extinguished?

She entered her room and pushed the door until it clicked, as if she could close the door on her feelings, as if she could shut out the words he'd just spoken. But the door was just a two-inch slab of wood, a useless barrier, and all of it stayed with her until the alarm blared bright and early.

25

*T*ravis was already gone by the time Shay was dressed and ready for the day. In the barn, she found the horses fed and the stalls cleaned. Leaving through the back door, she found him loading salt blocks into his truck bed. When he saw her, he stopped and watched her approach.

If only they could go their separate ways today. What was there to say? He'd kissed her, and she'd been a willing participant. She could've at least saved her dignity by pushing him away— before it got out of hand.

Travis shoved the blocks farther into the truck, then pulled off his gloves and tipped his hat back with the poke of a finger. " 'Morning."

He looked way too handsome in the golden morning light. Bright-eyed and bushy-tailed, like he hadn't lost a wink of sleep.

She remembered the sleep-swollen eyes that had stared back at her in the mirror minutes ago and tugged the brim of her hat lower. " 'Morning."

His eyes raked her form, and she knew he was remembering too. Remembering the feel of their lips moving together, the feel of their bodies pressed together, the feel of stirring desire. Embarrassment licked her cheeks.

He, on the other hand, looked her right in the eye, bold as a grizzly and twice as smug. *No regrets here,* they seemed to say.

He cocked a brow just to make it clear he'd welcome a repeat right here and now.

"I'll fetch my gloves." She scurried toward the barn as though her feet were on fire, longing for the days when she was trapped in the house with a splint on her foot.

Despite the awkward start, they fell into a rhythm as the morning progressed. She drove the pickup, and he put out the salt blocks. Before long, he was teasing her about dropping a block on her foot. After that chore was done, they hit leather, moving the cattle to better grazing territory—a job made simpler with two people.

The herd looked healthy, the calves well fed. They stuck to their mamas' sides like burrs on flannel and bawled when they were separated. By the time she and Travis returned to the house for dinner, Shay's stomach was rumbling.

Abigail's car was in the drive, and Shay spotted her friend on the porch with Olivia and Maddy.

When Shay dismounted, Travis took her reins. "I got it."

"I can do it myself."

"Go visit with your friend." He led both horses into the pen, leaving Shay to glare after him.

"Abigail brought pictures," Olivia said as Shay neared the porch.

"Birthday pictures." Abigail handed them to Shay. "They're not so good."

"Why not?" Shay lowered herself into the wooden chair.

"Let's just say I haven't gotten the hang of my new camera."

Shay opened the packet and shuffled through the pictures. The subjects were blurry more often than not, and random objects in the foreground were in focus instead.

"I don't know, Abs, this is a great picture."

"Yeah, of a Coke can."

They laughed.

"I like that one," Maddy said.

The burger in Shay's hand was frozen in time, crisply in focus—while Shay's face faded into the blurry background.

"I guess I need a little practice," Abigail said. "Sorry I ruined the only pictures of your surprise party."

Shay tapped her temple. "It's all up here."

"Can I go to Maddy's for the afternoon?" Olivia asked.

"I was hoping for an extra pair of hands in the garden," Abigail said.

Shay would be working anyway. "Don't see why not."

Seeming satisfied, Maddy and Olivia ran toward Travis.

Shay watched him work, noting his sturdy legs,

his muscular arms, his strong hands as they removed the horses' bridles. Hands rough with calluses. She could still feel them on her arms, on her face. A tingle raced down her spine.

Shay tore her eyes away. "Thanks for bringing these over."

Abigail lowered her chin and narrowed her eyes. "What happened . . . ?"

"What?"

"Don't be coy. Something happened."

Was she that transparent? Shay pursed her lips and sighed hard.

Abigail leaned forward, elbows on her knees. "Tell all. And quick, before they come back."

Shay toyed with the frayed edge of her shirt. "It was nothing."

If she told herself that enough, maybe she'd believe it. Kisses happened all the time. Meaningless, empty kisses that led nowhere. Kisses you forgot about the instant they ended.

"He kissed you."

Shay frowned. "What are you, a mind reader?"

Abigail snorted. "It hardly takes a mind reader. You should see the look on your face. Whoo-boy, that must've been some kiss."

"It was just a regular, old run-of-the-mill kiss."

"I'd like to run that mill awhile."

Shay tilted her head. "You're practically a newlywed. I'm sure your mill's just fine."

Abigail gave a furtive smile. "Well, true. But there's nothing like that first kiss."

"Hardly a first."

"Well, the wedding kiss didn't count, not really. And it's been a lifetime since the others."

A lifetime. It didn't feel like a lifetime. It was all so fresh, these feelings. She felt eighteen again, young and silly-in-love.

You are not in love with him. She had been once upon a time. This was just . . . nostalgia or something. She shook the uncomfortable thought away.

"Shay . . . ?"

"We're talking about Travis here. He's pushy and arrogant and—and he does my crossword puzzles."

"I didn't know you did crossword puzzles."

"Well . . . I don't, but still." It was her paper, wasn't it? Her house. He could've asked.

"Back to the kiss . . . ," Abigail said.

"The kiss was a mistake. A middle-of-the-night mistake of monumental proportions."

Abigail perked up. "Middle of the night?"

Shay gave a mock glare. "Middle-of-the-night *mistake*. We were half asleep." She lifted her chin. "My guard was down."

"You didn't . . ."

"Of course we didn't."

"Well, you are married—in the eyes of God and man."

"I wish everyone would stop reminding me of that."

"It would be perfectly natural."

"It would be perfectly awful."

Well, not the act itself. That would be . . . She shivered at the thought. Then she crossed her arms, pretending to be chilled lest Abigail make something of it.

"If you say so," her friend said.

Across the yard Travis lifted his hat and placed it on Olivia's head. Her daughter made a muscle, showing her guns. Travis laughed, the sound of it barely carrying over the wind. Olivia rose on tiptoe and put the hat back on Travis's head. He gave her ponytail a tug before heading toward the porch.

It wasn't butterflies that danced in Shay's stomach at his approach. It was hunger. Desperation welled up at the thought of being alone again.

"Wanna stay for lunch?" she asked.

Abigail's lips twitched. "Sorry, but we're meeting Aunt Lucy at the Tin Roof."

"You're not going to invite me?"

"No way. You're stuck here. Just you and your hubby."

Shay narrowed her eyes. "Some friend. Let me grab some money for Olivia."

Abigail waved her off. "I got it." She stood as Travis approached.

He tipped his hat. "Abigail."

"Travis. Nice to see you." She passed him, called for the girls, then turned to Shay and wiggled her eyebrows.

Traitor. Thank God Travis had his back to her.

"See ya later," Abigail called.

" 'Bye, Mom! 'Bye, Travis!"

"Tell Miss Lucy I said hello," Shay said.

"Will do."

Shay watched them slip into the car and roll down the lane, then she went inside to wash up. This was no big deal. They'd been alone all day. What was wrong with her?

Minutes later she and Travis were seated at the table, scarfing down the sandwiches and soup they'd put together. Shay shuffled through Abigail's pictures while they ate, avoiding eye contact with Travis.

"You and Abigail were deep in conversation," he said.

She made a pointed effort to prevent her face from heating. "So?"

The corner of his lip hitched up. "Good stuff?" His twinkling eyes said more than his words.

Arrogant. He *assumed* they were talking about him. About his kiss.

"You know, women talk about more than just men."

"That so?"

"Exactly so." She shot him a look, then stacked the pictures and handed them to him.

"Thanks for the insight." He looked through the pictures, frowning. "These are the strangest pictures I've ever seen."

"She hasn't gotten the hang of the autofocus."

"No kidding." He shuffled through the pile, smiling here and there. Not that she was watching.

For pity's sake, stop it, Shay. Think about something else.

The soup was good. Rich broth with chunks of chicken, cubed carrots, and slippery noodles. Just the right touch of pepper. Never mind that it was canned. It was something to think about. Something other than the man who took up a whole side of the table.

"Can I ask you something?" He turned a blurry picture of Olivia and Maddy toward her. "How come Olivia never smiles?"

"She's smiling."

"You know what I mean."

Shay shrugged. "Doesn't like her teeth. The bottom ones are a little crooked. It's not that bad, she's just self-conscious."

He frowned at the photo. "She need braces?"

Shay gave a wry laugh. "That would be helpful, yes."

"Doesn't she want them?"

"Sure she does." Shay had started saving for

them two years before, but then her transmission went out and the furnace needed repairing. Every time she saved a little, something went wrong.

"Let's do it, then."

Shay shot him a look. The man acted like money grew on trees. She hated to turn it down, but she'd already racked up a huge debt. How would she ever pay him back?

"Absolutely not."

"It's part of our deal—I said I'd provide the necessities."

"Braces are hardly a necessity."

"Last time I checked, a pretty smile was a necessity."

Shay looked at the picture of Olivia. She was laughing, but she'd pulled her lips over her teeth like she always did. She didn't want her daughter hiding her smile. Still, this was above and beyond. Would Travis expect something in return? Would she feel she owed him something?

"No strings attached," he said.

She was torn between her daughter and her pride. Not for the first time.

"Come on, Shay. I never had a child to spoil. Think I might enjoy it."

He did enjoy spoiling. The look on his face when she'd opened her boots was proof of that. And who was she to be wearing fancy boots while her daughter went around covering her smile?

She'd do it, she decided. For Olivia's sake. *But this is it, Shay. Don't go getting used to his help. This is only temporary.*

"All right." Just two words, and she felt like she'd lost a war.

Travis's smile broadened. "Let's tell her tonight."

When they finished for the day, Travis went to check on the Barr M while Shay started supper. He'd decided the night before, as he lay in bed wanting Shay, that he was going to buy her a real wedding band. Not the handed-down cheap piece of tin she was wearing, but a real, brand-new, fine gold one from him.

He couldn't buy it in Moose Creek without starting the rumor mill, so while he was at his folks' house, he did a little online browsing. He settled on a simple gold band with some fine beveling at the edge. It was made from quality materials by a reputable company, and the simple design suited Shay.

Travis filled out his credit and shipping info and clicked *Buy*. There. It was done. The timing wasn't right yet, but when the moment arrived, the ring would be waiting.

He printed out the receipt, then gathered the bills. He was just turning off the lights when his cell rang. Seth's name showed on the ID.

"Hey, buddy," Travis said.

"Did you hear?"

"Hear what?"

"We made it!" Seth let out a whoop Travis could've heard clear from Texas.

Travis pulled the phone from his ear, smiling. "The finals?"

"You and me, baby! Fourteenth place, but still. What do you expect when you deserted me halfway through the season?"

He smiled at his friend's teasing. "Well, don't that beat all. Your first finals."

"You finaled in steer and tie roping too, dude."

"What d'ya know. Congrats, man."

"You too. Gotta run. You'd better be practicing, partner."

"Don't worry, I'll be in top form."

Travis turned off his phone and locked up his parents' house.

The finals were the first full week of December. Since they had to arrive early, he'd have to leave just before Thanksgiving. He'd miss his parents' return by a couple days.

Worse, he'd be leaving about the time his and Shay's arrangement ended. He wondered how the news would hit her. Would she feel he was leaving her for the rodeo again? If it were just him, he'd gladly pass it up, but Seth was depending on him. He couldn't burst his buddy's dream.

He'd break the news to Shay later. Maybe he could invite her along. Just as quickly, he discounted the idea. Olivia would be in school, and there was no one else to run her ranch. Besides, she'd never leave the ranch or Olivia for a couple weeks.

Shay was glad for the respite when Travis went to the Barr M. She hoped Olivia arrived before he returned. But what if she didn't come home for hours? Last night had changed things. What were they going to do all evening, here, all alone? How was she going to manage for two more months? How was she going to avoid a repeat of last night, with Travis tossing her those sexy smiles?

The house felt stuffy and too warm. Too small. She made an impromptu decision to eat at the picnic table where the breeze would carry the manly smell of him someplace else.

She was setting the food on the table when she heard his truck rumble up the drive. Just a simple, quick little supper, then Olivia would be home and all would be well. No reason to end up in his embrace on the sofa again. No reason whatsoever.

She was entering the house for the plates and silver when Travis entered the front door with a stack of mail.

"Thought we'd eat outside," she said.

He grabbed the bottle of ketchup and the salad and followed her out the patio door.

After he said grace, Shay served herself and handed him the tongs. "Everything all right at your parents' place?"

"Running smooth. Jacob's got it under control."

Her cell rang, and she pulled it from her pocket and checked the ID.

"Hey, hon. You have a good day?"

"Yeah. We worked in the garden awhile, then Abigail let us cook supper. I learned how to make chicken and dumplings from scratch."

"Sounds fun."

"Can I spend the night, Mom? Abigail said it's okay."

She looked at Travis and found his eyes on her. She envisioned the quiet house. The empty house. The feel of his arms around her, his mouth on hers.

"No." Her answer was abrupt. "I mean, another time, okay, munchkin?"

"Awwww . . . ," Olivia said, and she heard Maddy in the background. "Please, please, please?"

Travis lifted a brow, and the corner of his lip kicked up.

She looked away. "Another time." Like three months from now.

"All right," her daughter said, heavy on the pout.

"You finished with supper?"

"Yeah." She heard Abigail's muffled voice in

the background. "Abigail said to tell you she was just trying to lend God an extra hand. Whatever that means."

"Tell Abigail—" She looked at Travis, chewing, still looking smug. "Never mind."

"Abigail said she'd run me home in a few minutes."

"Perfect. See you."

She turned off the phone and stuffed it into her pocket. She could feel Travis's eyes on her.

"Wanted to spend the night?" Travis asked.

"Mm-hmm."

"Why'd you say no?"

She didn't answer. She could already hear everything she needed to hear from the tone of his voice. She dipped her bite of meat loaf in ketchup and ate it.

"Chicken?"

She met his eyes boldly. "Really, McCoy?"

His eyes danced, silver sparks igniting in the evening light. A hint of a smirk tugged at his lips. His jaw bore the stubble of a long day. She could feel the graze of it against her palm, against her cheek. Feel the contrasting softness of his lips on hers.

The boldness oozed from her body, down the bench, and puddled beneath the table. She swallowed a lump of corn.

"Is it me you don't trust?" he asked. "Or yourself?"

She pulled her eyes away from his, cleared her throat. "I wanted to tell Olivia about the braces, that's all." She took another bite of cold corn, fixed her eyes on a crack in the table that ran all the way to the end.

"If you say so."

She didn't look again. His words repeated in her head. The swaggering tone ringing clear as a bell. She wasn't fooling anyone, least of all herself.

A week later Shay was doing the breakfast dishes, when a knock sounded on the door. Olivia was at school and Travis had run to the hardware store, so she dried her hands and went to answer. Through the window, she saw a brown UPS truck.

"Howdy, Shay," Morton Spencer said through his grizzly beard. "Got a delivery—for Travis." He handed over a small package.

Shay looked at the return address label. Signature Jewelers.

"Says to deliver it to his folks' place, but since he's living here now . . ." Morton shrugged and held out the form for her signature.

She looked at the package, felt a small square box inside. Who was Travis buying jewelry for? He didn't wear any himself, never had, except for the old wedding band he wore now.

Surely he hadn't bought something for her. Her

birthday was past, and Christmas was three months off.

But what if he had? What if he'd had it shipped to his folks' house intentionally?

"Shay? You gonna sign?" Morton shoved the form and pen toward her.

Instead, Shay handed back the package. "You know, maybe you'd better take this next door, Morton."

His bushy gray brows popped up. "You sure?"

She gave a friendly smile. "I'm sure. Thanks for bringing it by, though."

He shrugged his burly shoulders. "Suit yourself. Have a good one now."

"You too."

Shay closed the door and headed for the kitchen as a thread of happiness spiraled through her.

26

Travis watched Shay glide across the floor, her hips swaying with the line dance steps, thumbs hooked in her front pockets. The Chuckwagon was packed and noisy, their friends and neighbors ready for a fun night out after a full workweek. The lead singer of the Silver Spurs belted out the chorus.

Dylan sank into the chair across from him, bearing a heaping plate of nachos with the works. "Help yourself," his friend hollered over the music.

Travis waved the plate away and turned his eyes toward Shay again. Olivia misstepped, bumped into Shay, and they laughed.

The girl's braces sparkled under the lights. She'd had them on a few weeks and never once complained of the pain. She proudly showed off her pink and purple bands at every opportunity. It felt good to do something to help her, something far-reaching. He could get used to this.

"So, how's all that going?" Dylan gestured toward Shay with a loaded nacho in his hand.

Travis and Dylan had hit it off since his return, and Travis had confided in him about the real circumstances of his and Shay's relationship.

"Slow." Travis pulled his eyes from Shay and took a long drink.

Dylan smiled around a bite. "Not what I heard."

How did . . . Ah. Shay *had* told Abigail about their kiss. Then Abigail told Wade and Wade told Dylan. "Good to know the rumor mill's in working order."

Another month had passed, and he was no closer to winning her heart than he had been. If anything, he was further away.

"Think I scared her away," he said over the din.

"She doesn't strike me as skittish. Reminds me of another filly I know," Dylan said, looking across the room where Annie Stevens sat with her sister Sierra.

Shay might have come across as strong and fearless. But Travis knew her the way others didn't. "Not as tough as she seems." In fact, deep down she was downright soft and vulnerable.

The line dancers spun on their heels and faced the band, gliding to the right. He drank in Shay's form. Square shoulders, narrow waist, legs that went forever. He realized he was ogling and tore his eyes away.

But she was his wife, blast it—biblically and legally. Could he help it if he loved her? If he wanted her in every way? If he wasn't careful, Thanksgiving would arrive and he'd be out on his tail end, his chance gone forever.

The thought scared him spitless. It was the same fear that stopped him from broaching the topic of the rodeo finals. He was afraid of losing her. As much as he wanted her, he had to be careful. She'd had enough hurt for one lifetime. He had to earn her trust before breaking the news, but he was running out of time.

He had to woo her, which was what he'd been trying to do. *I could use some help here, God. I'm getting nowhere fast.* Just like that dream he'd had. On a treadmill, going nowhere.

Right now he just wanted to take her in his arms and hold her all night long. Protect her from all life's hurts, soothe away the ones in her past. He could almost feel her lean softness pressed against him.

The song drew to a close, and he watched her take a final twirl. The dancers began dispersing as the band kicked into a slow tune.

"Excuse me," he said, standing. "I have a woman to claim."

When the song ended, Shay turned toward the table and ran smack into Travis. She braced herself against the hard wall of his chest.

Instead of backing away, he set his hands at her waist. "Dance with me."

It wasn't a question, and he gave her no choice unless she wanted to make a scene.

She slid her hands up to his shoulders and stared at the second white button on his shirt. They moved together, swaying to the introduction of "Bless the Broken Road." *Not this song*. She always turned off the radio when it came on. The words always reminded her of Travis.

Focus on the button. The round, pearly button with the white thread sticking from one of the holes. She didn't have to think about footwork; they'd always moved well together, like two halves of a whole.

She had to remember the heartbreak, the pain, the weeping nights and red-eyed days. She had to remember how long it had taken to get over him.

Who was she kidding? She'd never gotten over him. Even Garrett had sensed it. He'd been jealous and suspicious. Little did he know, the only man he'd had to be jealous of was long gone.

"Relax." Travis's hands slid up her sides. "Not gonna bite."

Her hands had knotted at his shoulders. She released the fabric of his shirt and smoothed the wrinkles. His shoulders were warm and hard beneath her palms. So strong, so sturdy. So Travis.

She met his gaze and felt locked in time. The way he looked at her, with his heart in his eyes . . .

His lips began moving with the lyrics. *Every long-lost dream* . . . He was singing them to her, and she wanted to believe he meant them.

Believe he felt the way the song's writer had, that the other women had only been a sign pointing him back to her.

Stop it, Shay. Go back to the button.

But she couldn't seem to tear her eyes away. The chorus swelled, echoing feelings she'd tried to smother for years.

Travis tightened his embrace, pulled her close until her cheek was against the soft cotton of his shirt.

She shouldn't. She really shouldn't.

Her palms flattened against his shoulders, ready to push. A protest formed on her lips, and she inhaled to give the words wings. But his musky scent snuffed out the objection. Instead, her hands slid around his shoulders.

She heard his heart thudding inside his chest, deep booms. His chin came to rest on top of her head. It was just a dance. Just one dance. But it was heaven, and didn't she deserve just this little slice of happiness? Just one song, was all she asked.

She closed her eyes, giving in to the temptation. Oh, how she'd missed this. The way he made her feel. Like the rest of the world didn't exist. It was just the two of them and enough love to see them through.

The singer began the second chorus. She wanted to freeze time, wanted the song to last forever, because once it was over, things would return to normal. She couldn't afford for them not to.

She pulled in another lungful of Travis and nestled into the warmth of his chest, remembering all the other times he'd held her. In her parents' barn, in the cab of his rattly pickup. Behind the school bleachers. It never got old. Not when she was young and green, and not now, fourteen years and countless heartaches later. But she was no longer naïve. No longer believed this feeling led to happily-ever-after.

The chorus segued into the bridge. Almost over. She needed to start letting go. She was one tag and an interlude away from reality.

She remembered the jewelry package that had arrived nearly a month ago. He'd never mentioned it, and he sure hadn't given her anything. Maybe the jewelry had been for someone else. Maybe it was that Ella back in Texas. Maybe Shay was making a fool of herself over Travis McCoy all over again.

The words ended and the melody began winding down. When the song ended, she would go back to being the old Shay. The smart Shay. She was strong, strong enough to stand on her own two feet, strong enough to do what was best.

The final notes rang out. Travis pressed a kiss where his chin had rested.

She planted her palms against his chest and gave a gentle push, looking away.

"Shay . . ."

She shook her head and turned away. As the audience applauded the band, she headed toward the table where Abigail and Wade were cuddled into one lump.

Before she reached the table, she spotted Olivia in the back corner frowning at Katy O'Neil. She couldn't see the girl's expression, but she could read Olivia's. She detoured, winding her way to the back of the room, forgetting all about the dance with Travis as protectiveness surged inside.

As she neared the girls, she caught Katy's words.

". . . why you wear that stupid ponytail. It looks like—"

"Hello, Katy," Shay said.

The girl jumped, her expression changing from shock to an awkward smile. "Hi, Mrs. Brandenberger."

Don't you mean Mrs. Hoboberger? Shay stopped the words from leaking out. Barely. "Talked to your dad earlier today. He's bringing me some barbed wire tomorrow for my baskets."

Judging by her widened blue eyes, Katy got the hint. "Oh, that's nice." She glanced at Olivia. "Well, have fun, Olivia. See ya, Mrs. Brandenberger." Her blond hair swung saucily as she scurried toward the dance floor.

Shay turned to Olivia. "What was that about?"

241

She shrugged. "She was making fun of my hair."

"What's wrong with your hair? It's beautiful." Thick and naturally wavy and shiny to boot.

"Said it looks like a monkey cut it with a hacksaw."

Shay scowled. She took exception to that, especially since she was the one who trimmed it. Maybe it was time for a real cut, at least one to shape it up. She still hadn't used her birthday coupon for the Hair Barn.

Shay put her arm around Olivia, guiding her toward the tables. "How about a real haircut?"

"Could I?"

Shay smiled. "Sure. We'll do it this week, all right?"

She was rewarded with a metal smile. "Thanks, Mom."

Olivia trotted toward the dance floor where Maddy was dancing freestyle. She remembered Travis's caution about fixing everything for Olivia, but it was only a haircut. And if she could so easily help her daughter fit in, wouldn't it be cruel not to?

Shay headed toward the table where Wade and Abigail snuggled together.

She took a seat across from them and stiffened when Travis, out of nowhere, pulled out the chair beside her. He sank into it, his knee brushing hers.

She pulled away and sipped her watery soda, feeling suddenly exhausted. She wanted to run home and burrow under a thick pile of quilts.

"Look at the girls," Abigail said over the zippy country tune the band had started.

Shay watched her daughter and Maddy working out their own steps to the song, laughing as they botched them. Olivia seemed to have forgotten all about Katy O'Neil.

Maddy had discarded the ponytail for the night and added a few curls. Maybe Olivia would like a style like that. "I like Maddy's hair."

"She begged me to curl it." Abigail leaned forward. "I think there's a boy."

Beside her, Wade frowned. "What?"

Abigail smiled at him. "Settle down, Dad. I don't think it's fatal."

Travis was quiet, and Shay wondered what he was thinking, what he was feeling after that dance.

No, she didn't. She only wanted the night to end. She smothered a yawn.

"You can go on, if you want," Abigail said. "We can take Olivia home with us. Maddy's been wanting her to spend the night for weeks."

This again. Why did it always come up when Travis was there? She felt his eyes on her, felt her shoulders stiffening at the thought of a night alone. Especially after that dance. Apprehension raced through her veins, speeding her heart.

She tried for nonchalance. "Another time."

Abigail started to respond, then her eyes darted to Travis and back. "You sure?"

She wondered what Abigail had seen on Travis's face, and before she could stop herself, she looked. Just a glance. But it turned into something longer. His brow was quirked, but his lips formed a hard straight line.

Travis knew she was afraid to be alone with him. His question from weeks ago was written all over his face. *Chicken?* Only this time he didn't look amused.

He thought he knew her so well. That he could just read her mind any ol' time he pleased. That he knew what she wanted before she knew it herself. Well, he didn't.

She lifted her chin and shot him a look.

Then she faced Abigail. "Actually, tonight would be great. Thanks, guys."

Abigail looked between the two of them. "Sure, anytime."

It was settled. Olivia was going to Maddy's for the night, and she'd proven to Travis that she did trust herself to be alone with him. That resisting his charms was easy as pie. If her limbs suddenly quivered, if her shoulders suddenly felt heavy, it was only fatigue from a hard day's work.

27

*T*ravis gripped the steering wheel as he guided the truck toward home. Beside him, Shay huddled close to her door. A thick curtain of tension had fallen between them like fog on a cool autumn morning.

Less than an hour ago she'd been soft and malleable in his arms. He'd dared to hope, just for the space of one song, that things might change. That Shay might realize how much he loved her and give him another chance.

But as soon as the song ended, something shifted. She pushed him away, her guard as high as ever.

His fingers ached now, and he loosened his grip on the wheel. She regretted letting Olivia spend the night with Maddy. He knew she would as soon as she gave in, but she'd never admit it. Certainly not to him.

He drew in a deep breath and released it quietly. *Help me remember she's been hurt. That she's only trying to protect herself.* Hadn't he just been thinking earlier this evening how vulnerable she was? Of course she'd try to protect herself. It was human nature.

But having her in his arms for just those few

minutes had been bliss. She smelled of sunshine and citrus. She seemed so willing to give herself to him. And then—*boom!* She was gone, just like that. If only he could recapture what they'd had on the dance floor.

Or at least dispel this awkward silence. He flipped on the radio, and a slow country tune wafted from the speakers. Even with the music, tension thickened the air in the cab, swelling the molecules until it was hard to breathe. How long could this go on?

He'd been waiting to tell her what he'd done. This wasn't quite the moment he'd hoped for, but maybe it would soothe her worries, make her drop her guard a hair. He turned into the drive. Pebbles popped under the tires, loud in the quiet confines of the cab.

When he pulled up to the house, he shut off the engine and she moved to get out.

"Wait." He stopped her with a hand on her arm. "I have something for you."

He felt her eyes on him while he gathered his thoughts. It was too dark to read her eyes.

He reached into his pocket and pulled out his wallet. He pulled out a paper, unfolded it, and handed it to her.

"What's this?"

He turned on the dome light. "Read it."

Her eyes squinted as she read, her brows going low. Her lips tightened.

What was she thinking? Surely she'd be relieved to have the monkey off her back awhile.

"You paid up my mortgage."

Her tone was flat, not what he expected. Maybe she was overwhelmed.

"For six months. Through March. Thought it might help you breathe a little easier."

She aimed a smile in his direction, not quite meeting his eyes. "Thank you. That was very generous."

Her smile seemed forced. She reached for the handle.

"Wait."

Shay stopped, her hand still on the lever.

"Why are you sore at me?"

She cleared her throat. "I'm not. How could I be—it was very thoughtful. I'm obliged."

She was out the door before he could move. Couldn't get away from him fast enough. He tried not to feel hurt.

He followed, catching up with her on the porch steps. "Can we talk?"

She sighed. "About what?"

"Shay . . ."

"I'm tired."

So was he. Tired of trying to read her mind and being wrong. Tired of trying to figure out what was going on behind those green eyes.

He shook his head. "I don't know what you want from me."

"Don't want anything from you."

Maybe that was the problem. She'd seemed to want something from him during that dance. But now . . .

"You're like a faucet, Shay. Running hot one minute, cold the next."

She glared at him. "I am not frigid."

He frowned, watching her open the door, her jaw set.

"Never said you were." Shoot, frigid was the last word that came to mind when he thought of Shay. She was full of passion and life. "Is that what your ex-husband said?"

"None of your business." She entered the house and flipped on a lamp.

"Shay, I'm trying to understand."

She turned in the kitchen doorway, heaving a deep sigh. "Just leave me alone, Travis."

He dragged in a breath and blew it out silently. Patience. He needed patience.

He crossed the living room, emptied his pockets. A handful of coins, his wallet and cell, a ponytail holder Olivia had handed him halfway through the night.

He heard the cupboard door fall shut, the faucet running in the kitchen. He heard the abruptness of her movements. Was she cross because he'd paid her mortgage? Maybe so, but she'd been distant before that.

Had she felt forced into the dance by the crowd

of neighbors? Her body had seemed willing enough, but maybe he was wrong. Or was it his clumsy comment on the porch?

He didn't know, but he knew he didn't want the evening to end on this note. He reached the passage between rooms just as she did.

She stopped short, and the water in her glass sloshed over the rim and onto her shirt.

"Sorry."

She tried to step around him, but he blocked her way. "Shay, wait."

She shot him a look.

He was getting that look a lot these days, and he felt his patience draining. "What? What did I do?"

"Move."

He could be stubborn too. "Not till you tell me what's wrong."

"Nothing's wrong."

"You could freeze water with those looks."

She shoved him with her palm. "Stop saying that."

"Is that what's bothering you? I didn't mean it like that. Blast it, Shay, you're the furthest thing from frigid there ever was. If your ex called you that, he was an idiot."

"He never called me that—now move."

Travis sighed hard. "Then what's the problem?"

"There is no problem, Travis. Not a single one. Everything is just hunky-dory!"

"You're yelling."

"Well, you're blocking my way."

He moved aside, rubbing his jaw. "Fine, go on."

"Fine."

She took her half-empty glass and passed. He ran his hand over his jaw. That woman was gonna be the death of him. He watched her enter her room and give the door a shove. It hit the frame with a slam.

"You can't hide forever, Shay," he called.

If she had the last word, he didn't hear what it was.

28

*O*ctober morphed into November. The leaves no sooner turned vibrant than the wind tugged them from their branches. Shay watched them fall with equal measures of anticipation and dread. They lay on the cool, spongy ground where they faded to drab earth tones, then curled into brittle skeletons.

November swept across the valley, bringing snowstorms and gusts of frosty wind. Maddy spent the night with Olivia during one such storm, and the next morning Travis helped them build a snowman that didn't melt away until the middle of the month when an unseasonable warm front moved through the area. Warm, down-filled coats were happily traded for lined jackets for several days before winter claimed the valley once again.

Shay and Travis had reached an unspoken truce. They worked efficiently together, shifting to the chores required by the colder season. He'd made no overtures since the night they'd danced, and he never mentioned the jewelry he'd purchased. But Shay couldn't help but wonder what he'd bought and for whom.

Working together required closeness, and sometimes his hand or knee would brush hers and she'd retreat. Each night Shay struck another day off her mental calendar.

When they were one month from the end of their arrangement, a nervous anticipation climbed onto her back and rode with her everywhere. She was glad. Relieved. Only one more month, and Travis would be gone from their lives.

But as soon as the thought surfaced, dread and fear sank like heavy weights into her unwanted backpack. He'd leave and then what? They'd never see him again?

Lying in bed at night, listening to the quiet strum of hymns on his guitar, Shay wondered how deep her feelings had grown. She worried about how attached Olivia had become to him.

Travis seemed to sense her trepidation as the month slid by. Either that or he had apprehensions of his own. Tension mounted with each day that melted off the calendar, accumulating like snow on the ground outside.

Shay was checking Olivia's school papers on Monday evening after supper when she found a crinkled blue paper in the bottom of her daughter's book bag.

"What's this?"

Olivia looked up from the game of Scrabble she and Travis were playing at the kitchen table, her new layered haircut framing her face. She tossed her swingy hair over her shoulder. "Oh, that."

"You have a group project due tomorrow? Is it done?"

"Uh . . . not exactly."

"What does that mean?"

"Well, me and Rachel Lewis were supposed to do this science experiment with her horse, but we didn't have everything we needed, and now . . ." Her shrug was the sentence's final punctuation mark.

"Says here it's 40 percent of your science grade. Olivia, you have to do it." Shay was surprised she hadn't heard from Rachel's mom, but maybe she didn't know about the assignment either.

"Isn't that Tina's daughter, from the coffee shop?" Travis asked.

"Yeah."

"I can run her over there," Travis said. "Can you finish it in one night?" he asked Olivia.

She shrugged. "Guess so, but we'd be up pretty late."

Shay got on the phone and made arrangements for Olivia to spend the night with Rachel. She took the list of supplies to the market, then dropped Olivia at her friend's house.

It was only on the way home that she realized what she'd done. The last thing she wanted a week from the end of their arrangement was to spend a night alone with Travis. Well, she'd just stay busy and out of his way. She'd work on some barbed wire baskets for the tourist shops. She'd have less time to work on them once she was working part-time for Hank. Travis would be gone, along with his financial support, and every basket would help. She'd work late tonight, until Travis was asleep, then she'd creep into the house. Before she knew it, it would be morning.

Upon returning home, she went straight to the barn. The sturdy timber-framed barn held back the bite of the cold wind. Inside, the straw provided insulation from the cold, and the body heat from the horses warmed the space. Even so, her breath fogged in front of her.

She worked with the used barbed wire, winding it into basket shapes, careful of the barbs, even with the work gloves. She made each one a little different. Later she'd lacquer the baskets, tie raffia on the handles, and attach the price tags with her simple logo.

The animals had quieted behind her, giving in to sleep despite the clicking sounds of the wires knocking together and the loud clips when she cut through them. She told herself each basket would be the last one, but then she'd find herself picking up another strand of wire and bending it into shape.

She liked the one she was working on now. It was oval shaped, and she wrapped the handle round and round with barb-free metal. Maybe she'd keep this one for Abigail's Christmas present.

"Getting late."

She dropped the wire cutters. They hit the dirt floor with a clunk.

"Sorry. Thought you heard me come in."

"I was busy." She shot him a look, taking in his long, sturdy frame in that split second. Her heart galloped in her chest, and she wasn't entirely sure it was from the fright.

It didn't slow as he approached.

"I see that." He picked up a basket and looked it over while Shay finished the one she was working on.

She hated the tension that had crawled into the barn with him. The way it had continually these last several weeks. Only now it wasn't daytime, and Olivia wasn't waiting at home. Now they faced a long, quiet night, and Shay wondered how she'd get any sleep with Travis lying so near in the empty house.

He touched her on the shoulder, and she jumped.

Why was he out here? He was supposed to fall asleep on the sofa and let her sneak in later. He was ruining the plan.

"Talk to me."

She shrugged. "Nothing to say."

"You're strung tighter'n these wires."

"You scared me, is all."

He hooked a finger under her jaw, turning her face. "It's more'n that."

She pulled away. "You haven't exactly been Mr. Easygoing lately either, you know."

He was quiet so long she almost looked at him. Almost. In the quiet, she could feel her pulse throbbing in her neck.

"Reckon you're right," he said.

She could count on one hand the times she'd heard that from a man. One finger.

"It's harder than I thought."

"What is?" she asked, then pressed her lips together, suddenly sure she didn't want to know.

"Loving you."

She looked at him, feeling the tug of two emotions. Pleasure at his declaration of love, offense at his implication. It was easier to focus on the latter.

She dropped the basket and jerked off her gloves. "That's an awful thing to say." She turned to leave.

If she was so hard to love, why didn't he just stop it? Why didn't he just leave now?

"I didn't mean it that way," he called.

She made it as far as the third empty stall before he stopped her, turning her around.

"Blast it, Shay, why are you always twisting my words?"

She pulled her arm away. "I didn't twist anything." She was surprised by the sting of his words. How did he have the power to hurt her? When had she surrendered that to him?

"It's easier to fight than admit the feelings, isn't it?"

"You're delusional." She turned to go.

He pulled her to him, and she smacked into the hard wall of his chest. Their breath tangled in the air between them for an instant.

"Am I?" A storm surged in his eyes, gone almost black in the dimness of the barn.

Then his lips claimed hers.

Panic descended on her, a torrential downpour. This couldn't happen. It couldn't. She pushed at his chest.

Three heartbeats later a fog of desire moved in. The fight slowly drained away.

His lips were so warm, so strong and capable. Her arms slid around him, her fingers forked through his hair.

At her response, his kiss grew more urgent, and she felt months of need building inside her. Years of need. No one had ever taken Travis's place in her heart. How could she give him up again? She couldn't. Not when she had a choice. She wanted him now, forever.

He lifted her from her feet. Her body pressed against the warm length of his. She was scarcely aware of moving, and then she was lowered onto a bed of fresh-smelling straw.

Travis broke the kiss, and she heard herself whimper. She didn't want to open her eyes. She was afraid of what she'd see. *Don't leave me. Oh, God, don't let him leave me now.*

He pressed a kiss to her forehead. His breaths came quickly, bathing her with warmth. His heart thudded against her side.

She opened her eyes. He was a heartbeat away, his eyes as serious as she'd ever seen them. The clouds were gone, and in their place were all the things she needed from him.

"Shay . . . ," he whispered.

She didn't want to talk. Talk would ruin the spell that had wound itself around them.

"Shh." She pulled him closer and toyed with his lips. His breath caught, and the heady feeling that assuaged her took her own breath away.

He pulled back and looked at her. "I love you, Shay."

Something swelled inside her, big and powerful. Her own declaration clawed for release and caught like a rock in her throat.

"If you don't hear anything else, hear that," he said. And then his lips were on hers again, and she was floating in a sea of rapture.

29

Consciousness slowly claimed Shay. She felt warm and snug, as if she were wrapped in a cozy cocoon. She didn't want to open her eyes, didn't want to check the time. Dawn would arrive soon enough, if it hadn't already.

Her body felt like liquid, languid and relaxed. The mattress was warm and soft against her belly. Her arm was under her pillow, and her leg was entwined with another.

Her eyelids fluttered open.

Travis stared back from the pillow beside her.

" 'Morning," he said.

She sucked in a breath and clutched the sheet to her chest. The night before came rushing back. The kiss, the stall, her clothes . . . where were they?

Heat flushed her face even as something stirred in the pit of her belly. "What are you doing?" she croaked.

"Watching you sleep." His voice was deep and raspy. Dawn's light leaked through the sheers, bathing the planes of his face. He looked so peaceful. At ease.

What they'd done last night was beautiful and perfectly permissible. They were married, after all. He was her husband.

She relaxed into the softness of the bed,

unclenched the bedding from her fist. She stared into his eyes, soaking in some of his peace.

"If I'm dreaming, don't wake me," he whispered.

She felt like she was dreaming too. But she wasn't. This was real. He was here, in her bed, looking at her with forever in his eyes. A touch of panic swept through her.

He touched her hair and came away with a piece of straw.

She remembered last night. His hands, soft and capable. The look in his eyes, the sound of his voice whispering things in her ear. Things she'd never heard from any man, things she knew she'd replay in her mind a million times.

The panic drained away, replaced by something else. Contentment? Yes, she felt strangely content to stay here with him all day.

But she had responsibilities. Hungry livestock. She sighed. "What time is it?"

He brushed the hair from her face and trailed his thumb along her jaw. "Chore time, unfortunately."

She wished they had a little time. Just an hour or so. She had little doubt what they'd do with that hour. At the thought, gooseflesh pebbled her skin.

He pressed a kiss to her forehead. "Talk later?"

"Mm-hmm."

He pushed himself upright and left the bed.

Shay turned her face into the pillow, suddenly shy. A moment later the shower kicked on.

She got out of bed and slipped into her warm terry robe. Her body felt sluggish and achy as she entered the kitchen and started the coffee. A few minutes later she filled two thermoses, adding cream to her own.

She carried hers to the living room window and sipped the hot brew, looking out over the fresh white landscape, her thoughts churning. What did last night mean? He'd told her he loved her so many times.

And she loved him too. She wasn't so stubborn she couldn't admit it, though she hadn't verbalized it. He had to know. She'd never have made love to him if she didn't.

What now, God? I took a step of faith, but I'm not sure the ground is stable.

"It snowed." He slipped his arms around her and pulled her into his chest.

Shay leaned back and folded her arms around his. The clouds on the horizon had brightened. Fingers of periwinkle and pink stretched across the sky.

"Pretty," she said.

He kissed her temple. "Beautiful."

He smelled good, all musky and clean. And way too distracting. "Better get my shower." She turned, but he didn't let go. He pulled her closer and kissed her softly.

"Stay here," he said. "I got the chores."

It was tempting to stay inside, all warm and cozy. But they'd get it done faster, the two of them. "I'll be out in a few minutes."

"Run a bath. Have a long, hot soak. You work too hard."

On the other hand, a bath sounded heavenly, and he was offering so nicely. "If you insist."

"I do." He gave her one last kiss before tugging on his boots and coat and hat. The wind blew a chill through the room before he could shut the door. Shay watched him through the window, wonder swelling inside at the sight of him, her mouth lifting in a smile.

30

*T*ravis would've been in heaven that week if it weren't for the secret he'd been keeping. He had to tell Shay about the rodeo. He needed to leave the day their arrangement officially ended if he was going to make it to Vegas in time to practice with Seth.

Four nights ago had been the beginning of everything he'd dreamed. The way Shay had surrendered made his heart race. She loved him. Maybe she hadn't said the words, but she'd said it in other ways. If she trusted him with her body, she trusted him with her heart.

But with his departure only three days away now, he had to tell her soon. Like today.

She'd understand. Now that he thought about it, he was sure of it. They'd worked so well together all week. The looks she'd tossed his way made it hard to concentrate on work. Each night after Olivia fell asleep, he'd curled up with Shay in the warmth of her bed and shown her how much he loved her.

He looked forward to being alone with her tonight. But first he had to check on his parents' ranch. He'd bring back the wedding band he'd been waiting to give her, and then, after supper, he'd tell her about the rodeo. They'd laugh about how nervous he'd been, then he'd present her with the ring.

He entered the kitchen where Shay was cooking. "I'm gonna go check on the Barr M."

He wanted to gather her in his arms right now, but Olivia was at the table doing homework. They were trying to take it slow.

Shay looked up from the skillet. "I'll keep things warm," she said with a secret glimmer in her eyes.

"Can I ride along?" Olivia asked.

He pulled his eyes from Shay. "Homework done?"

"Yep!" She closed her book and stuffed it into her book bag. "Just finished."

"All right with you, Mom?" Travis asked.

"Yep."

"Mind if I take yours? I'm on E."

"Keys are on the peg."

"Thanks." Travis went for the keys, then rooted through the junk on his table. "Anyone seen my cell? I haven't seen it since yesterday." He'd missed it all day, that lump in his pocket.

"You could call it," Olivia said.

"It'll have to wait. I wanna get back before supper's cold."

"You check the barn?" Shay called from the kitchen. "Third stall on the left?"

Travis smothered a smile, remembering their return to the third stall the day before. He peeked into the kitchen. "Maybe you can help me look there later."

Shay hiked a brow. "Maybe I can."

The smile she put on his face carried him out the door.

"Buckle up," he told Olivia when she got in the passenger side. He put the truck in gear and headed down the lane. "How's school going? You get that project turned in?"

"Yeah, we did. School's okay, I guess. I'm ready for Thanksgiving break, though."

"And then Christmas right after that." The realization that he'd be there for the holidays buoyed his spirits. He nudged Olivia playfully. "How're things on the boy front?"

She groaned. "Boys stink!" She turned an innocent look on him. "Except you, of course."

"Oh yeah, of course."

Olivia bared her braces. "How old were you and Mom when you met?"

"Your mom and I went to school together from the time we were little. Barely knew each other, though. We hung in different crowds."

"How'd you get together?"

Travis smiled, remembering. "Well, after the summer of our sophomore year, I was walking through the hall and saw this tall, stunning girl—from the back, see, so I didn't recognize her. Thought she was a new student. 'Bout that time, your mom, she turns around, and I saw who it was."

He'd felt like lightning had struck. Shay had

grown a good four inches over the summer, and her face had matured. She had a tan that set off her green eyes and a mysterious smile that kicked him in the gut.

"What happened next?"

He chuckled. "Well, she turned and saw me gawking, so I looked away and walked right past her."

"You chickened out."

"Guess I did."

"Did you ask her out?"

"For a while we just kept making eye contact. Over our books in study hall, across the cafeteria, down the hallway. Then another girl started flirting with me a lot, and I guess your mom thought I liked her. She wouldn't look at me after that."

"What'd you do?"

"Rode over to her house and asked her out."

"Just like that?"

Actually, they'd exchanged words in her folks' barn. It had escalated, passion sparking a fire the way it always did with Shay. In a fit of anger, she'd dared him to kiss her, thinking he wouldn't, thinking he really cared for Marla.

Boy, had she been wrong.

He smiled. "Just like that." Nothing he loved more than thinking about Shay. What a long journey they'd had.

"Why didn't you marry her back then, when you ran off together?"

He shook his head. "Well, squirt, I let another dream get in the way. Never stopped loving your mom, though. Not for a minute." He turned into his parents' drive. "I regretted it soon after, but by then your mom was married. I thought I'd lost her for good."

"Were you crushed?"

He traded a smile with Olivia. "Sure was. But God brought us back together, didn't He? 'Sides"—he winked at her—"if I hadn't left, there wouldn't be you. And you, kiddo, were meant to be." He ruffled her hair and watched her duck her head.

Travis guided the truck down the lane, then pulled up to the house. "Gotta go grab some bills and stuff. You can run to the barn if you want. Bitsy had her pups a couple weeks ago." He turned the key and exited the truck.

"Cool." Olivia hopped out her side and started for the barn.

"Meet me back here in twenty," he called, shutting the door.

" 'Kay, Dad!"

He froze, the title catching him right in the gut. He watched her disappear into the barn, a smile of wonder lifting his mouth.

Shay added salt to the pasta, lowered the heat, and set the timer. The past week with Travis had been different from all the weeks before. The glances, filled with meaning, the not-so-accidental touches . . . not to mention the necking in the barn when the chores were done.

She waved her hand in front of her face. It wasn't the steam that flushed her skin. She stirred the ground beef, unable to wipe the silly grin off her face. That an accidental wedding had morphed into a full-fledged marriage was just . . . amazing. That Travis was back in her life, loving her, was nothing short of miraculous.

She'd looked at him numerous times that week with wonder. *My husband. Travis McCoy is my husband.* He'd asked what she was thinking when she looked at him like that.

"Nothing," she'd say, smiling each time. A little mystery never hurt anyone.

Shay gave the beef a final stir and turned the heat down before setting the table. She was laying down the napkins when she heard a buzzing.

Travis's cell. She followed the sound, moving quickly. In the living room. No, in her bedroom. She walked around the bed. Under the bed? No, under the damp towel lying on the floor.

She picked up the phone, glad she'd found it for him. The screen was lit, and a text stared back.

Miss u, T! Only 3 more days. Can't wait 2 see u! XXOO Ella

An ache bloomed inside her.

Ella? The woman from Texas? Three more days? What did that mean? Was she coming here? Shay set her hand on her chest where her heart kicked against her ribs.

She looked at the text again. Hugs and kisses? She wandered into the living room and dropped the phone on the sofa, wanting it out of her hand. What was going on? Maybe there was a rational explanation.

But how else could she take the message? Friends didn't use Xs and Os. And she said she missed him. That she was going to see him in three days. Three days would be . . . Monday.

The day their arrangement ended.

Shay's stomach twisted into a hard knot. It couldn't be true. Everything he'd said this week, it couldn't all be lies.

But what else could it be? Why else would he be seeing this woman the very day their arrangement ended? Why else would he be in contact with someone who signed her notes with Xs and Os?

He's leaving.

The realization hit her with sudden surety. He wasn't even sticking around a single extra day.

The memory of the jewelry package flashed in her mind like a beacon. He'd bought jewelry, all right. It just hadn't been for her. He'd bought it for Ella, whatever it was.

What have I done? Oh, dear Lord, what have I done? She palmed her forehead. She was such a ninny! She'd fallen for it all, hook, line, and sinker. When was she going to learn?

Why had Travis done this? Why had he lured her into bed just before he reunited with his lover?

It doesn't matter why, Shay. What matters is that you fell for it again. Fell for him, head over heels. You've made a fool of yourself all over again.

She sank onto the sofa, remembered it was where he slept. *Used* to sleep, she reminded herself. She leapt to her feet again. She was in love with him. Hadn't she admitted it to herself just this week? And if that wasn't enough to convince her, this terrible ache in her midsection was proof enough.

The timer went off, and she went numbly to turn it off, setting everything to simmer. She returned to the living room, pacing like a caged cougar.

What now? What should I do, God?

She had to confront him. He had to leave, the sooner the better. If only she'd found out sooner, before she'd given herself to him. What had felt beautiful and right before now only felt cheap and wrong. So wrong.

She crossed her arms over her stomach. How could he do it? How could he take her that way, shower her with words of love, when he had another woman in the wings? It didn't make sense.

But then, did love ever make sense? Not for her, it hadn't.

She remembered the way Travis had reacted to Beau, all jealous and possessive. She gave a wry laugh. Wasn't that funny, when he'd been carrying on behind her back the whole time? Hadn't Garrett been the same way? Accusing her of flirting with other men while he came on to the waitresses at the Chuckwagon?

Either she had the worst luck, or she was the worst judge of character this side of the Mississippi. She had a special talent for finding real winners.

And now she supposed an annulment was out of the question. They would have to get a divorce. Shay felt the sting of tears. Twice divorced! Unthinkable for a woman who believed so strongly in till-death-do-us-part.

She paced and thought and paced some more. She added sauce to the beef and gave it a stir.

By the time the truck rumbled up the drive, her legs were limp and wobbly. *Buck up, Shay. You have to do this. Be brave. Get through supper, then you can confront him alone.*

He'd know something was wrong. She wasn't that good an actor, and he knew her too well. But he'd wait until they were alone to press her. She pulled in a deep breath and blew it out just as the front door flew open.

Olivia shut the door and pulled her boots off. "It's cold out there!" She had flurries melting in her hair. "Travis said go ahead with supper. Your truck's making a funny noise, and he's checking it out."

Shay hoped it took awhile. She got supper on the table and had Olivia say grace.

"I'm starving." Olivia ladled sauce over her pasta. "Travis said it's supposed to be colder than usual this winter. They use solar patterns to make the predictions, know that?"

"No, I didn't."

"Travis said the almanac's pretty accurate. He's a good cowboy, don'tcha think, Mom?"

"Very good."

"Jacob Whitehorse said Travis can rope like nobody's business. I guess that's why he did so good on the circuit, huh?"

"Guess so."

"He's teaching me, but I'm not too good. I'm gonna practice and then by next fall, maybe I can help with roundup."

Next fall? When had Olivia started looking at his stay as long term? *Maybe since you started looking all goo-goo-eyed at the man.*

"Olivia . . ."

"Mom, I was thinking." Olivia played with her

pasta. "You know I loved Daddy . . ." She looked up at Shay with a question in her eyes.

"I know, hon." Garrett hadn't been much of a father, but children were sometimes blind to that. Especially when they had nothing else to compare them to.

"But he's gone, and he's never coming back," Olivia said. "And I really like Travis, and he likes me too."

Shay forced a smile. "You're easy to like."

"Is it okay if I call him Dad?" The words burst from Olivia like a bull through barbed wire. "He's more of a dad than my real dad ever was. He's teaching me things and spending time with—What's wrong?"

Shay felt her food congealing in her stomach. How had this happened?

She thought of the bedtime readings, the ride-alongs, the games of Scrabble. That's how it happened.

"Oh, hon," Shay said. "I don't think that's a good idea."

"But, Mom—"

"No, Olivia." Her words shot out like bullets, propelled by fear. "I'm sorry, it's just—"

"That's not fair. Maddy has a dad, all my friends have dads, and Travis is here, and he's married to you and everything."

"You know this was a temporary arrangement."

"But things are—you've been getting along good. I thought . . ."

Shay closed her eyes. This was all her fault. "I'm sorry. I should've made sure you understood. There's something else we need to talk about."

"Well, it doesn't matter." Olivia dropped her fork on her plate. "I already did it."

Shay frowned, a feeling of dread snaking up her spine. "Already did what?"

"I already called him Dad." Olivia lifted her stubborn chin.

Shay's food sank like a lead weight in her stomach. She set her fork down. "When?"

"Tonight at his folks' place. I want him to be my real dad!"

Shay stood, her chair squawking across the floor. She carried her half-full plate to the garbage and dumped it. Her thoughts swirled like flurries in a blizzard.

She had to talk to Travis. Had to tell him to go. This had gotten way out of hand. Olivia would be hurt when he left, but she couldn't help that. Better now than later when she'd come to love and trust him as her dad.

"Why are you being this way? I thought you liked him."

Shay put her plate in the sink. "We'll talk about this later. Finish up."

She grabbed her coat off the hook and tugged

on her boots. She had to take care of this now before things got worse.

The cold air smacked her face as she left the house. The sun had vanished behind the mountains, and twilight marched across the sky. Travis leaned over the engine of her truck, the hood propped over his head on a crooked spindle.

She took the porch steps slowly, then crossed the lawn, the blades of grass crunching like brittle sticks of ice under her feet.

"I love you, sweetness." His words from the night before flashed, unbidden, in her mind. *Stop it, Shay.*

She had to forget it. It was a lie. He probably said the same thing to Ella. Would say it to her on Monday when he saw her again.

Her thoughts flew like rabid bats around her head. She stopped a safe distance away and pulled her frame upright. She was strong. She could do this.

"Going somewhere?" she asked.

"Not in this bucket o' bolts." He turned, a teasing smile on his lips.

The grin fell away slowly. A crease formed between his brows. "What's wrong?" Then his brows lifted and his head tipped back. "Oh. Hey, if you're not cool with the Dad thing, that's fine, Shay. I didn't expect her to—"

"When were you gonna tell me you're

leaving?" She jabbed her hands into her coat pockets.

He jerked at the abrupt change in topic, then slowly lifted his hands, palms up. "Tonight. I was gonna tell you tonight."

Sure he was. "Before or after you slept with me?"

He winced. "I should've told you before—was afraid you'd be upset . . ."

"You were right."

He took a step forward.

She stepped back.

He stopped. "I didn't expect to make the finals, and I wouldn't go at all except my friend Seth is my team roping partner. He's never been. It's his dream."

The rodeo? This was about the rodeo again? Her breath came out in a wry laugh. She couldn't even compete with the rodeo, much less another woman. She felt the sting of ancient tears and blinked them back.

"I'll be back in a few weeks at most."

Like heck he would. "You need to leave, Travis. Tonight."

His mouth opened, then closed.

She forced herself to meet his eyes. *Be strong. You can do this, Shay. You have to do this. For Olivia. For yourself.*

"What?" He took a step, reached for her.

She stiffened. "Don't touch me."

His hand fell to his side. He pushed his hat back. "It's just one competition, Shay. I know I should've told you, but when it's over, I'm coming back."

She swallowed against the hard lump in her throat. "Don't bother."

He looked away, at the barn. Then he looked at her again. "You don't mean that."

She steeled herself against the hurt in his eyes. She repeated the text message in her head, right down to the Xs and Os. She toyed with the idea of tossing it in his face. But this was humiliating enough.

"Tonight, Travis."

He exhaled, his breath fogging in front of him. He pulled his hat and rubbed his jaw. Set his hat back on his head. A shadow flickered on his cheek. "Our agreement is through Monday," he said. "I have a right to stay till then."

"I don't give a fig about the agreement."

He rubbed his jaw. "We had a deal."

"I'll pay back everything I owe you."

"I don't care about the stinking money, Shay!"

Maybe she could get that in writing. He sure wasn't worth his word. If she were smart, she would've learned that fourteen years ago.

She walked past him, pulled the rod, and set the hood down. "I'm taking Olivia for hot chocolate. Pack up and be gone before we get back." She met his gaze. "Don't call, don't write, and don't come back."

When she passed, he took her arm. "What about—my gosh, Shay, didn't it mean anything to you? What about everything we did—everything we said?"

She pulled her arm from him and looked him square in the eye. "Yeah, Travis. What about it?"

31

*T*ravis stared aimlessly down the dark Mojave Freeway. Ahead, a semi's taillights led the way, and darkness pressed in from every side. His grip was loose on the steering wheel. It was late and had been a long day of traveling, but he wasn't so much tired as bone-weary.

Weary and empty. The emptiness started three days earlier, when Shay drove off with a tearful Olivia. He'd gone to the Barr M, hoping Shay would see reason once the dust settled. But her phone had gone to voice mail each time he'd called, and she hadn't been at church. He'd come around Sunday evening, hoping for one last chance to talk, but she and Olivia were gone.

They'd been the slowest three days of his life. But then Monday came calling, and the farther he got from Moose Creek, the more riled he became. Didn't she know he planned to return? He'd left messages saying as much, but she either didn't buy in or didn't give a hoot.

It was only three measly weeks. One lousy rodeo—and not even for him, but for his friend. But the longer he drove, the more time passed with no word from Shay, he wondered if there were any point in returning.

All day he'd had nothing but time to think, remember, and regret. It seemed cruel that he'd finally won Shay's heart back only to lose her again. Why couldn't she trust him? Why couldn't she give him a chance? Didn't she know he'd changed?

God, I was patient, wasn't I? What happened? Why have I lost her all over again?

His cell phone pealed and vibrated in his pocket. Hope flooded through him, kicking his heart into high gear.

He checked the lit screen and saw his parents' cell number. He let out a deep breath and answered.

"Howdy, son," Wyatt McCoy said. "Hope we didn't catch you at a bad time."

"Not at all, Dad. Just heading down to Vegas for the finals."

"Everything okay at the Barr M?"

"Fine, just fine. Jacob keeps it running like a well-oiled machine. How're things in Guatemala?"

"Good, good. Fact is . . . that's why your mom and I are calling."

"Hi, honey," Mom said. "We're sharing the phone. We wanted to tell you about something that happened yesterday."

Travis got the feeling something big was coming. "Okay, shoot."

"During the service, Pastor Gomez preached on knowing God's will for your life. And during the invitation, well, your dad and I just looked at each other, and we both knew what that was for us."

"Let's just tell him, Doreen," Dad said.

"Okay, well, the bottom line is, we feel God calling us to stay here, honey."

"Permanently," Dad said.

"I'll be darned." It was all Travis could think to say. His folks had ranched all his life. But they were nothing if not obedient to God.

"We've both been feeling it," his mom said. "But we didn't mention it to each other until last night during the service. It's been weighing heavily on me our whole time here."

"On me too," Dad said. "We want to serve the people of Guatemala."

"We've come to love them very much," Mom said.

"That's something else. I'm happy for you, that you both agree and want to go where God's leading you. Are you still coming home for a while? What about the Barr M?"

"We're returning just long enough to pack our things," Mom said.

"We're wondering if you'd be interested in running the Barr M now that you're back in Moose Creek," Dad said. "Maybe even owning it."

Travis squeezed the wheel, regret rising in him so fast it threatened to suck him under. If they'd asked a week ago, how different things would've been. But now . . .

"That means a lot to me, Dad. Mom." How could he commit to living the rest of his life next door to the woman he loved? He wasn't into torture.

"I hear a *but* coming," Mom said.

He hoped this wouldn't ruin their plans. "Thing is, it didn't work out between me and Shay. I don't know if I'm going back after the finals."

"I see," Dad said.

Travis heard the disappointment in his voice.

"I'm sorry to hear that," Mom said. "Are you okay, honey?"

"I'll be fine." Eventually. He'd lost her before and survived it. If you could call the life he had before surviving.

"You and Shay," his mom said. "I thought for sure . . . Are you certain it's over?"

"It didn't work out like I thought. I—I wish it had."

"Have you prayed about it, honey?"

"Yeah, of course, I—" He had prayed before he returned to Moose Creek. Had felt peace about returning with hopes of reuniting with his soul mate.

He frowned at the windshield. But when the wedding certificate had come, when the crazy arrangement idea had occurred, had he even stopped to get God's take on it?

He didn't think so. He'd known Miss Lucy was praying for them, but what kind of Christian was he, letting the elderly woman pull his spiritual weight?

"Maybe I didn't," he said. "Not like I should've." Regret settled into a spot in his heart, just below the empty space Shay had left.

"Maybe you can work it out with her yet. She's your wife, whether either of you intended it or not."

"I don't think so, Mom. Right now I'm just going to focus on getting through the finals. After that I may end up back in Texas."

"You sure about that, son? I know how much you love the ranch. And you've always wanted a spread of your own."

"Don't press him, Wyatt. Honey, you take some time and think it over. At least a couple weeks, okay?"

He promised he would, though his hopes weren't high. They talked for a few more minutes, then wrapped up the call.

For the remainder of the drive, he found himself dreaming of owning the Barr M. Of Shay and him running the whole spread and raising a family. Then he'd wake from his daydream and scold himself for letting his thoughts get away.

By the time he reached the hotel, it was nearly midnight. He checked in and took the gilded elevator to his room. Once there, he tossed his suitcase on the hotel bed and went to look out the window. Twenty floors down, the streets teemed with cars and people. The glitter of Las Vegas stared back, mocking him with its promise of pleasure and thrills.

There would be no pleasure or thrills for him in this city. He glanced at the lump in his duffel bag where Shay's new wedding band nested in a bed of velvet. He felt like all kinds of fool now for having hoped. For having thought it could last forever.

A knock sounded on the hotel door, interrupting his thoughts.

There was only one person who'd visit him at this hour. Seth was probably bursting at the seams to get started. He forced a smile and opened the door.

But it wasn't Seth standing in the hall. Ella wore her trademark red cowboy hat and Crest smile. Her perfume was sweet and cloying.

"Travis!" She drew him into a hug. "It's so good to see you."

He'd ignored the flirtatious text she'd sent three days ago, and now he was paying for that. But he'd already told her he was married, told her he loved his wife. He hated to be rude, but she was leaving him no choice.

Ella stepped back, her smile unwavering. "You look the same." She grabbed his left hand and looked at it. "No wedding band . . . Were you just puttin' me on, Travis McCoy?"

He pulled his hand away and stuffed it in his

pocket. He'd removed the band somewhere between Ogden and Salt Lake City.

" 'Fraid not," he said.

The sparkle in her eyes dimmed, more at his action than his words, he suspected.

She propped her smile back up. "Well, we have a long three weeks ahead of us and plenty of time to . . . catch up." She winked. "You look tired as a Thanksgiving turkey. If you get bored, I'm in 1620, and Seth's across the hall from me."

She'd never been subtle. "See you tomorrow." He pushed the door shut.

" 'Night, Travis."

He locked the door and fell into bed, weariness creeping over every muscle in his body.

32

*S*hay finished her chores and headed into the house to warm up. December had blown frigid air into the valley. The snow from November had melted off on Thanksgiving, leaving Paradise Valley the bleak and barren shade of old straw.

Shay knew all about bleak and barren. When Travis left, it felt like he'd taken part of her with him, whether she wanted to admit it or not. She tried not to think about him. Tried not to think about the fact that he was with Ella now, that he'd run back to his first love—the wretched rodeo. Why was she always a distant second? Music for Garrett and the rodeo for Travis.

It seemed the more she tried not to think of him, the more her thoughts went there. Olivia was barely speaking to her. Apparently Shay was to blame for Travis's departure, for ruining the marriage.

Ha! Some marriage. It started as an accident and ended with a betrayal. But telling Olivia that would do no good. Despite Shay's anger with Travis, she didn't want to spoil Olivia's perception of him. She'd learn soon enough that people weren't always as they seemed.

Shay entered the house, shrugged off her coat, and pulled off her boots. The boots. An unwanted souvenir from life with Travis. If she had another pair, she'd give these away, no matter how comfy they were, just to be rid of the constant reminder.

But she didn't have another pair, and shedding him from her life wouldn't be as easy as discarding a pair of boots. That much she knew. He was everywhere she turned.

Her eyes caught the back of the *Moose Creek Chronicle*. She could hardly bring herself to pick it up anymore. When she did, she saw news of the national finals or even the crossword puzzle waiting to be filled in. She tore her eyes from the paper and rubbed her hands together, warming them.

The phone vibrated. She pulled it from her pocket, hating the jittery anticipation that filled her. She read the screen, then told herself that the sinking feeling was relief.

"Hey, Abigail."

"You're meeting us for lunch at the Tin Roof at noon."

Abigail had been trying to get her out of the house for days, but facing all the questions about Travis's whereabouts at church had been hard enough. When others asked where he was, she'd told them he was at the finals. But the finals ended today. Now what would she say?

"Shay?"

"Who's us?"

"Aunt Lucy and I, and we're not taking no for an answer. You've been cooped up too long."

Shay checked her watch. "Noon's twenty minutes from now."

"Better hurry."

"Fine, fine, whatever." She was tired of putting up a fight. Between tiptoeing around Olivia and putting off Abigail, she was fresh out of energy.

She hung up, changed into clean jeans, a clean undershirt, and a warm sweater, and headed toward the Tin Roof.

The diner was packed with retired folks and moms, trying to shake the winter doldrums. Abigail waved from the far corner booth. Shay wove between tables, an uncomfortable feeling spreading through her bones. Her neighbors' looks glanced off her as she met their eyes. She knew pity when she saw it. But why?

Did they already know Travis had left? That he wasn't coming back after the rodeo? But how could they know that? She fixed her eyes on the back of Miss Lucy's head.

They'd know soon enough, but the comprehension would come slowly, and by the time they realized it, maybe it wouldn't be such a big deal. Maybe it wouldn't spin the rumor mill for months on end like the last time he'd left her. Maybe there wouldn't be awkward pats on the shoulder and pity-filled glances this time.

Please, Lord.

She reached the booth and was forced to slide into Abigail's side by Miss Lucy's enormous purse.

Miss Lucy gave her a smile, her kind eyes enlarged through her coke-bottle glasses. "Shay, dear, so glad you could make it."

"Not like I had much choice." She opened her menu and tossed Abigail a put-upon look.

Abigail shrugged, all innocence.

Shay turned her mug over. Mercy, did she ever need coffee. She peeked at her neighbors over the menu. Ida Mae stared over her coffee mug rim. The woman looked away when her eyes met Shay's. Mayor Wadell's wife gave her a sad smile. And Mrs. Teasley's eyes tipped down at the corners before she looked away, sipping her coffee.

Shay fastened her eyes on the menu, on an image of a juicy hamburger, and slunk down in her seat. "Why's everyone staring?"

Mabel Franklin, the owner, appeared at her side, wielding a welcome pot of coffee. She filled Shay's mug, leaving room for cream.

"Darlin' . . ." Mabel leaned closer, whispering. "Didn't you see the paper?"

Dread wormed through her body as Shay looked at Abigail, then at Miss Lucy. They seemed equally oblivious.

"What—what's going on?" Shay asked.

"I have a paper right here." Miss Lucy pulled the *Moose Creek Chronicle* from her purse.

Mabel patted her on the shoulder. "You just keep your chin up, honey." She winked at Shay and then walked away, her pink uniform skirt swaying against her thin form.

Her words, intended to soothe, sent a bolt of panic through her instead.

"Oh, dear." Miss Lucy frowned.

"What is it?" Abigail flipped the paper around.

Shay read the headline above the fold on the cover: "Founders Day Wedding One Big Mistake."

No. Please . . .

Of their own volition, her eyes continued to the column.

This year's Founders Day wedding reenactment was anything but the tedious ritual of years gone by. Local rancher Shay Brandenberger and Moose Creek native Travis McCoy stirred up conversation when they announced in June that the ceremony had been legitimate. It seemed the once-engaged couple had at last decided to tie the knot. But recent discoveries refute this idea.

Turns out, the wedding was all a big mistake.

The couple's original wedding license—somehow saved for fourteen years and brought to the scene of what was supposed to be a wedding reenactment—was mistakenly filed by Pastor George Blevins.

"It got mixed up with a couple other licenses I had to file," Pastor Blevins said. "I sent it by mistake. The whole thing was an accident—it was all my fault."

But that didn't stop the couple from taking advantage of Providence. Brandenberger and McCoy, who've lived as husband and wife since the wedding, apparently decided that sometimes destiny just needs a little help.

"Oh no." Shay's face felt like a furnace. She was finished reading, but she couldn't look up.

"It's all right, Shay." Abigail put her hand over Shay's. "There's nothing bad in there, not really. So what if people know it was an accident?"

"If it were no big deal, people wouldn't be staring at me like I'm a charity case."

"They care about you," Abigail said. "Besides, they'll forget all about this as soon as the next rumor comes rolling along."

"That might be true if Travis was still here. But he's gone. *I'll* be the next rumor." The words blurred in front of her.

"They know he's at finals," Miss Lucy whispered.

Shay blinked hard. She had to get it together. "But it ends today. And he's not coming back. It won't take long for everyone to figure out . . ." That he didn't love her. That she'd been left again. That Shay Brandenberger was still the same old fool she'd always been.

"That he's not coming back?" Abigail asked.

"And that he didn't marry me by choice." She looked into Miss Lucy's sympathetic eyes. "That he left me not once, but twice. I'm such a fool."

"You made him leave," Abigail said.

"Nobody knows that. They all feel sorry for me."

"They're just concerned for you," Abigail said. "You've done nothing wrong—have nothing to be ashamed of."

This was just like before. She might as well be in her wedding gown, arriving home alone on the seven-thirty bus from Cody.

"You don't understand," Shay whispered.

"Well, I do," Miss Lucy said. "You're thinking it's just like it was before, but it's not. And anyway, dear, Abigail is right. You've only got to worry about pleasing One—and He's known all along about the wedding."

She hardly heard Miss Lucy's words. Everyone was staring, she could feel it. Shay pulled her purse into her stomach.

"I have to go." She flickered a look at Miss Lucy. "Pray for me."

"Always, dear."

"You haven't even eaten," Abigail said.

The thought of food made her stomach turn. She fished in her purse for enough change to cover the coffee she hadn't drunk.

"I'll come with you," Abigail said.

"No, stay. I'll be fine." She gave what she hoped was a reassuring smile. But inside, her heart felt hollow.

The eyes followed her all the way through the diner, and when she reached the door, it flew open before she could reach for the knob.

Pastor Blevins stopped short, looking windblown in his wool coat. His eyes widened upon seeing her, then softened. The door fell shut behind him, and the bells tinkled over their heads.

He smoothed a tuft of hair over his bald spot, then set his hand on her arm. "Shay, I'm so glad I ran into you. Sit down with me. I'll buy you a coffee."

So close to escape, she couldn't bring herself to stay. As it was, she felt every eye in the diner on her back.

"I—I can't, Pastor. I'm sorry, I have to go." She reached for the door.

He stopped her. "Please, Shay." His eyes turned down at the corners. "You've read the paper, then." His pastor voice seemed to boom through the diner. "I owe you an apology. I never meant to embarrass you."

"I know, I—it's okay." She moved past him and twisted the knob.

"I'm so sorry, dear."

"It's fine, really." She tossed a simulated smile in his general direction and walked out of the diner. She could feel the eyes on her as she crossed the street and slipped into her truck, and all the way home she wondered how she could survive this again.

When she reached the house, she pulled her truck to the barn. She needed to put out minerals for the cattle. That would keep her busy for a while. Too busy to think about her nosy neighbors.

She put on her gloves and collected the first salt block. She was setting it on the tailgate when Abigail's car pulled alongside.

Her friend shut off the ignition and left her vehicle. "Need some help?" Her breath fogged on release.

Shay took in her flimsy red peacoat and soft-soled shoes. "You're not really dressed for it. I told you to finish your lunch."

"You seemed upset. I didn't want to leave you alone."

Shay shoved the block deep into the bed. "Yeah, well. I'm fine."

"You're not fine. You miss him."

"I'll get over it."

"Why don't you just ask him to come back?"

Shay crossed her arms. "And why would I do that?"

"Because you love him."

Shay clamped down on her teeth. It was hard to argue when Abigail was right. Her friend knew it too. It was there in the tipped chin, the direct look.

"Love doesn't fix everything." Shay started for the barn, for her next block of salt. If Travis loved her at all, it sure wasn't the same way she loved him.

"It's a start . . ." Abigail had followed her.

Abigail didn't know about Ella. Didn't know how it felt to be rejected in favor of a rodeo. "I don't want to talk about this. Got enough to worry about with that stupid article." She picked up a block and started for the truck.

Abigail darted out of her way, following. "Why does it bother you so much what everyone thinks?"

"You don't understand."

"So tell me."

Shay sighed hard. How could Abigail understand? She'd never experienced poverty. She'd come from Midwestern suburbia.

"You don't know what it was like, growing up poor. It was humiliating. I ate on the government program and wore jeans that were always inches too short. Kids are cruel, and the only thing worse than that was the pity from the adults."

"Must've been hard."

"All I ever wanted was to make a decent living, to give my daughter more than I had so she never had to feel that way. And look at us." Shay shoved the block into the bed, her breaths coming hard. "Still scraping by."

"But Olivia's fine. All her needs are met. She's a lovely, happy girl."

It was true, despite their lack of material things.

"It just seems like no matter what I do, I'm continually being humiliated. First Travis dumps me in Cody on our wedding day, then that farce of an accidental wedding, and now a newspaper article declaring to the world that Travis never intended to marry me at all. Now he's gone, and everyone will know he left me—again! Do you have any idea how that feels? What did I do to deserve this?"

Abigail reached out. "I'm sorry, honey."

Shay leaned against the tailgate. "I've done nothing wrong, have I? Why do I continually feel embarrassed? I want to hide in my house and never come out. It feels just like it did when I was a kid, and I hate it." Shay hit her palm on the tailgate, and the metal sound rang out. "I wish I didn't care what anyone else thought."

Abigail perched on the truck beside her and folded her arms against the cold. "When my sister and I were in high school, we were obsessed with being popular. My dad quoted this verse so much, it still sticks in my head. 'For am I now trying to win the favor of people, or God? Or am I striving to please people?'" She snorted. "We used to get so sick of hearing that. But he was right. Life would be a lot simpler if we only aimed to please God, wouldn't it?"

The verse struck the center of Shay's heart like an arrow to a bull's-eye. *Is that my problem, God? That I care too much about what other people think and not enough about what You think?*

Before the thought was complete, she knew it was. Hadn't she even married Garrett to prove to her neighbors that she was worthy of a man's love?

"You're right. What is wrong with me?"

"We all care to a degree, honey. It's kind of like those pictures I took at your birthday, remember? I focused on the wrong objects, and the photos came out all wrong. The main subject was blurry while some random object was in focus."

"You're right, Abigail. I've been focusing on the wrong subject. How could I miss something so obvious?"

"Hey, we all have our issues. Shoot, I chose my career out of guilt. I had to do a major turnaround because of that. Here I am back in school again."

Abigail had told her about witnessing her childhood friend being abused and keeping it a secret. Her guilt had driven her into journalism to expose truths via her magazine column.

"I've been so focused on what everyone else thinks, I rarely even consider what God thinks of what I'm doing or who I am."

Abigail gave her a sideways hug. "He thinks you're pretty great."

"Yeah?"

"Yeah."

Or maybe God thought it was about time she got her life in focus. Maybe He'd even allowed all those things to happen to teach her what now seemed so obvious. Life's lessons did rise from the deepest hurts.

Abigail hopped down. "He also thinks I'm turning into a Popsicle out here." Her nose was already red.

"You really should get a decent coat."

Abigail posed. "But this one's so pretty."

"Never mind the frostbite."

"Coming from Chicago, you'd think I'd know better."

"Go home," Shay said. "I'm sure Wade'll have you warm in no time."

"I just might do that." Abigail rounded her car. "Call me if you need to talk."

Shay watched her friend pull from the drive, then began loading the blocks again.

Help me figure this out, God. I don't want to care so much what everyone thinks. I want to care what You think. Show me how to do it, Lord, because I don't think I can do it on my own.

33

The country music was almost as loud as the rowdy cowboys and cowgirls in the Las Vegas restaurant. They'd chosen a Texas-style steakhouse to celebrate the end of the National Rodeo Finals.

Travis pulled his phone from his pocket and checked the screen. Why did he bother? Shay wasn't going to call . . . hadn't called once since he'd left. It was time to face facts.

She didn't want him back, didn't love him. Not like he loved her. If she did, she wouldn't have put him out so easily. Maybe her heart wasn't turned inside out like his.

"Hey, cowboy." Ella sidled into the seat beside him and flipped her silky blond hair over her shoulder. "Congratulations on your finish."

"Thanks. You too." Across the room Seth laughed, taking the hand of the new filly he'd meet several days earlier. He was glad for his buddy. Somehow they'd finished first, though Travis wasn't sure how he'd focused long enough to secure the record time.

"When ya headed back to Montana?" Ella asked, bumping his shoulder.

"Not sure."

"I'm leaving tomorrow, bright and early." Ella

took a swig from her bottle, then turned a coy smile on him. *Last chance,* her eyes said.

"Safe travels."

She laughed, a high-pitched sound that grated on his nerves. Across the room, two bull riders gawked at her from their spot by the blaring jukebox.

"All right, McCoy, be that way," she said. "We could've had something. But you go back to wifey and have a nice little life together." She stood. "There's plenty of other cowboys in the corral, you know." She smiled toward the two bull riders, then sauntered off in their direction.

Travis wanted to leave, but he'd already ordered. He didn't feel like celebrating. He felt like going back to his room and losing himself in sleep. It was the only time he felt at peace. The only time this hole in his gut stopped aching.

His phone vibrated in his pocket, and his heart held its breath as he pulled it out and checked the screen.

Dylan. He stuffed the disappointment and slipped away from the table, seeking the quieter cove at the front of the building.

"Hey, buddy," Dylan said when he answered. "Hear congratulations are in order."

"Thanks."

"News'll be all over town tomorrow."

He wondered if Shay had heard. If Dylan had seen her lately. If she'd asked about him.

"Saw your ride on TV. You two had a great time. I was almost jealous."

"You've got your own trophy buckles. I don't feel sorry for you."

"Yeah, well . . . I miss it sometimes," Dylan said.

It was ironic. Travis was where Dylan wanted to be, and Dylan was where Travis wanted to be. But being in Moose Creek wouldn't help matters. He'd been there six months, and for what?

"When ya coming home? We might throw a party or something."

"Any ol' excuse to get together," Travis said.

"Well, it is winter. So tomorrow? Next day?"

Travis sighed hard, walked to the window, his boots crunching the peanut shells strewn on the planked floor.

"I'm not coming back, Dylan." It was the first time he'd said it aloud, the first time he'd even admitted it to himself. He'd have to call his parents in the morning. They'd need to put the ranch on the market soon.

"Why not?"

"Come on, you know why. She doesn't want me there."

"She's your *wife*."

"My accidental wife. She never chose this, clearly doesn't want to be married to me."

"And you're giving up, just like that?"

"No, it's not just like that, pal. I've loved Shay

for years. I came home—shoot, I even married the woman—lived with her for five months. I showed her I loved her in every way I know how, and she kicked me to the curb. She doesn't want me in her life—nothing I can do about that."

So he'd go back to dreaming, go back to his regrets, his memories. He closed his eyes against them.

"What are your plans?"

Travis sank onto the waiting bench. "Don't know. Going back to Texas. Maybe I'll buy a ranch or something. I'm done with the rodeo."

"Too bad. Good money in it for someone with your skills."

"Yeah, well." Travis leaned his head against the wood siding. "The rodeo cost me more than it ever paid."

34

Shay looked at her refrigerator calendar. One week until Christmas. One full week since the rodeo ended.

And no word from Travis. She told herself she was glad he'd stopped calling. He'd probably gone back to Texas after his big win in Vegas, which she'd purposely not watched. It was hard enough just remembering him. She didn't need to see him showing his stuff on horseback in living color.

Yes, he was probably in Texas with Ella, getting ready to celebrate the holidays together. Maybe that piece of jewelry was her Christmas gift. Maybe he'd catch her under the mistletoe and lay a big one on her. She closed her eyes against the thought.

She expected to receive papers any day. He'd surely want a divorce soon, and as long as he was paying, she'd give it. God knew she didn't have the money to throw away on something so pointless. What did she need a divorce for? She was sure never marrying again.

She looked at the calendar, frowning. How long ago had her last cycle been? She always circled the day. She flipped back to November. The ninth was circled in blue ink. She flipped back to December, her pulse racing.

She'd just forgotten. Surely she had. She didn't remember having a period recently, but then she'd been so distracted by Travis's departure, by the newspaper article, by the Christmas preparations.

She had been tired lately, but that was because she wasn't sleeping well. And she'd had none of the nausea that had plagued her during her pregnancy with Olivia.

Shay let loose of the calendar pages and retrieved her nightly glass of water. *No way.*

She turned off the multicolored Christmas tree lights, wandered to her bedroom, and climbed into bed, setting her alarm numbly. She tried desperately to remember a period in December and couldn't. Her thoughts spun frantically. She couldn't be pregnant. She just couldn't.

There was no discreet way to buy a pregnancy test in Moose Creek, Montana. Shay drove all the way to Bozeman, wasting gas and time, to preserve what little privacy she had left.

She was trying to get a grip on the verse Abigail had shared with her—had been meditating on it for over a week. But her potential pregnancy was no one else's business. And besides, God didn't care where she bought the test.

She perused the vast selection and decided on an expensive brand—this was no time to be cheap—then she returned to a home that had grown chilly in her absence. After donning a thick sweater, she read the directions, took the test, then propped the stick on the bathroom counter next to her toothbrush.

She set the kitchen timer and started another pot of coffee. She checked the timer. Wiped down the table. Checked the timer.

Was it broken? She frowned. Time had never crawled so slowly.

You're being silly, Shay. You are not pregnant. For heaven's sake, it had taken eleven months to conceive Olivia. She and Travis had only been together four measly days. If she'd missed her period in December, it was just because of stress. That happened sometimes. Not to her, but still. That's probably what had happened.

She was going to check the stick, then she'd have a good, long laugh at her own silliness. Then she'd bury the test in the trash barrel so Olivia never found it.

When the coffeepot gurgled, Shay poured herself a cup, adding cream until the dark brew turned caramel. She sipped the hot liquid, letting it warm her throat. Outside, flurries danced in the air, driven by the winter wind. There were already a few inches of snow on the ground and more to come.

She looked at the vacant spot in the yard where the snowman Olivia, Maddy, and Travis built had stood for half of November. She could almost picture them now, rolling snowballs, tussling in the drifts. They'd come into the house, laughing and stomping snow from their frozen jeans, flecks of flurries melting in their hair.

It seemed like yesterday. Now the house was quiet as a tomb.

Olivia had cooled her heels, but things weren't the same between them, despite Shay's best efforts. She wished she could give her daughter a better life, but she was doing the best she could, wasn't she?

The buzzer sounded and Shay shut it off, her heart thudding like a drum in her chest. She walked toward the bathroom.

It's fine. You're not pregnant. Relax.

But the frantic butterflies beating their wings against her stomach didn't mind her soothing reassurances.

She opened the door and grabbed for the stick. *Help me, God.*

A bold pink line streaked across the white background.

"Oh, God." The prayer left her body on a breath. Her legs went weak, crumpling like a melting snowbank. She slid down the wall and onto the linoleum.

Oh, God, what have I done?

She was pregnant!

Pregnant and *single!*

Not quite true. She was married, all right. To a man who was chasing his dreams and another woman clear across the country. She banged her head against the wall.

What was she going to do? They were barely making ends meet. How would she manage now? Pregnancy and livestock didn't mix. There were risks of falls and kicks from the animals. She'd stayed off horseback through her pregnancy with Olivia, but she wouldn't have that luxury now.

And what about after the baby was born? She couldn't do chores with a baby slung to her chest. She couldn't run her own ranch, much less work at Hank's part-time. There was no way she could manage.

They'd have to move. And then how would she provide for them?

She sure couldn't count on Travis. He was with someone else. The last thing she wanted was him coming back out of obligation. Her eyes burned at the thought. She'd rather never see him again than have him pitying her.

She could hardly wait for word to get around town. Hardly wait until her pregnancy was apparent for the whole world to see. She always managed to give them something to talk about.

"For am I now trying to win the favor of people, or God?"

The scripture formed in her mind without thought.

She was doing it again. For pity's sake, when would she learn? It was always the first place her mind went.

She looked at the stick in her hand, the pink line bright and bold as a shiny new dime.

I'm pregnant.

Okay, God, so what do You think about this?

She closed her eyes and tried to grow still, but her heart kicked at her like a wild horse.

"I knew you before I formed you in your mother's womb."

The scripture came from nowhere. He did know her. And He knew this baby. Had known this baby before He formed him or her in Shay's womb.

God formed this baby. He or she wasn't an accident, like their wedding. This baby was part of God's plan for her life. She didn't know what the future held, but He did. She just had to take one step at a time. She had to trust Him through this.

Shay laid her hand on her abdomen. There was really a baby in there. A baby brother or sister for Olivia. A son or daughter for her.

"Hello, baby," she whispered as a tear slipped down her cheek.

35

$\mathcal{S}$hay wadded up the Christmas paper and dropped it into the bag Abigail held. Her friend's living room looked like a Christmas factory had exploded.

They'd filled their bellies with a tasty supper and exchanged gifts. Aunt Lucy had left awhile ago, Maddy had taken Olivia upstairs to paint their nails with her new manicure kit, and Wade and Dylan were outside plugging in Wade's new battery charger, probably jawing about man-stuff.

Shay'd had a week to come around to the idea of being pregnant. She'd seen Dr. Garvin two days earlier to have the test confirmed. The night before she'd told Olivia, who'd been giddy at the prospect of a new brother or sister, though she was clearly hoping for a girl.

"You're quiet tonight." Abigail picked up Wade's stack of gifts and set it on the stairs.

Shay supposed now was as good a time as any. She'd been waiting to deliver the news in private. "I got an early Christmas present."

"Oh yeah? What's that?"

"I'm pregnant."

Abigail stopped, lowered the garbage bag, her jaw going slack. "You're pregnant?"

"Yep." Shay crumpled up another sheet of paper and held it out.

Abigail took it. "Holy cow. How are you doing? How are you feeling?"

"Scared silly." Shay gave a wry grin. "Other than that, all right."

Abigail smiled and pulled her into a hug. "It's going to be fine. Congratulations, honey."

"Thanks."

"Does Olivia know?"

Shay retrieved the last stray bow and sank onto the sofa. "Told her last night. She wants a sister." And she wanted Travis to come back. She'd left no room for doubt about that.

"What are you going to do? You can't— you're not supposed to ride in your condition, are you?"

Shay had done little other than think about their future the last week. "I'll have to sell."

Abigail frowned. "But your ranch . . . it's been in your family so long."

It would break her heart. She'd worked so hard to keep the place. "Don't have much choice, I'm afraid."

"Maybe Wade and I could help out—"

Shay set her hand on her friend's arm. "That's sweet, but no. I've given it a lot of thought. I'll sell it and rent a place. I'm hoping to find work in town."

She had a little equity in the property and was paid up through March. She'd pay Travis back and use the rest as emergency funds.

"What about . . . ?" Abigail's eyes turned sympathetic.

Travis. Shay folded her hands in her lap. "I don't know. I don't know what I'm going to do. For now, nothing."

"You have to tell him."

"Eventually. I don't want him coming back for the wrong reasons. Who am I kidding? He won't come back at all. Maybe I don't want to face that fact." Shay shook the thought away. "Our relationship was nothing but a series of accidents. I don't want to think about it right now."

"You're a great mom. That's a very blessed baby you're carrying."

Shay swallowed against a lump in her throat. She hoped so. Sometimes she wished she had more to offer.

"I hope this isn't a bad time . . . ," Abigail started.

Shay could tell her friend was bursting to say something. "What is it?"

Abigail winced. "I'm pregnant too."

Shay sucked her breath. "Seriously?"

"Seriously."

Shay let out a whoop and hugged Abigail. "Congratulations! Oh, I can't believe this."

"Wade and Maddy are totally stoked. And I'm just—well, an emotional wreck."

Abigail let out a tearful laugh.

"I know the feeling." She'd teared up more times in the last week than she had in ten years.

Abigail smiled through her tears. "I guess we're in this together, friend."

"I guess we are," Shay said.

Except Abigail's baby had a daddy. Shay returned her friend's smile, pretending that the tears sliding down her own face were happy ones.

36

Shay heard the door slam from the patio where she'd dragged the browning Christmas tree. She dropped her load and entered the house, rubbing her hands and feeling the sticky tar of tree sap. Her stomach let out a loud rumble. She was hungry all the time, yet it seemed all she did was eat.

"Olivia?"

It was her daughter's first day back to school after Christmas break, but judging from the banging she heard from Olivia's bedroom, it hadn't gone well.

Shay tapped on the closed door. "Olivia?"

The sound of footsteps on the hardwood floor ceased. *"What?"*

That didn't sound like her daughter at all. Shay eased the door open.

Olivia stood at the foot of her bed, her chest heaving. Pink splotched her cheeks, and Shay didn't think it was from the cold walk up the drive.

"What did Katy say now?"

Olivia crossed her arms and pressed her lips tight. But the actions weren't enough to stop the inevitable tears. They welled up, thick and heavy, then flowed down Olivia's face. She swiped them away.

"Nothing." Olivia turned toward her window and looked out at the white landscape.

Shay walked toward the window and put her arm around Olivia's stiff shoulder. "Come on, now. What is it?"

Olivia looked cute as a bug in a new sweater, and her cut still looked nice, though she was overdue for a trim. What could Katy possibly find wrong now?

"Why did Dad leave?"

The question, so out of the blue, startled Shay. "What?"

"Why'd he leave us? It was my fault, wasn't it? And Travis too! They both left because of me!"

"What? Honey, what are you talking about?"

"Katy said I've had two dads, and they both left because I'm a pain in the butt."

Shay pressed her lips together, then reached for her phone. "That's it. I'm calling her mom."

Olivia grabbed her arm. "No, don't! That'll only make it worse." Tears filled her eyes again. "It's true, isn't it? They left because of me!" Olivia turned into Shay and sobbed.

Shay embraced her daughter. "No, hon, that's not true. Nothing could be further from the truth. You're a wonderful girl, the daughter of my dreams."

"Then why'd they leave?" Olivia's words were muffled.

Shay drew in a deep breath and let it out.

"Marriage is complicated, munchkin. Your dad and I—we just weren't a good match. He loved you very much, though. Didn't he call you every week after he left? He missed you. He would've come back to see you if he were still alive."

Olivia shuddered in her arms, and Shay tightened her grip.

"Travis loved you too, and his leaving had nothing to do with you. It was my fault, remember?" She knew she risked Olivia's wrath by saying it, but it was better than her daughter blaming herself.

Olivia sniffled. The tears hadn't let up. Shay wanted to make everything better, but what could she do? This wasn't something she could fix with a shopping trip or an appointment at the Hair Barn. This was something Olivia had to believe.

She remembered Travis's reservation when she'd solved Olivia's problem by buying her a new wardrobe. What had he said? *"You don't want her thinking her worth comes from clothes. Or that those girls' opinions really matter."*

But that's exactly what Shay had taught her, wasn't it? Not only by her reactions to the teasing, but by how Shay was handling her own problems. By the way she avoided anything that might cause gossip, by the way she reacted when she'd sent the rumor mill into action, by the way she'd left church and hidden in the ladies' room when she'd felt the judgment of her neighbors.

Oh man, she'd really blown this. Had passed on her own issues to her daughter.

She pulled Olivia from the hug and dried her cheeks. "We need to talk, hon. I'm afraid I haven't done such a great job."

Olivia sniffled and frowned. "Not true, Mom."

"Come here." Shay tugged her toward the bed, and they sank onto the edge. *Where to start?*

"Listen, this is something I struggle with. We care when people say things and do things that hurt our feelings. That's totally natural. But I think I did you a disservice when I reacted to Katy's teasing the way I did. I shouldn't have rushed out to fix the things she teased you about."

"But I like the new clothes and haircut. You said we could afford them."

"We could. It's not that. And it's not that there's anything wrong with having those things. I just think it's a mistake to arrange our lives around other people's opinions. It's something I'm still learning myself. Abigail reminded me of a scripture recently—" She took Olivia's white Bible from her nightstand. "Here, I'll show you."

She flipped it open to Galatians. "Here it is. Read this one." She pointed to chapter one, verse ten.

Olivia wiped her eyes clear. " 'For am I now trying to win the favor of people, or God? Or am I striving to please people?' "

"That verse really helps me put things in

perspective. Whenever I start worrying what people think, I say this to myself. It reminds me to focus on God's opinions, not other people's."

"I get it. It's still hard, though."

"It's absolutely hard. Especially at your age. But it's something to hang on to and remind yourself of." She gave Olivia a sideways hug. "And, hon, you can be sure that God thinks you're awfully special, just like I do."

Olivia leaned into her.

"Your dad thought you were special too, and so did Travis. So don't let Katy O'Neil convince you otherwise."

"I'll try."

"Are you sure you don't want me to call her mom? Maybe it'll make her stop."

"She'll just tease me about it. Or her friends will do it for her. I need to handle this myself, Mom."

Shay studied her daughter, then gave her a final squeeze. "All right. But if you change your mind, let me know, okay?"

Olivia nodded.

"Now go get cleaned up and come help me with supper, okay?"

Olivia frowned. "It's only three forty-five."

Shay shrugged. "What can I say? Your brother or sister is hungry again."

That got a little smile from her daughter. It was a start.

37

$\mathcal{T}$ravis stood under the spray of birdseed, watching his buddy Seth and his new bride dart across the church's lawn toward the stallion that waited, saddled and ready.

Seth gave Hanna a long kiss before lifting her onto the horse and mounting behind her. One final wave, and the pair rode off into the sunset—literally. They'd only met three months earlier at the rodeo finals, but the two had been inseparable ever since.

Travis loosened his tie and slipped away from the crowd, walking toward the back lot where he'd parked his truck. His boss had given him leave for the evening, but he felt like working anyway. He had a little time before he lost daylight, and the temperature was mild enough. At least Texas didn't have the cold springs Montana had. It was a small consolation.

He pulled off his tie as he walked, unbuttoning the stiff dress shirt. Standing by his friend through the ceremony had been torture. All he could think about was the last ceremony he'd been in—his own.

He could still see Shay's eyes, spitting fire at him while Pastor Blevins droned on about the sanctity of marriage. He smiled a little, thinking of it. He'd thought she was going to bite him when he kissed her. But no. His lips seemed to tame the wild beast. At least for a few seconds. A few very pleasurable seconds.

The smile fell from his lips.

I miss her, God. I can't believe how much.

He missed the way she looked at him with wonder sometimes, like she couldn't believe he was there. He missed the way she smelled like sunshine and citrus, the way her eyes danced when she smiled, the way her hair looked all rumpled in the morning. Shoot, he even missed the way she put ketchup on every blame thing she ate.

He missed Olivia too, and wondered if she'd finished the book they'd been reading. If she'd built any snowmen without him. He wouldn't see her when her braces were removed, wouldn't see how pretty she looked when she stopped hiding her smile.

Travis slid into his cab and started the vehicle. He was so tired of this ache in his gut. When would it go away? He pounded the steering wheel.

The night before, in a moment of weakness, he'd started a letter to Shay. This morning he'd read it, then wadded it up and tossed it into the nearest garbage can. Shay didn't want to hear that. She wouldn't believe him. Didn't trust him. When would he get that through his thick skull?

The phone vibrated in his dress pants pocket. He didn't feel like talking to anyone. But it might be Seth. Maybe he'd left something at the church, forgotten to pay the pianist or save the wedding cake top. He was the best man, still on duty, he supposed.

He checked the screen. Miss Lucy? Travis started to return the phone to his pocket, then stopped. What if something was wrong with Shay? Maybe she'd dropped a salt block on her other foot.

"Hi, Miss Lucy."

"Hello, young man. Am I interrupting anything?"

"Not at all. Just leaving my friend's wedding. Headed home now." Travis put the truck in gear. "Everything okay?"

"Oh, just fine, dear. How's your job?"

"All right. I'm staying busy enough." Working someone else's land wasn't the same as having your own. Not even close.

"Dylan said you were looking for a place of your own. Any luck finding a spread?"

Travis pulled onto the street. "Not yet. I've looked at a few, but nothing that's calling my name." He'd started wondering if anything would appeal to him.

"Heard about one you might be interested in."

He sighed. "Not buying my parents' place, Miss Lucy."

"Oh, I wasn't talking about that. Shay's ranch is up for sale."

Travis gripped the steering wheel, frowning. "Shay's place?"

"As of last month."

Shay would never willingly sell her place. She'd go to any lengths to keep it. Shoot, hadn't she let him move in, agreed to live as husband and wife for five months just to keep it?

"Why?" Travis said. He'd gotten her through a rough spot, had even paid up her mortgage a few months ahead.

"I don't know the particulars, dear. Just saw the sign one day and asked Abigail about it."

"What'd she say? Is Shay moving away?" Travis asked, then scolded himself for caring.

"Said she was moving into town. Word has it John Oakley put in a lowball offer."

Travis pressed his lips together. Didn't the man make enough money at his bank? He had to take advantage of a single mom too? "She accept?"

"Abigail said she countered high. Bet he'll come back just as low as before."

What if she didn't have a choice? How were they going to make ends meet without the ranch? Those baskets she made were great extra income, but that wouldn't support them.

"Why don't you just come back, Travis?"

His gut tightened. He missed Shay so much he ached for her. He wondered if Miss Lucy felt like that when she'd lost her husband. He'd thought it might be easier here, hundreds of miles away. But it wasn't. Who was he kidding?

"I feel just awful about my part in all this," Miss Lucy said. "And call me crazy, but I still think it was all part of God's plan. At least think about coming back."

"Sure." Travis wanted off the phone. Talking about Shay wasn't helping. Now he only felt worked up and frustrated.

"That didn't sound very sincere, young man."

"Sorry, ma'am."

"You'll think about it, then?"

"I will."

They talked a few minutes more, then said their good-byes.

Why was Shay selling her ranch? He couldn't come up with any reason other than she had to. Things were tough right now. It was hard for ranchers to make ends meet, much less a single mom trying to run her own spread.

He supposed she'd finally just had enough of stretching her dollars. Moving to town . . . He couldn't picture it. Couldn't picture Shay anywhere but out in the country, the sun on her face, the wind in her hair. It was where she belonged.

Travis turned into the ranch drive and headed down the long dirt road toward the bunkhouse he shared with two other cowboys.

And now that weasel from the bank was trying to take advantage of her.

Everything in him wanted to step in. He had the money just sitting in his account. He wouldn't even miss it. But who'd died and made him her knight in shining armor? She didn't want his rescue. Would probably spit in his face if he tried.

All right, God. Last time I just jumped right in and did what I wanted. This time I'm asking. What am I supposed to do? I want to do Your will, and I want to help Shay.

But was that all he wanted?

No. He wanted her to hear him out one last time. He wanted her to listen and believe him when he said that he loved her, that he wanted those vows they'd shared to be permanent. He wanted to slip that band onto her finger and tell her she was the love of his life, his first and only. But was that what God wanted?

Travis pulled up to the house and shut off the engine, an idea already forming in his mind. He shrugged the thought away. It wouldn't work. He'd only have his heart broken again.

Jesus, show me the way. I don't want to go off half-cocked, and I don't want to hurt Shay. I want Your will this time, even if that means losing Shay for good.

The idea surged to the front of his mind again. He remembered his mom's words. Shay was his wife. Surely God wanted them to keep their vows, even if they had been accidental. It seemed pointless to end the marriage when they still loved each other. If Shay still loved him.

He looked around the barren barracks. He didn't want to share his life with a couple stinky cowboys. He wanted Shay back. He wanted them to be a family, Shay, Olivia, and him. He wanted to share Shay's bed, to wake up and see her face every morning for the rest of his life. He wanted to hear Olivia call for "Dad" again and know she was calling for him.

Peace settled over him like fog on a spring morning, and he felt God's blessing clear down to the tips of his cowboy boots. His breaths grew shallow as his heart kicked into gear. The idea took shape, making more sense with each minute that passed. It was a risk, but life was a risk. And besides, God was in control this time.

Travis pulled the cell from his pocket and dialed.

38

$\mathcal{S}$hay watched Olivia and Maddy two-step across the dance floor, laughing when they bumped into each other. Her daughter looked especially happy tonight, and Shay knew it had everything to do with her triumphant moment the day before.

Across the room, Katy O'Neil sat with her mom and dad, her chin propped on her palm. Shay smiled. She was glad she hadn't called Katy's parents. Olivia had handled herself just fine.

"What's that smile about?" Abigail said over the music.

"I was just thinking about something Olivia told me yesterday. She stood up to Katy at recess in front of some other girls, and they took her side."

Abigail smiled. "Maddy told me."

"Well, I just hope this puts an end to the teasing. It was getting out of hand."

"I think it will. Maddy seemed sure of it."

The loud band made conversation difficult. Shay wondered if it was too loud for her baby's developing ears. She folded her arms over the bump of her growing belly just in case.

The smell of grilled steak stirred her appetite. She wished she could afford it, but the burger basket would have to suffice. It seemed all she'd done lately was eat. Especially beef. Even Olivia was tiring of grilled burgers.

Two tables over, Ida Mae and Vern stared at her. Shay looked away, her cheeks warming, and caught the eyes of Pappy Barnes. Or was he looking at her? Maybe he was looking at someone over her shoulder.

No doubt word had circulated that she was pregnant. And since three and a half months had passed since the rodeo finals, everyone knew Travis wasn't coming back. Shay straightened in her chair and sucked in a breath of courage.

"For am I now trying to win the favor of people, or God?"

Facing her neighbors hadn't been easy. She carried the verse wherever she went, her security blanket, ready to be whipped out at a moment's notice. And she'd been finding plenty of those moments lately.

Abigail leaned in on her elbows. "What's wrong?"

"People are staring."

Abigail looked around. "No, they aren't. And even if they were, it doesn't matter, right?" She patted Shay's hand. "I'm so proud of you."

"I'm trying."

"I can tell, and so can God. That's all that matters."

She gave a wry grin. "That's what I keep telling myself."

Abigail looked over her shoulder, then back at her. "There is one person who can't take his eyes off you. Poor Beau."

He'd approached her last month after hearing about her pregnancy. Offered to step in and marry her, be the father of her children. "I am married, Beau," she'd told him before kindly turning down his offer.

"He'll get over it," Shay said. "Never would've worked." He deserved someone who loved him the way she loved—

Do not go there, Shay Brandenberger.

"Did you decide what to do about John's offer?" Abigail asked.

Shay was glad to think of something else, even if the insulting offer on her property did raise her hackles. "I countered. Just a little under asking price."

"Good for you. It's a fair price."

Shay nodded. "I'll bet he doesn't counter back."

And that worried her. Other than John's offer, there hadn't been so much as a nibble since she'd put it on the market a month ago. If she didn't sell it soon, she'd be in trouble.

The baby was due August 7, just a week before her own birthday. What was she going to do with cattle to care for and a newborn baby? It had been hard enough over the winter, keeping the livestock fed. There seemed to be no end to their appetite. They ate and ate and bawled for more hay, and every day it started over again. Now calving season had arrived, and nighttime calving had cost her more than one night's sleep.

"What's John Oakley want a ranch for, anyway?" Abigail asked. "Never even seen the man in a pair of jeans."

"He doesn't want a ranch, he wants a deal."

Abigail snorted, then tossed her blond hair. "More like a rip-off."

"Well, I can't afford not to take the offer seriously. Not like they're flying at me from every direction."

The server set her burger basket down. Shay said grace and dug in.

"How are your classes going?"

"Great. I'll be ready for a break this summer, though. Not sure what I'm going to do once the baby comes." Abigail eyed Shay's fries.

Shay shoved the plate forward. "Help yourself. Believe me, I totally understand."

"Thanks. I ate a nice nutritious meal at home and told myself that was it. But Junior has the appetite of a grizzly, and salad doesn't seem to be his thing."

Abigail had had an ultrasound two weeks ago and knew she was having a boy. Shay preferred to be surprised.

"Tell me about it. I keep telling myself *no more fried food,* and look at me."

Her phone vibrated in her pocket. Shay pulled it out and saw a text from her realtor. She read it and clamped her jaw. Selfish man.

"What's wrong?" Abigail asked.

"Oakley countered. Five grand more than his first measly offer."

Abigail's brows pulled together. "I could just smack that man."

"Get in line. He knows I owe more than that on it." She'd be way upside down. Would be better off renting the property, though who'd rent it out for the price of her payments?

Her phone vibrated in her pocket, a call this time. Shay looked at the screen. "It's Joann. Probably wants to advise on that wonderful counterbid."

Shay hurried to the exit and answered the phone as she stepped outside into the cold spring air. "Hi, Joann. I got your text."

"Oh, that. Never mind that offer . . . We have a new one."

"Hallelujah. Please tell me it's reasonable."

"Better than reasonable. They offered list price."

Shay caught her breath, unbelieving.

"That's right. And better yet, it's a cash offer."

"I'll take it!"

Joann laughed. "I thought you might."

"Wait, who is it? Anyone I know?" Not that it mattered—an offer was an offer.

"It's Wyatt and Doreen McCoy."

Travis's parents? But why . . . "They're selling their place. Why would they want mine?"

"I didn't ask their realtor, but I can guess. Their property is adjacent to yours, and a bigger spread will be more appealing to corporate investors. Plus you have all those springs on your property and river frontage, which theirs lacks. It adds value to their property."

The bass thumped through the Chuckwagon's walls. "Well, I'm not looking a gift horse in the mouth."

"It'll be a mail-away transaction, but since it's a cash offer, that makes things simpler. Oh, and Zach said there's no hurry on evacuating the property. Closing will probably be in thirty days, but since the McCoys aren't moving in, they wanted to know if you'd stay until the property sells."

"I can for a while. That's very kind of them."

Shay had to be out of there before the baby came, but at least the ranch was settled. They wouldn't have to rush out, and she had ample time to find a rental and a new job. She pushed down the dread that spread through her at the thought of leaving.

"I'll get the offer over first thing Monday, if that's okay."

"Fine, of course."

They said good-bye and Shay turned off her

phone. She'd been so afraid she'd have no choice but to accept John's offer. But now she'd gotten more than she dreamed—list price.

Thank You, God. It's so much more than I hoped for.

She'd have cash coming back to her, enough to pay off Travis and then some. Enough to pay for medical care when she delivered her baby. She put her hand over her slightly rounded belly.

She wouldn't let herself think about losing the place where she'd grown up. The only home Olivia had ever known. The place where she and Travis had first kissed, the place where they'd made love and conceived this baby.

She wouldn't let herself think about any of that. If she did, she'd fall into a million pieces right there on Main Street.

39

Travis eased up on the gas as he entered town.

Moose Creek, the sign read. Gateway to Yellowstone.

His heart raced at the sight. He'd driven half the night, but all weariness fled now. The day had finally arrived, and he was here. Mere miles from Shay.

It had been so long, a full five months since he'd left. Since she had tossed him from the property. What would she say when she saw him?

He feared she'd kick him from her land without giving him a chance to explain. Travis wiped his sweaty palms down the length of his thigh. She'd hear him out whether she wanted to or not. He'd tossed her over his shoulder once before, and he'd do it again. He loved her, and it was time she believed it.

He stopped at the office on Main Street and collected the envelope before heading toward the Barr M. Buck had been cooped up in the trailer since Texas. He'd ride the horse over to Shay's and allow him a little hard-earned freedom.

Spring was dragging its feet in the valley. Gray clouds stretched across the expansive sky. The vegetation had yet to green, and snow still clung to the rocky peaks of the Gallatin Range. In the distance pine trees added dark splashes of green to the landscape, otherwise still clothed in the drab colors of winter. Alongside the road, the Yellowstone ran quick and deep, flushed by snowmelt off the mountains.

When he arrived at his folks' ranch, he fed and watered Buck, saddled him despite the slow drizzle that had started, and turned toward Shay's place. He'd catch up with Jacob later. Right now he only had one thing on his mind.

Shay was probably nearing the end of calving season. He wondered how many nights she'd been up, assisting in births. Hopefully not too many. He'd used light birth-weight bulls with her first-calf heifers.

He missed working her ranch. Missed working with her. He wondered if she missed his help. Wondered if she missed him.

She hadn't filed for divorce at least. He told himself it wasn't because of the costs involved. Maybe she held out hope that they'd work it out.

He'd find out for sure in a few minutes. He'd know when he saw her. Shay was good at hiding her feelings, but he wasn't just any old neighbor. She was his first love, his soul mate. He'd know when she saw him how she felt about his return. For better or worse.

Travis patted the envelope in his shirt pocket, reassuring himself that it was there. He felt for the lump in his jeans pocket as he crossed the shallow spot of the creek.

40

Shay washed off in the barn tub. The last heifer to calve had gone into labor that morning. An hour ago Shay had pulled a healthy newborn calf from the relieved mama. Now the heifer was on her feet and licking her calf clean in the fresh bed of straw.

Shay was glad to have the last birth behind her, relieved she'd managed without getting kicked. Branding was on the horizon, but she wasn't fool enough to try that in her condition. Her neighbors would pitch in even if she couldn't return the favor.

She dried her hands and went to the house to change into clean clothing. There was little that fit her now. She was down to two pair of jeans she could wear unfastened.

She finished the buttons on her flannel shirt. Gray—the exact color of Travis's eyes. Her rounded belly pressed against the buttons, and she promised herself she'd go to the thrift store the next day with the equity check from the sale of her ranch.

"Either that," she said, looking in the mirror, "or you'll have to wear your bathrobe to church Sunday." That would get the neighbors talking.

Shay grabbed her coat off the tree and left the house. She wanted to check on the pair again, make sure the heifer was accepting her calf. Gray clouds rolled across the valley, promising rain. The sun peeked out through a gap, warming the air for a moment, making her believe spring really was on its way.

Feeling optimistic, she tossed her coat on her truck as she passed. Maybe it would warm up today. Maybe the rain would green up the grass.

She entered the barn and walked to the stall where the heifer was licking her scrawny calf. Shay hitched a foot on the gate and leaned into it, watching. She never tired of this, her favorite part of the job. The births could make for some sleepless nights, but it was always worth it when the calf arrived safe and sound.

Now the mama began nursing her calf. She eyed Shay suspiciously, seeming to have forgotten who it was that had just helped her baby safely into the world.

Shay understood that protective gleam in the heifer's eyes, though. Wouldn't she do anything for her own daughter? For the baby that grew inside her? Wouldn't she give up the only home she'd ever known? Give up the cowboy way of life to provide for her own?

She'd found a little apartment in town, and a job awaited her at Pappy's Market after the baby was born. Marla said she could bring the baby to work the first few weeks. After that, Shay would have to figure out something else. She might have to sell her truck to pay for day care, but she could walk to work. She'd do whatever it took. She'd spent every spare minute of the winter making barbed wire baskets. Those would provide extra cash over the summer.

She shifted her weight, and the cow rolled her huge eyes toward her.

"Relax, mama. Your baby's safe."

The calf stopped nursing a moment, then continued. The mama would keep the calf at her side, feeding her, caring for her every need. It was her job, and hers alone. They had more in common than the cow could ever know.

The wind whistled through the cracks in the barn, and the rain began a tap dance on the roof. She'd miss this place. She breathed in the smell of rain, fresh straw, and horseflesh, meandering over to Brandy's stall.

She ran a hand down her horse's nose. There was no way she could keep her in town. Maybe the new owners would let her and Olivia visit from time to time. Hard to say, since a big corporation would probably buy the place. Until then, the McCoys would have to hire out help to run the place.

She wondered if they'd told Travis, then checked her thoughts. Why would he care? He and Ella were probably cozying up somewhere in Texas, riding tandem, waking up next to one another. He was picking straw from her hair and whispering sweet nothings in her ear. Calling her "sweetness."

Her gut clenched hard at the thought as her eyes, of their own volition, swung to the third stall. She'd raked out the straw, leaving the floor bare, a week after he'd left. She didn't want the reminder of their secret rendezvous.

But reminders were everywhere she looked. In the shower they'd shared on one occasion, in the bedroom where they'd made love, inside her swollen belly where the evidence of their affection had culminated in life.

When she lay in bed at night, she missed the quiet strum of his guitar. She missed how protective he was, even missed the way he rubbed his jaw when he got fed up with her.

Mostly, she ached for his arms around her. Wondered, if he was still here, if he'd put his hand on her belly and dream with her about what their baby would be like. If it was a boy and if he would have Travis's gray eyes and dark hair. Or if it was a girl and she'd have Shay's coloring and stubborn streak.

Shay would correct him: strong-willed, not stubborn. Then he'd chuckle and give her a kiss that would start quick and easy, then grow slow and desperate.

Brandy whinnied softly.

None of that was going to happen. Shay shook the wandering thoughts away, blinked the moisture from her eyes. She had to stop this. Had to stop thinking about him, dreaming things were different. It was unhealthy.

You got over him once before, you can do it again.

But even as the thought surfaced, the truth bubbled up with it. She hadn't gotten over him before. She'd never loved Garrett the way she loved Travis.

Is this just the way it's going to be, God? Am I going to have to live with this aching hole inside for the rest of my life?

The only answer was the soft patter of rain, the faint rustling of the calf in the bed of straw, the distant creaking of leather.

She frowned at that last sound, turning toward it. The wind swung the barn door on its hinge, making it squeak. But that wasn't the sound she'd heard.

A moment later a familiar silhouette filled the doorway. Her heart stopped beating, her breath caught in her lungs. She'd know the set of those shoulders, the contours of that body, anywhere.

Travis scanned the barn until he saw her.

Saw her.

She turned her back to him, leaned into the stall door, hiding her pregnant belly. Panic surged through her like a lightning bolt. He couldn't see. He couldn't know. Not like this.

"Hello, Shay." His footsteps grew closer.

Her heart started again, made up for lost time. Why was he here? Was he trying to torture her? *Help me, Jesus*.

He put his hand on the gate beside hers, facing her. She leaned into the gate, propping her elbows so the top of her shirt ballooned out. Why, oh why, had she ditched her coat outside? She wanted to run, but there was nowhere to hide. She was trapped. If she tried to run for the house, he'd stop her. She'd be out in the open, in full view, and then he'd see.

"Shay . . ." He pulled his hat, and the movement sent a waft of his musky scent her way.

"What are you doing here?" Her voice sounded like she'd swallowed a coil of barbed wire. She tried to swallow and found her throat swollen and achy.

"We need to talk."

"We have nothing to—"

A terrible thought hit her like a sledgehammer. Had someone told him about the baby? His parents didn't know, but Travis had friends. Dylan, Wade . . . but surely they wouldn't have meddled. This was her matter to handle, and hers alone.

"Have something for you." He didn't sound cross.

Maybe he didn't know. Maybe he'd come back to box up his parents' things and ship them off to

Guatemala. That had to be it. She sneaked a peek at him—a quick one. His face was relaxed, his eyes sparkling with something . . . hope?

"Go for a ride with me," he said.

She couldn't go for a ride—she couldn't even step away from the gate. She had to get him out of there. "It's raining."

"In the house, then. I'll fix some coffee."

"Why don't you call me later?" She could put him off until he left town again, which would hopefully be soon, before someone mentioned her pregnancy. "Maybe tonight?"

Olivia would be home. It had taken months for her to forgive Shay for making Travis leave, and they'd be back to square one, but it couldn't be helped.

"You look good." The deep tone of his voice roused something in the pit of her stomach.

She could feel his gaze on her face, and her skin heated under his perusal. Why had he come here? It wasn't fair that he could stir her up this way. She was just beginning to forget, and now he was here making her remember what she was missing. She felt the sting of tears and swallowed hard.

"I've missed you," he said.

She'd bet he had. A wry laugh escaped. Her feet itched to run. Only her swollen belly, pressed against the wooden gate, kept her still.

"Don't believe me?" he asked.

He had no idea what missing was. Missing was lying in the dampness of your tears night after night. Missing was a constant hollow spot in the center of your chest. Missing was a yawning ache that was never satisfied.

"Go away, Travis. *Please.*"

He moved beside her, and she heard a crackling sound. He handed her an envelope. She stared at it, frowning.

"Go ahead." He pushed it toward her. "Open it."

He wasn't going away until she did. Sighing hard, she took the envelope, slid her finger under the flap, and removed the folded paper.

It was an official document. A deed of some kind. She scanned the paper and found her ranch's address.

"What is this, Travis?"

"The deed to your ranch."

She studied the paper, confused. "I don't understand. Your parents bought my place."

"Actually, *I* did."

She looked at him then, frowning. The flecks in his gray eyes sparkled. He'd bought her home? For what purpose? And why'd he hide behind his folks?

"They were my nominees," he said. "Perfectly legal." He looked rather pleased with himself, his chin tucked, a tiny smile playing at his lips.

He was taking her property away? Kicking her

out the way she'd kicked him out? What was this . . . revenge? The flesh under her arms heated, prickling. She felt angry tears gathering in her eyes. She had to get away, was not going to crumble to pieces in front of him.

She shoved the envelope into his chest. "Congratulations."

She darted away, her feet moving quickly. How could he have done this? He of all people knew what this place meant to her. It was her home. Their home. She could barely stand the thought of strangers living here, much less Travis.

"Shay . . ."

She left the barn and passed Buck. The drizzle cooled her skin, but not her temper. He'd said he loved her, but she knew better, didn't she? Last time he'd loved her, he'd deserted her. This time he'd taken away her home.

"Wait, Shay." He sounded close behind.

She had to make it to the house. She'd slam the door in his face and lock him out. But it wasn't even her house now. It was his.

His footsteps pounded the dirt behind her. He was catching up.

"Shay."

So close.

She grabbed her jacket from the hood of her truck just as he took her arm and whipped her around. She clutched the damp coat to her belly, breathing fire.

"You don't understand," he said. He no longer looked pleased. A flicker of fear flashed in his eyes. He held out the folded paper. "It's yours. I bought it for *you*—it's all paid for."

All hers? She was afraid to believe it. Why would he—

"Take it." He thrust it at her.

She clutched the coat against her belly. Why was he doing this? Guilt for all the pain he'd put her through? She didn't want his charity. Besides, she couldn't run the ranch now, not like this and not after the baby was born.

"It's yours," he said.

"I don't want it."

His eyes narrowed thoughtfully. His hair was plastered to his head. A drop of rain ran down the crease between his brows. His eyes had gone the color of a summer storm.

"No strings attached—it's yours free and clear. But I came back to see . . . I've missed you, Shay. I love—"

She whipped around and jogged for the house.

"Shay, blast it, why do you have to be so stubborn?"

She had a childish urge to put her hands over her ears. But her hands were full of coat, and running was easier. She didn't want to hear his declarations of love. She didn't believe him, refused to believe him, and if she stood there for a second more, she'd be tempted. Tempted to believe him, tempted to fall right back into his arms like a fool.

She was so close, nearly to the porch, almost to the first step.

He tore the coat from her arms, spinning her around.

Her arms were empty, her belly exposed. Her shirt was wet, no doubt plastered to her form. She folded her arms.

Too late. Travis's eyes had fallen to her swollen belly and fastened there. His brows knotted, a crease between them.

She froze, couldn't move if she wanted. Her breath caught in her lungs and held there, thick and heavy.

Travis's eyes widened as they fastened on hers. He searched her face for answers. She could see the wheels turning and wondered where they'd stop.

He opened his mouth to speak, then closed it again. His head tilted. His eyes filled with wonder. And then moisture. He ran his hand across his jaw.

She wanted him to say something. Anything. What was he thinking? What had moved him to tears? Was he sorry? Did he feel trapped? It was the last thing she wanted.

A look of hurt passed across his face. "Why didn't you tell me?"

So he could feel torn between what he wanted and what he was obliged to do?

"I don't want to be an obligation, Travis." She raised her chin and gathered her strength. "You're off the hook."

"Off the—for crying out loud, Shay, how can you say that? Didn't I just tell you how I feel?"

She didn't want to go there, but he was giving her no choice. "I know about Ella, Travis. Do you tell her how you feel too?"

The crease was back, doubled. "Ella . . . Ella Reynolds?"

She wiped the rain from her face. "I saw the text, Travis. I know you were meeting her in Vegas. I know there's something between the two of you, so you can just go back to Texas and take that deed with you. Clearly, I'm in no shape to run this place."

His eyes looked slate gray under the storm clouds. "What text? There's nothing between me and Ella. We dated a few times, before I came back here. That's all. Yes, she was interested, but I told her I was married."

Shay crossed her arms over her chest as if to prevent any of his words from sinking into her heart. It was lies, all lies. She lifted her chin. "You communicated with her while you were here. You met up with her in Vegas. You've probably been with her since then."

"I texted her from here, but only to tell her I

was married—that I loved my wife. And once to congratulate her on finaling. That's it, Shay." He pulled his phone from his pocket and held it out. "Check for yourself. I probably haven't deleted any texts since then. I never think of it."

Shay took the phone and held it against herself, shielding it from the rain.

What if it was true? He wouldn't hand over his phone if he had something to hide, would he? And if she'd been wrong about Ella, what else had she been wrong about?

He took a step closer and reached out, framing her face. His palms were warm against her damp skin.

He looked deep into her eyes. "I know I let you down before. I know I hurt you, and I'll have to earn back your trust. I'll be as patient as I need to be, only please let me prove it to you. Let me prove that I'm here to stay. I've never wanted anything so badly in my whole life."

His voice, his words, reached deep into her heart. She still had one reservation—his first love, the thing that had taken him from her before.

"What about the rodeo, Travis?"

His thumb glided over her the corner of her mouth. "I'm done with the rodeo. Haven't ridden competitively since the finals, and I don't miss it, Shay. What I miss is *you*. I miss us. I miss Olivia."

He reached into his pocket again and pulled out a velvet box. "This isn't the way I planned this last fall when I bought it." He opened the box, and a gold wedding band sparkled in the center.

The jewelry package. It had been for her after all.

He met her eyes. "I love you so much, Shay Brandenberger. I want you to be my wife because you choose to be, not because of some cockamamie accident. I want to love you the rest of your life. I want to be a father for Olivia . . ." He reached out and palmed the side of her belly, a tiny smile hitching up his lips. "A father for our child."

Her eyes burned, her heart thundered in her chest. She swallowed past the lump in her throat. She wanted to believe it.

Can I trust him to stay this time, God?

"I bought my parents' place too."

She frowned. "Why?"

"I'm here for good this time, Shay. Please don't make me settle for being your neighbor." He pulled the ring from its velvet nest and held it in his fingers. "I want so much more."

He looked on her with love, his eyes promising more than his words. "I'll earn your trust back, every bit of it. But the first step is yours."

She looked down at the band, circular and perfect, a droplet of rain glistening on its surface.

She wanted nothing more than to be his forever wife. She'd never wanted anything but that. All she had to do was take this one step and trust God to carry her through. He'd never left her side. Hadn't He led Travis straight back to her—twice?

She uncrossed her arms, held out her hand. It trembled in the air before he caught it in his own.

Gazing into her eyes, Travis slid the ring into place. The metal was warm against her skin. The weight of it familiar and right.

He cupped her chin, lifting. "I love you." The warmth of his breath was a whisper on her lips.

"I love you too. So much."

His eyes softened. She drank in the look, savoring it. She'd missed it, the way he could love her with a look. The way he could send chills down her spine with a touch.

He pulled her close and took possession of her lips, softly at first, then more urgently when she wrapped her arms around him and pressed closer. He was Travis, her first love, her husband, the father of the baby that nestled in her womb.

He pulled away and pressed kisses to her closed eyes, then folded her into his arms. "Forever and ever," he whispered. "As long as we both shall live."

Her eyes stung at his tender words, and her

heart was near to exploding from her chest. His promise rang true in her ears. A smile tugged her lips as she pressed into the warmth of his embrace.

As long as we both shall live.

Epilogue

*S*hay pulled the rake, piling the old straw at her feet. When the stall was clean, she set the rake down and rubbed her back, catching her breath. The backache she'd woken with had only gotten worse.

Of course, the chores weren't helping. If Travis knew she was working out here in the August heat, he'd come home, sweep her off her feet, and carry her right back into the house. But she couldn't stand seeing him work so hard while she sat on the sofa with her swollen feet propped on the ottoman, watching her belly grow larger.

As if that were possible. She looked down and eyed the protrusion. It seemed impossible she had another week to go. She was already big as a barn.

Abigail hadn't gotten nearly this big. Her friend had delivered a healthy baby boy three weeks earlier, following a long, difficult labor. Shay had brought Olivia to the hospital and watched rugged cowboy Wade blink back tears as he held his newborn son. Maddy was positively gaga over her baby brother.

A spasm seized Shay's back, and she froze until it passed. *Yeeow.* Maybe Travis was right. She shouldn't be raking out stalls in her condition. She took the rake back to the tack room and replaced a couple tools that had been left out.

The last four months had been busy ones and full of change. After a lot of conversation, they'd decided to move into Travis's house at the Barr M. With a baby on the way, they needed the extra room. Besides, Shay reminded herself, a house was just a house. Her home was where her family was. Olivia had claimed Travis's boyhood room, and they'd made it girly with lavender paint and floral rugs. The nursery, adjacent to the master bedroom, had been readied as well.

Soon after Travis's return, Shay'd had her last name changed to McCoy. Last month Travis had told her he'd like to formally adopt Olivia. When they'd told her, she'd whooped with excitement. The adoption process was now in motion and would be completed soon.

Shay was smiling as she started from the tack room. When she reached the doorway, another spasm arced through her back, wrapping around her abdomen.

Oh.

Her legs wavered under her, and she braced herself against the door frame, her stubby fingernails digging into the splintered wood.

How long had it been since the last pain? Two minutes? Three? Was she in labor?

With Olivia, her water had broken—it was nothing like this. The pain subsided, but she was afraid to move. She reached for her cell and found her pocket empty. She'd left it charging on her nightstand. Olivia had gone with Travis to make his circle, and Travis had only agreed because Shay had promised to stay close to the phone.

Well, I am close. It was only a few hundred yards away. But the distance to the house had never seemed so far.

She was fine now, though. Her legs, though wobbly, could support her weight. She started for the house, making plans to prepare. Her bag was already packed, and Miss Lucy was on alert to expect Olivia overnight if necessary.

She was halfway to the house when another spasm buckled her legs. She sank down to the grass on all fours, gritting her teeth against the pain until she remembered to breathe. She pulled in one shaky breath after another.

Finally the spasm began to recede. It was nearly gone when she heard the clopping of horses' hooves. Travis was bearing down hard, Olivia a ways behind. He dismounted before Buck reached a full stop.

"Shay!" His face was tense.

Shay pulled her hands from the dry grass, sitting back on her haunches, and gave a dry smile. "I think the baby's coming."

"Olivia," he called over his shoulder. "Run in the house and get my keys."

"And my overnight bag," Shay said.

Olivia dismounted nearby. "The baby's coming?"

"Ready or not." Shay wiped the sweat from her forehead while her daughter ran into the house.

Travis called Wade and asked him to take care of their horses, then put in a quick call to Miss Lucy.

"What were you doing out here?" he asked when he turned off the phone. "I couldn't reach you."

"I was in the barn. The stalls needed—"

His glower stopped her. She put her hands down, preparing to stand, but he swooped her up in his arms and stood.

"I can walk just fine."

"Yeah, I see that." He carried her to the truck. As he deposited her gently on the seat, another contraction overtook her.

Pain ripped through her abdomen. Her breath caught in her lungs, the pain stealing all voluntary function.

Travis took her hand. "Breathe, baby. Breathe."

She sucked in a tremulous breath and blew it out.

"Again," he said. "That's it, you're doing great." He pushed the hair off her face and crooned gently until the spasm passed.

Shay took a cleansing breath and opened her eyes. "They're getting closer."

Olivia arrived with the keys and bag. "Here, Daddy."

"Hop in, kiddo," Travis said. "Your baby brother or sister is in a hurry to meet you."

Shay sagged against the hospital bed, her muscles still quivering. The nurse had their baby boy in the bassinet and was doing all the newborn procedures.

Travis pocketed his phone and perched on the bed, facing her. "My parents said to tell you congratulations. Dad got all choked up when I told him the name. He was honored."

They'd decided on Austin Wyatt McCoy, Wyatt after his dad. "Think they'll come back soon for a visit?"

"Mom said they'll come next month one way or another. It's killing her that she can't be here." Travis brushed Shay's hair back from her damp forehead. "You did so great, sweetness." He kissed her, his lips lingering for a long second. "You amaze me."

She choked back a laugh. "Sorry about, you know, all the yelling. I didn't mean a word of it." Truth be told, she didn't remember much of what she'd said.

Travis smiled. "I sure hope he doesn't have your temper."

As if on cue, their baby boy let out a screech.

"Uh-oh," she said.

One of the nurses raised her bed while another bundled their baby in a hospital blanket and brought him over.

He was light as a feather in Shay's arms. She cradled him against her, shushing him.

Travis leaned in, smiling at Austin's red, wrinkled face.

"It's okay, little guy," Shay said. "Mama and Daddy are here."

The infant hushed his crying, searched for the voice, and fastened his glassy blue eyes on Shay. He had a healthy patch of Travis's dark hair, but the shape of his eyes was all Shay. He was beautiful. A wonderful mixture of the two of them. Love for this tiny being filled her to overflowing, making her eyes burn.

Travis touched the baby's hand with his finger. "He's so perfect. Look at his tiny hands, his paper-thin nails . . . his little nose . . ." The baby's eyes swung toward his dad, and Travis smiled. "He knows my voice."

Shay moved the bundle toward him. "Your turn, Daddy."

Travis took Austin with utmost care, his eyes never leaving his son's face. His eyes filled. "I can't believe I have a son," he said, blinking back the moisture.

Shay set her arm on Travis's and squeezed. The labor had been hard, but worth the reward. So worth it.

"Knock knock," the nurse said, peeking in. "Big Sister's out here, eager to meet her little brother."

"Oh, send her in," Shay said.

Olivia moved into the room tentatively.

"Come on in, kiddo." Travis turned on the bed. "Meet your little brother."

Olivia reached out and touched his cheek with the back of her hand. "He's so little . . . and he has so much hair."

"Want to hold him?" Shay asked.

Olivia nodded. "I already washed my hands."

Shay had her sit in the nearby chair, and Travis placed the bundle in her arms.

"What do you think?" Travis asked, squatting beside her.

"He's light. His eyes are so blue. Will they change color?"

"Probably," Shay said. "Maybe they'll turn brown just like yours."

"Or gray like Dad's." She looked down at Austin and smiled. "Hey, baby brother. I'm your big sister, Olivia."

Austin made a funny little peep, and Olivia chuckled.

A knock sounded on the door. "It's just us," Abigail said.

Shay adjusted her covers. "Come on in."

"We won't stay—we just want to take a peek." Abigail and Miss Lucy entered the room. They went straight to the chair where Olivia sat with the baby.

"Oh, Shay, he's beautiful," Abigail said. "He favors you, Olivia."

"He does," Miss Lucy said. "And Big Sister's doing such a good job holding him."

"Have you been here long?" Travis asked.

"Are you kidding?" Abigail said. "You no sooner called and told us you were in labor than we heard a squall coming from the room." She gave Shay a mock glare. "I'm trying not to hate you."

Shay shrugged, all innocence. "He was in a hurry."

"All right, Mama," the nurse said as she entered the room. "Time to feed baby McCoy."

"Awwww . . ." Olivia pouted as she handed over her brother.

Abigail gave Shay a peck on the forehead. "I'm happy for you, friend."

Miss Lucy kissed Shay's cheek. "Congratulations."

Where would she be without her elderly friend? "Thanks for praying for me, Miss Lucy."

She patted Shay's hand. "Always, dear."

Miss Lucy hugged Travis, then framed his face and whispered, "See? It all worked out—just as God intended." She gave him a big hug, patting his back.

Abigail and Miss Lucy left, promising Olivia a

late supper. The nurse placed Austin in Shay's arms, and her son latched onto her.

"Well, that was easy," the nurse said, chuckling. She showed Shay how to position her arms to prevent fatigue and gave her a few reminders. "If you need anything, just press the button."

"Thanks, I think we're fine."

When she left, Travis perched on the edge of the bed and stared in wonder at his son. Soon Austin fell asleep, and Shay propped him against her shoulder. Travis scooted beside her, gathering her in his arms.

As she patted the baby's back, Shay thought back over what she'd heard Miss Lucy say. "What was all that about—what Miss Lucy said?"

Travis looked into her eyes, nostalgia sweeping over his face. "Back when I discovered what happened with the wedding, I called her. I was a little frazzled. I mean, I loved the idea of being married to you, but I knew you were gonna blow a gasket."

"I didn't blow a gasket."

Travis tilted his head and gave her a look.

"Okay, maybe a little."

"Miss Lucy said it would all work out as God intended." His eyes grew serious, and a smile played at the corner of his lips. "She was right." He leaned in and pressed a kiss to her temple.

His breath was warm on her skin. "I couldn't be happier, Shay," he whispered.

She drank in the love that shone from his eyes. "Me neither."

Travis pulled her close, and she nestled in the safety of his arms. Outside the window, night fell. A heavy drape of blue fell slowly over the Gallatin Range, swaddling the valley in stillness.

Reading Group Guide

1. Shay was afraid to marry again after having her heart broken twice before. How does fear play into our ability to love fully?
2. Because of Shay's background, she tended to worry too much about others' opinions. Galatians 1:10 says, "For am I now trying to win the favor of people, or God? Or am I striving to please people?" What does that mean to you?
3. How were Abigail's blurry pictures a metaphor for Shay's outlook?
4. Olivia picked up on Shay's issue with pleasing others. Are there any issues that were handed down to you from your parents? What can you do to break the cycle?
5. Travis made the selfish decision to leave Shay at the altar when he was a young adult. What price did he and others pay as a result? Discuss the ways in which poor choices can sometimes have far-reaching consequences. How can we best recover?
6. How did Shay's tendency to please others impact her decision-making? What events caused her to see her sin? What changes did

she make as a result of this revelation?

7. When Travis lost Shay, he realized he hadn't sought God's will during a critical point in his life. Instead, he'd relied on Miss Lucy's prayers. Do you ever foist your spiritual responsibilities onto someone you feel has a closer walk with God?

8. Miss Lucy supported Shay in prayer for years. Is there someone who lifts you up in prayer faithfully? Whom do you pray for?

9. Were you more frustrated at Travis or Shay for the way each of them handled every new obstacle? His not telling her about the rodeo competition? Her not asking about the jewelry package? His not returning right after the competition? Her not telling him she was pregnant? Or do you think both were accountable for what kept them apart?

10. Ranching is hard work, and money is often tight. Why do you think families continue this way of life?

Dear friend,

I hope you enjoyed the special love story of Travis and Shay. These characters wormed their way into my heart and became like close friends.

When I decided this story would have an accidental wedding, I had no idea what a challenge I'd set out on. Turns out, it's not so easy to become accidently married!

To pull off such a feat, I had to bend the rules a little—we like to call that "artistic license." While artistic licenses are valid indefinitely, Wyoming wedding licenses are not, nor are they mailed to the newlyweds after the ceremony. So rest assured, an accidental marriage is not likely to happen to you or anyone you know!

I hope you enjoyed the story, despite these two improvisations, and I hope that walking in Shay's shoes (boots!) somehow drew you into a closer walk with God. Thank you for joining me on the journey to Moose Creek, Montana. I value each one of you more than you can know!

In His grace,
Denise Hunter

Acknowledgments

I'm so grateful for the many people who helped shape this story. *The Accidental Bride* wouldn't exist without the Thomas Nelson fiction team. I'm so grateful for the entire team, led by Publisher Allen Arnold: Amanda Bostic, Eric Mullett, Natalie Hanemann, Dean Arvidson, Jodi Hughes, Ami McConnell, Heather McCulloch, Becky Monds, Ashley Schneider, Katie Bond, and Kristen Vasgaard.

Thanks especially to my editor, Natalie Hanemann, who helped shape this story, notified me of gaping holes, and otherwise helped me fashion this into a more enjoyable read. I'm forever grateful to the talented LB Norton, who fine-tuned this manuscript, finessed my prose, and saved me from more than one embarrassing mistake!

Authors Colleen Coble and Diann Hunt are my brainstorming partners. Thank you, friends! And thank you, Colleen, for always being my first reader.

I'm grateful to my agent, Karen Solem, who handles all the left-brained matters so I can focus on the right-brained stuff.

To Billy and Marci Whitehurst, who opened their Montana home and ranch for a city girl and her husband. Thanks for taking the time to show me the cowboy way of life.

A research trip to Montana would've been impossible without my sister-in-law Gina Sinclair, brother-in-law Mark Sinclair, and niece Mindy Sinclair. Thanks so much for coming to take over our daily lives for a few days so Kevin and I could gallivant all over Big Sky Country. We're so grateful to call you family.

Thanks to my Facebook friends at Denise Hunter Readers Circle who helped me name the town of Moose Creek and the series itself. Thanks for all your input!

To my family, Kevin, Justin, Chad, and Trevor. I love each one of you so much!

Lastly, thank you, friend, for letting me share this story with you. I've enjoyed getting to know so many readers like you through my Facebook group. Visit my website at www.DeniseHunterBooks.com or just drop me a note at Denise@DeniseHunterBooks.com. I'd love to hear from you!

About the Author

Denise Hunter is the best-selling author of many novels, including *The Convenient Groom* and *Driftwood Lane*. She lives in Indiana with her husband, Kevin, and their three sons. In 1996, Denise began her first book, a Christian romance novel, writing while her children napped. Two years later it was published, and she's been writing ever since. Her books contain a strong romantic element, and her husband says he provides all her romantic material, but Denise insists a good imagination helps too! Visit her website at DeniseHunterBooks.com.

Center Point Publishing
600 Brooks Road ● PO Box 1
Thorndike ME 04986-0001 USA

(207) 568-3717

US & Canada:
1 800 929-9108
www.centerpointlargeprint.com